Praise for *The Dead Beat Scroll*

"Slick, sardonic and suspenseful—everything a great thriller should be."

—Lee Child, bestselling author
of the Jack Reacher novels

"Fast-paced excursion into the remnants of San Francisco's lost bohemia…Alternately comic, sad, lurid, impossible, blasphemous, and just plain fun."

—Domenic Stansberry, Edgar Award-winning
author of the North Beach Mystery Series

"Glorious potpourri of violence, black humor, sex, and a hunt for a lost manuscript… Read *The Dead Beat Scroll*, and enjoy again the type of mystery novel that defined this genre."

—*New York Journal of Books*

THE DEAD
BEAT SCROLL

ALSO BY MARK COGGINS

The August Riordan Series
The Immortal Game
Vulture Capital
Candy from Strangers
Runoff
The Big Wake-Up
No Hard Feelings
The Dead Beat Scroll

Other Titles
Prom Night and Other Man-made Disasters (essay collection)
The Space Between (photography monograph)

MARK COGGINS

THE DEAD BEAT SCROLL

An August Riordan Mystery

Down & Out Books
3959 Van Dyke Road, Suite 265
Lutz, FL 33558
DownAndOutBooks.com

The characters and events in this book are fictitious. Any similarity to real persons, living or dead, is coincidental and not intended by the author.

Cover photograph by Mark Coggins
Cover design by Lance Wright

ISBN: 1-64396-031-8
ISBN-13: 978-1-64396-031-9

献给周琳
(for Linda)

*My story is endless. I put in a teletype roll, you know, you know
what they are, you have them in newspapers, and run it through
there and fix the margins and just go, go—just go, go, go.*
—Jack Kerouac

1
GOLDEN FINGERS

The theme music for the quiz show *Jeopardy!* makes an unsettling ringtone. Although originally composed as a lullaby, its relentless, tick-tock, time-is-running-out associations can't help but impinge upon your dreams if you've already nodded off.

Other things that can impinge are a hip flask full of Old Grand-Dad and memories of a turbulent flight from Palm Springs to San Francisco earlier in the day. Now, as I dozed on a couch in my old apartment on the corner of Post and Hyde, the inexorable march of tinny notes from my cellphone turned my vague dreams about flying into lucid nightmares about crashing.

The caller went to voice mail and redialed. I fumbled the phone out of my suit coat and held the glowing screen to my face. The blurry characters told me three things: I was still drunk. It was two twenty-three in the morning. And someone with a 415 number I didn't recognize was calling.

I swiped my finger over the touchscreen to answer. "Riordan," I tried to say, but it came out like a sea lion clearing phlegm.

"Riordan?" repeated the caller.

"That's what I said. Who is this?"

"Kittredge."

Kittredge. Lieutenant "Smiling Jack" Kittredge. That showboating asshole from SFPD Homicide was at least part of the reason I'd thrown in the towel on my PI business and left the city.

"Where'd you get this number?"

"It's the same fucking number you had when you lived here."

"Oh." I sat up on the couch and brought a hand to my throbbing forehead. It came away greasy with sweat.

"I talked to your secretary," said Kittredge.

"Ex-secretary."

"Whatever. I know why you're back."

"So?"

"Don't make this any harder than it already is, Riordan. You and I are never going be on each other's Christmas card list, but I'm trying to do the right thing. You need to get over here."

I drew in a ragged breath. "Where's here?"

"A rub-and-tug place called Golden Fingers. It's on Stockton, just before Bush."

"You mean just before the tunnel under Bush. I remember it. But if you know why I'm back, you know that doesn't make any sense. Duckworth wouldn't be caught dead in a place like that."

There was a long pause. "You're going to regret saying that."

"He's there?"

"Yeah."

"And he's—"

"I'm sorry, Riordan. Yeah, he's dead."

"Fifteen minutes."

I tottered to my feet and felt around in the dark for the floor lamp. I squeezed my eyes shut against the flood of light—and the spinning room—and stood braced against the arm of the sofa. My dinner auditioned for a return engagement, and more sweat popped from my forehead. More moisture welled at the corners of my eyes.

Chris Duckworth had been my best friend and sometime assistant. In the last case we'd worked together, I'd convinced him to participate in what could most charitably be characterized as vigilante justice. Together with a former cop, we had ambushed and killed a gang of psychopaths from Argentina. I had no doubt that they deserved it, just as I had no doubt that Chris's guilt over his involvement destroyed our friendship. It was another reason I had left San Francisco. The main reason—if I was being honest with myself.

I thought my leaving would be the best thing for him. That it would allow him to move on. What I didn't anticipate is that he would pick up where I left off, taking over my old business, my old office, and my old apartment. When Gretchen—my old secretary—called me in Palm Springs to tell me that Chris was missing, it had been more than five years since I'd seen him.

My wing tips lay on the floor by the sofa. I stepped into them, not trusting my equilibrium enough to bother with the laces. I cinched the knot of my tie closer to my throat—it still had inches to go—speared my overcoat from the sofa, and shrugged it on.

I tottered around the black granite megalith Chris used for a dining-room table, brushed past the Andy Warhol prints in the entryway, and lurched out the door. The building elevator was every bit as decrepit as I remembered, and the ride to the ground floor still felt like an extended toilet flush.

I pushed through the building's door out onto Post Street. A thick mist hung in the air, making the walk up the hill toward the massage parlor feel like wading through applesauce. It was less than three-quarters of a mile, so calling a cab or an Uber would have taken more time than it was worth—especially since I didn't know how the hell to summon an Uber. I made it to Stockton without seeing a car or a pedestrian, but when I turned left for the short block to where the street ran under Bush, an old guy with shiny hair, a shimmery track suit, and a towel around his neck materialized out of the mist doing an awkward racewalk. He elbowed past me without a word.

Up ahead, a pair of SFPD cruisers blocked the left lane of the tunnel, their red and blue emergency lights filling its mouth with an eerie luminescence. I was nearly beneath the towering Golden Fingers street sign before I noticed it. A TOUCH OF ECSTASY, it promised. MASSAGE, SAUNA, WHIRLPOOL—INCALL OR OUTCALL. A smaller neon sign next to the entrance still glowed. OPEN.

A bald patrol cop with a chest puffed out by body armor stood in the doorway. "The establishment is closed, sir," he said.

My throat had gone froggy again. "I know," I managed to croak. "Kittredge called me."

He frowned. "You're Riordan?"

"Yeah."

"You look pretty green. I thought you were a drunk looking to sweat off a bender." He paused. "No offense."

"None taken."

"They're in the back, past reception. It's room number four."

I wobbled by him into a dinky reception area painted red with gilded wainscoting. Gold bric-à-brac bulged from rosewood curio cabinets, and a Sputnik fixture overhead projected searing glints of light into my occipital lobe. I plunged through a beaded curtain to the left of the reception desk and walked down a corridor that was mirrored on one side and upholstered in red velvet on the other. A detective leaned against the door frame of the only room that was open, peering inside with a bored expression.

The squawk of a walkie-talkie burst from the room. "I just sent Riordan back."

"Roger that," said a voice that sounded like Kittredge's.

The detective in the door frame turned to look down the corridor, and seeing me, stepped away. "Stand just outside, sir. Don't contaminate the scene."

I nodded and came up to the doorway. The room was just large enough to hold a narrow massage table with space around the sides to maneuver. A rosewood pedestal with a collection of massage oils stood at the back, a pair of big round mirrors reflected infinite views, and a paper lantern with a gold bulb dangled from the ceiling. Everything that could be painted was painted red.

Kittredge was at the side of the massage table, his hands protected by latex gloves and his shoes covered in paper booties. The walkie-talkie I'd heard earlier hung from his belt. He looked as ill at ease as I'd ever seen him.

The source of his unease was on the table. Facedown in the headrest with a black flannel sheet draped over him from midcalf to upper back was my friend Chris. There were no obvious signs of violence, and from where I stood, it looked like he was sleeping.

I glanced up at Kittredge, but he avoided my eyes. "Again, Riordan, I'm sorry. I wouldn't have dragged you down here, but I didn't think you'd take my word for it."

"Yeah. You're probably right. What happened?"

Kittredge brought a hand up to loosen his tie, thrust his chin out, and pulled his lips back in a chimpanzee grimace, showing off the perfect white choppers that had earned him his nickname. "We got a call from the janitorial service that cleans this place."

"What a job, huh?" said the detective behind me. "Imagine the amount of jizz that gets squirted out here."

I turned back to look at him, and something in my face made him cough and turn away. "Right," he mumbled.

"So the janitor found him?" I asked Kittredge.

"Yeah."

"What time do they close?"

"Ten."

"What time does the janitor come to clean?"

"According to him, he got here around midnight and there was no one in the building when he arrived."

"Did he find Chris right off?"

"No. He cleans the sauna and the whirlpool first because they're the most work. He doesn't wear a watch, so he doesn't know exactly what time he found him, but he called the owner at about one-thirty. Then she called us."

"Any chance he's involved?"

Kittredge made an elaborate shrug. "It's possible. We'll question him more to be certain, but I doubt it. He's from El Salvador, probably illegal, and doesn't speak much English. What would he want with Duckworth?"

"I don't know." I cleared my throat and asked the question I intended to ask from the get-go. "What killed him?"

Kittredge's eyebrows crept up in surprise. "I guess you can't see. A bullet to the back of the head. Base of the skull, execution style. Looks to be small caliber. It's a small entrance wound, not much bleeding and no exit wound."

"Any other marks or wounds on him?"

Kittredge reddened. Chris had been gay, and it was clear that Kittredge felt uncomfortable acknowledging that he had pulled off the sheet to examine the body. "Ah, no, nothing we could see. The medical examiner will do a full workup. In fact, the lab guys are coming, so you're going to need to clear out."

I looked down at my friend Chris. He had always been a slight man, but laid out cold under the light of the dim gold bulb, he looked smaller, almost childlike. I wanted to see his face—perhaps to get some insight into what he was thinking as he died or maybe feel less guilty about abandoning him here—but it was obscured by the padding around the headrest. I took a step forward to touch the back of his head. Kittredge flinched but did nothing to stop me.

"Goodbye, Chris," I said.

I turned abruptly and headed back up the hallway. The other detective jumped out of my way, and I heard Kittredge growl behind me, "Just a minute, Riordan."

I stopped, and he came up to me, some of the old toughness creeping back into his demeanor. "What do you know about this?"

"Just what you told me."

"I mean about why he went missing."

"Nothing more than you. Gretchen called to tell me that he hadn't been to the office for several weeks and wasn't living in his apartment. She was worried about him and wanted me to find him."

"What was he working on?"

"I don't know. She didn't know."

Kittredge pointed a gloved finger at me. "Homicide is police business. You find out anything about what he was working on or where he was, you bring it to me. No vigilante stuff, Riordan. I know you were involved in the massacre of those Argentines even if the DA couldn't pin it on you. You try to avenge Duckworth's murder, and I'll wreck you."

I took hold of his hand, intending to push it away from me, but I was in no condition to get physical. He shoved me backward into a tangled heap on the floor.

"You're too late, Kittredge," I said to the ceiling. "There's nothing left to wreck."

2
OLD HOME WEEK

At eleven-twenty that same morning, I stood outside the door to my old office on the twelfth floor of the Flood Building at the corner of Market and Powell streets. The door was pebble glass, and it used to have my name and the suite number painted on it in black. The Flood Building, the door, and the suite number were all the same, but DUCKWORTH INVESTIGATIVE SOLUTIONS was painted on the glass instead. I brought a hand up to knock, thought better of it, and reached down to turn the knob.

Gretchen Sabatini, my old secretary, confidant, gal Friday—and one-time fiancée—glanced up as I stepped through the doorway. She looked exactly as I remembered: shoulder-length auburn hair, lightly freckled skin, and gorgeous cornflower-blue eyes, which, seen without makeup, looked touchingly like those of a young child. As always, she was dressed in black—a designer pantsuit that accentuated her narrow waist.

She jumped from behind her desk and ran to embrace me. "Why didn't you call?" she nearly wailed into my ear. Then, in a panicked undertone, as if she had said something she shouldn't: "Did you hear?"

I pulled her closer to my chest. "Yes. Kittredge saw to that."

"I heard on the radio. Kittredge phoned, but I couldn't bring

9

myself to answer. I haven't even listened to his message." She paused. "Did you see Chris?"

"Yeah, the lieutenant did me a favor—if you can call it that. He brought me to the scene before they took the body away."

I felt her tense in my arms. "How was he? I mean—"

"I know what you mean. He wouldn't have suffered. It was quick. He may not have known it was happening."

She took hold of my arms above the elbows and gently pushed me away. Twin rivulets of mascara streaked her cheeks. "But why was he there? It doesn't make any sense."

I shook my head. "I was hoping you'd have some clue."

She sniffed and reached for the tissue box on her desk. "I don't," she said, as she dabbed her eyes. She threaded a lock of hair around an ear and stared at me solemnly. "You look tired, August."

I took that to mean "You look old, August." The five years since I'd seen Gretchen had been rough ones—for me, at least. "Well, 2 a.m. play dates with the cops can take it out of you."

"You also smell—of booze *and* BO."

"I'm blaming Chris for that."

"Don't you dare—"

I held up my hands. "Hold on. It's not what you think. He redid everything in the apartment, including the bathroom. He's got some flossy European shower fixture in there. I couldn't figure how to get hot water out of it, so I did what I could with a washcloth at the sink."

She smirked and shook her head, and for the first time, it felt like it used to between us. "At least you managed to get inside the building."

The building had been switched to a keyless entry system. Gretchen had supplied the codes for the lobby door and the apartment when she called me in Palm Springs, but the truth of the matter was I'd had to throw myself on the mercy of the building super when I arrived.

"Not a problem," I lied. "But speaking of remodeling, look at this place." The suite had been gone over from stem to stern. It was lighter, brighter, and hopelessly mod. "And where's Bonacker? Not in the private office with Chris?"

Gretchen slipped behind her chromium-and-glass desk and settled into her Aeron chair. She gestured for me to take the one in front of her desk. "Bonacker retired. It's just been Chris and I the last three years."

Ben Bonacker was the buffoon of an insurance agent I'd shared the space with. He told terrible jokes and hectored my clients with pitches for whole life, but having him in the office reduced my overhead considerably. "How did Chris cover the rent without him? And what about you? Most of the secretarial work came from Bonacker."

"I wasn't Chris's secretary."

"Sorry. Administrative assistant."

"I wasn't that either. I was a full partner."

"A full partner in Duckworth Investigative Solutions?"

She nodded. "Chris wasn't doing the kind of work you did, August. Most of his cases involved computers—cybersecurity, identity theft, and online reputation. He trained me to help him, and we rarely left the office. Keyboard and phone replaced shoe leather and muscle. And it was a lot more lucrative. The rent wasn't a problem."

I put my elbow on the ergonomic armrest of the Aeron chair and dropped my chin into my palm. To me, Chris had always been an overenthusiastic amateur. Half the assignments I gave him were simply to get him out of my hair. The idea that I was living in exile in the desert while he outearned and outclassed me in my own town was hard to swallow. "Why'd you call me, then? Why didn't you just sit behind your keyboard and cyber-google him back when he went missing?"

Gretchen didn't waste any time responding. She threw the box of tissues straight at my head. "*You* were the one who abandoned us—who left without a word. Whatever it was that drove you away, it had more to do with *your* demons than us. But we adapted. We learned what we were good at and made it the focus of the business. It wasn't about showing you up. It was about getting on with *life*."

I rubbed the place on my forehead where the corner of the tissue box had hit. "I deserved that."

"And more." She sat forward and clutched both her knees through the silky fabric of her pantsuit. "I don't know what happened to Chris. But when you discover the details, when you find out how he came to be shot execution-style in a massage parlor in the middle of the night, I know it will be because of the things that made him what he was—his enthusiasm and love of adventure."

She released her knees and looked up at me. "And when you do solve the mystery, when you catch and punish Chris's killer, I know it will be because of the things that make *you* what *you* are—your loyalty and your relentless focus on finding answers."

I held her eyes for a moment. It was the nicest thing she'd ever said to me, so naturally I had to ruin it. "Not my youthful looks and pleasant odor?"

She laughed. "Maybe if you learn to work the shower faucet."

I shifted in my chair, somehow failing to find the webbed back and lack of upholstery to be all that comfortable. "Well, what can you tell me, then? Was he working a case that was less virtual and more dangerous back alley?"

"No, he wasn't. He wasn't working on anything as far as I knew. We finished a case a few weeks ago, and he said he wanted to take some time off. He stayed out longer than I expected, and when I tried to contact him to ask why, I struck out. All my phone calls when to voice mail, and he wasn't at his apartment any of the times I went there."

"Why'd he move from the Castro, anyway? Moving into the office I can see because you were here and it went with the business. But my old apartment is nothing special. It's in a worse part of town far away from the neighborhood he loved."

"He claimed that he did it because of the commute, but that wasn't the real reason. You were his model, August, his hero. By slipping into your old life as completely as he could, he felt like he was donning your mantle."

"Christ, I wasn't Batman. I don't know whether to be flattered or weirded out."

"Some of both, I expect."

"All right. What about the last case you worked? Anything about it that could have blown back on Chris or the firm? A disgruntled client, for instance?"

She pushed a manila folder across the desk toward me. "I figured you were going to ask, so I printed out the file. To answer your question, no, the client was happy with the resolution, and I really doubt she would be the sort to kill anyone, much less Chris."

I reached over to snag the file and started flipping through the pages. The client was a coed at UC-Berkeley, and the assignment had to do with determining the identity of someone she met on a website called Looking for Daddy. "Is this site what I think it is?"

"What do you think it is?"

"A service to reunite adopted children with their biological fathers?"

"Please. It's a sugar-daddy site. It matches wealthy older men with so-called sugar babies who want an arrangement."

"Wealthy older *married* men?"

"Usually, but not always. In this case, the person our client was talking to was married."

"Did she hire you to find that out?"

"Not really. The daddy acknowledged he was married in his profile. Our client—Ivy is her name—wanted to know more about his background and personality before getting involved with him. The site doesn't use real names, of course, so finding the real-world identify of someone involves reverse-engineering it from the details they do reveal."

"Huh." I slumped back in my chair. What Gretchen had suggested earlier was right: I was a dinosaur from another era. I wouldn't know the first thing about using the internet to find out that sort of thing. "The file says you identified him. May I ask how?"

"Chris figured it out. Daddy had a picture posted on his profile."

"You pretty much have to, don't you? How do you go from a random picture to a name?"

"He made the mistake of using a picture he had posted on social media before. One that he thought made him look athletic, I guess. Chris used an image-search program to find the photo on the guy's page, then we had his name and a bunch of other stuff about him from his account."

It was exactly the sort of clever trick Chris would come up with. In spite of myself, I felt a little sympathy for the daddy. He wasn't the only one out of his league. "What did Ivy do with the information?"

"I don't know. We gave her the report and she seemed happy, but she didn't say if she was going to pursue the relationship."

"So it's possible she cut him off, daddy somehow found out that Chris was involved, and then he went looking for revenge."

Gretchen made a face. "I suppose. But listening to you lay it out like that, it seems pretty far-fetched. The ratio of women to men on these sites is three to one. I think daddy would have just moved on."

I closed the folder and set it back on the desk. "You're probably right, but I'm going to look into it anyway. What about other cases? Any others stand out as having a possible connection?"

"I've started a search. I'm looking for anyone who complained about an outcome, failed to pay their bill or was involved with anything criminal."

"Sounds about right. Can I help you dig through the files?"

She smiled. "You could, except Chris moved everything to the computer…"

"And I'm a Luddite." I stood abruptly, sending the chair wheeling backward. "Okay, how about tossing his office for clues? That's something we old-school detectives can really sink our teeth into."

"I don't think you'll find it much of a meal."

"What do you mean?"

"I'll show you." She retrieved some keys from her desk drawer and used them on the door leading to the suite's private office— my old office. I had filled the space with furniture I bought at an auction when a grade school burned down and hung a couple of black-and-white photos of my favorite jazz bassists on the walls. All of that was gone. In its stead was a motorized standing desk, a motorized treadmill to walk on while you worked at the motorized standing desk, a sleek laptop connected to an enormous monitor, and several pop art prints by the guy who painted in a comic-book style. The famous one of a fighter pilot shooting down another plane with WHAM! written in bright yellow next to the exploding plane was behind the desk.

"That's it?"

"That's it."

I walked over to the computer and ran my finger over the trackpad. A password screen flashed up. "You'll include his computer in your search?"

Gretchen nodded.

I sighed and stepped onto the treadmill. If you weren't expending shoe leather the old-fashioned way, I guess you needed another way to do it during your virtual investigations. I glanced back up at the colorful prints. "What's with all the pop art? His apartment is full of it, too."

"It wasn't just pop art. He was on a whole sixties kick. He spent nearly every weekend shopping in retro clothing stores."

"Men's or women's clothes?"

Gretchen laughed. "Both. But he looked better in the miniskirts than he did in the bell-bottoms."

I looked over at her and thought about what she had said about Chris's enthusiasm for life. We both teared up again, and I stepped off the treadmill to wrap her in another hug. "Relentless," I said softly.

3
SUGAR BABY

It's hard to be relentless when you are hungover. As much as my heart wanted to jump immediately into the search for Chris's killer, my splitting head and the rest of my sleep-deprived body were more interested in getting horizontal. I went back to the Post Street apartment, washed down four aspirin with some "oxygenated alkaline" water I found in Chris's refrigerator, and crashed on the couch.

It was three-thirty when I woke up. My head still throbbed, and my mouth had taken on the piquant flavor of penny loafers worn without socks, but at least I felt strong enough to re-engage with the world. I tormented the shower fixture into producing some hot water and used Chris's equally complicated electric toothbrush—with a new brush head I found under the sink—to eliminate most of the taste of worn loafer. I changed into the last clean shirt and underwear I had brought from Palm Springs and threw on my suit. Saint George was ready to do battle, but where was the dragon?

The only real leads I had were Ivy, the UC-Berkeley coed, and her would-be sugar daddy, a guy named Nate Schlein. I paged through the file Gretchen had given me until I found Ivy's number. My call immediately went to voice mail. I left a long, carefully worded message that I rerecorded several times to get just the right tone of urgency without mentioning Chris's murder and hung up. I was paging through the file again to find the contact information for Schlein when my phone buzzed with a text message. It was from Ivy's number.

who r u?

I was all thumbs—or no thumbs—when it came to texting, but there didn't seem to be any way to avoid it.

August Riordan. I left a voicemail to explain why I'm calling.

This led to an exchange with much backspacing and cursing on my part, and judging from the speed of her responses, no effort at all on hers.

Ivy: no one uses vm. is this nate? how did u get this number?
Riordan: No, it's August Riordan. I'm from Duckworth Investigative Solutions. We need to talk about your case.
Ivy: bioya. ur nate
Riordan: Bioya? What?
Ivy: blow it out your ass, om
Riordan: Look, I'm not Nate. I'm really from DIS. Om?
Ivy: old man. prove it
Riordan: You worked with Chris Duckworth. He identified Nate Schlein through an image search.
Ivy: cld b
Riordan: If Schlein is still bothering you, we definitely need to talk. My vm has more.
Ivy: hmm. why didn't chris call
Riordan: He only does computer investigations. I do the other stuff.
Ivy: If u r trying to get me to pay more, forget it
Riordan: No, no charge.

Ivy: k. lmirl. can u come to berkeley?

Riordan: Yes, where and when? Lmirl?

Ivy: let's meet in real life. u really r an om. Starbucks on Oxford at 5:30

Riordan: Okay, I'll be there.

Ivy: sus

Oxford Street was the western border of the UC campus. The Starbucks was probably across the street from one of the entrances. I wasn't entirely sure Ivy intended to meet me, but I knew I wasn't going to get any further with texting or calling. Worst case, I figured I could stake out the Berkeley address in her file if she stood me up.

Driving to Berkeley was out of the question. I had left my car in Palm Springs, and creeping across the Bay Bridge in a taxi would cost a bundle in heavy traffic. I hoofed it down to the Powell Street BART station and caught a ride on a train heading under the Bay via the Transbay Tube.

There's a 1972 newspaper photo of Pat and Richard Nixon riding BART just after the system opened. Back then, the subway was shiny and futuristic, and Nixon was so impressed that he compared the BART control room to NASA's Mission Control. Now, the cars looked like an abandoned Disney attraction from Tomorrowland. I sat on a seat with the same snot-green upholstery Pat and Dick admired in 1972, sandwiched between a dozing homeless man and a hipster standing in the aisle with a folded electric scooter.

The scooter dude mistook my desire to avoid being impaled by the scooter's handles with a genuine interest in his toy. "Kickstarter project," he said. "Goes thirty miles on a charge."

"That's nice." I pointed down the aisle. "Can it go two feet that way and get the hell out of my face?"

He grumbled something and moved away.

I got off the train at the Downtown Berkeley station and rode the escalator to a street-level entrance that looked like a gigantic Slinky frozen in midslink. Topside, it was hard to forget you were in a college town. Millennials in hoodies with book bags were everywhere, as were canvassers for the environment, LGBTQ rights, marijuana laws, and an old guy balanced precariously on a bucket yelling, "Happy, happy, happy" while holding a poster with tiny print that said something about American imperialism.

I went up Center Street toward Oxford and quickly located the Starbucks on the corner. I was running about ten minutes late and was worried that Ivy had bailed when she hadn't found me— if she had even shown up in the first place. Stepping through the door didn't make me worry any less. It was wall-to-wall millennials with their shiny aluminum laptops open. Many were Asian and well over half were female. I stood self-consciously by the door, try-ing to make eye contact with young women less than half my age who were not the least bit interested in having contact made.

Finally, I heard a half-chortle by my left elbow. I twisted to find an Asian girl with shoulder-length black hair in a 1960s flip sitting at a two-spot table. "You're not going to find any sugar babies dressed like that," she said, and laughed.

I pulled out the chair across from her and sat down. "I thought the wallet was more important than the wardrobe."

She took a sip from her orange juice and tilted her head back to look at me through her lashes. "Well, as my econ professor says, for some markets there are table stakes. Nice clothes are table stakes for sugar daddies."

I lifted the lapels of my jacket. "It's a suit. How much nicer do you want?"

She shifted her legs to one side, and I saw that she was wearing some sort of workout skirt made of synthetic material. Sneakers and a nylon bomber jacket completed her ensemble. It dawned on me then that she wasn't what I was expecting. She was clearly smarter than a wannabe Mrs. Donald Trump, and even with all the talk about clothes, she wasn't obsessed about her appearance.

"You really want to know?" she asked.

"Sure."

"It's both too nice and not nice enough. It's too nice in the sense that it's almost an anachronism. No one wears suits these days except investment bankers."

"And what makes you an expert on investment bankers?"

"I interned at Goldman Sachs in Hong Kong last summer, and I have an offer to join the firm after graduation. I saw plenty of suits there. Where I don't see them is in the Bay Area."

"Okay."

"And I don't intend to be mean, but your suit needs updating. It's cheaply made, it's way out of style, and it doesn't even fit you. It's much too tight across the shoulders."

I felt heat rising in my cheeks. It's hard to be lectured about your clothes by someone who is younger than you are. "You make some good points," I managed to concede.

She tilted her head back again and gave me a playful look. "You did ask."

"I did—I surely did."

"I find Americans—at least ones my age—are too sensitive. They are used to praise and affirmation, and when they get honest criticism, they are quick to take offense."

"And you are from…"

"China—Hong Kong."

"And your parents raised you differently?"

"Definitely. I have a *tiger* mom." She emphasized the word tiger with a mock pounding of her fist on the table. "Just today she told me I was getting too fat."

"I see. How would your tiger mom feel if she knew you had enrolled in a sugar-daddy site?"

"How do you know I didn't already tell her?"

"Did you?"

"No. But if I found a boyfriend through the site, she would be happy to hear it. Not having one is another thing she criticizes me for."

"Wait a minute, you were using the site to find dates? I thought you were trying to find an arrangement to make money."

"I don't need money. My parents are well-off, and I got a good offer from Goldman."

"But most of the men on the site are already married—and they are much older. Why not date someone from school? Or use one of those apps I keep reading about?"

She looked down at her orange juice and took a tentative sip. When she looked up, she said, "Did you have trouble finding me here?"

"Well, sure. I didn't know what you looked like, and there are a lot of girls..."

"That's right—there are a lot of girls in college now. More girls than boys. And at Berkeley, there are a lot of Asian girls. It's hard to find a boyfriend. I signed up on Looking for Daddy to find someone nice to be with. I knew I was going back to Hong Kong at the end of the year, so I didn't expect to get married. I just wanted..."

"A short-term relationship."

"Yes, a short-term relationship." She nodded cheerfully, as if I'd helped her come up with a word for a crossword puzzle, but there was a sadness behind her eyes.

I softened my tone. "So you hired us to help you make sure the person you found was nice."

"Yes. You can tell right away that most of the daddies are assholes. Nate's profile seemed nicer, but I didn't want to get too involved until I knew more about him. Once a daddy begins spending money on you, they have pretty definite expectations."

"I can imagine."

A barista shouted an order behind me while another pounded a filter holder to clear it of coffee grinds. Ivy glanced over my shoulder, then back at me. "I called your office," she said abruptly.

"You did?"

"To make sure you were really who you said you were."

"I understand."

"I spoke to Gretchen. She explained that you were the one who started the business, but even after talking to her and listening to your voice mail, I still don't see why you want to talk. Has Nate done something?"

I chewed my lower lip. I didn't want to lie to the girl, but I didn't want to explain what happened to Chris until I'd heard an unbiased version of her story. "Humor me for a minute, will you? Let me ask you a few more questions and then I'll give you the full background. Okay?"

She nodded.

"Nate seemed nice," I said, "but you wanted more information, so you hired us to find out more about him. We discovered his full name and a few other details and passed on the information. What happened then?"

"I googled him, of course. He has an MBA from Stan*furd*, a wife, and two sons, and is CEO of a start-up in San Francisco. The bio on his company website mentioned that he was a varsity swimmer in college and that he could do sixty push-ups in one minute."

"I'll bet he dressed well, too."

She slid me a grin. "Oh, yes, the standard daddy uniform: gray wool dress pants with a crisp pastel dress shirt—sleeves carefully rolled to three-quarters length. Sport coat and Rolex optional."

"I'll note that for future reference. Did you bite?"

"Bite?"

"Did you decide to see him?"

"Yes, we met for dinner at the Tonga Room at the Fairmont hotel. I guess he thought I would like it since I'm Asian. It seemed to go well—at first. He looked like his pictures and could carry on a conversation although he talked mostly about himself. He told me about his company and his plan to climb Everest next year. He showed me a video of his sixty push-ups, which sounds bad, but he made a joke about it. I laughed. Eventually, he mentioned he had a condo I could live in. I said I wasn't ready to discuss arrangements yet, but I don't think he realized I wasn't interested in the condo at all. He thought I was negotiating for something better."

"He still saw it as a transaction?"

"Yes, I guess I can't blame him. I found it hard to talk about what I really wanted. After dinner, he told me he'd gotten a room at the hotel, and would I like to go upstairs to have a little champagne?"

"Wait, are you even old enough to drink?"

"Sure, I'm twenty-two."

"I guess the drinking's not the point. Should I ask what happened next?"

She shifted in her chair and brought her hands down into her lap. "I was hesitant at first, but he promised no pressure for anything else. To tell the truth, I was enjoying the attention, and while he isn't that attractive, he *is* athletic. I was maybe even looking forward to the something else. Anyway, we went to the room and had some champagne. We started kissing and it was nice." She looked away and lowered her voice. "But then he unzipped his pants and pushed my head into his crotch. He forced me to give him oral sex."

I wasn't surprised, but I was angry. "Privileged little shit," I said louder than I intended. "I'm sorry, Ivy."

She pressed her lips together in a thin bloodless line. "It was my own fault," she nearly whispered. "I was stupid."

She did seem a curious mixture of worldliness and naiveté, but I felt guilt by association because of my sex. The fact that we had been joking earlier about what it took to be a daddy somehow made it worse. "You know it's not your fault. What he did was a crime, plain and simple. Did you report it to the police?"

"How could I, given the circumstances? I don't think he even understood I was upset. Later, when I didn't return his texts and emails, he knew something was wrong—but he still thought it was a negotiating ploy."

"Did he try to see you? Come to your home?"

"He couldn't. I never actually told him my real name or where I lived. Even the phone I used to talk to him was a cheap prepaid. He didn't have my regular number."

"Did you happen to tell Chris what happened?"

She frowned. "Why don't you ask him?"

"Humor me a little longer. I'll explain in a moment."

"I mentioned it to Chris. When we met to discuss the results of the investigation, we got to talking about fashion and became Snapchat friends. He also told me about Marlo Thomas."

"Marlo Thomas?"

"*That Girl.* He sent me a picture of her hairdo from the TV show and said it would be perfect for me." She held her hand up to her hair.

"He's right. It suits you perfectly. What did Chris say when you told him? Was he going to talk to Schlein?"

"No, I made him promise not to." A beat went by. "Something's happened to Chris, hasn't it?"

I nodded slowly. "He was killed."

"You think Nate was involved?"

"I don't know, but based on what you told me, I'm going to see him."

She drew herself up in her chair. The flirty, jovial girl I met a few minutes ago was gone. "You know what my tiger mom would say?"

"What?"

"Castrate him. Castrate him if he's guilty."

4
SUGAR DADDY

Nate Schlein's start-up was in an old bank building on Montgomery Street. An orangutan in a spacesuit adorned the double glass doors of the entrance, and the tagline KEEP YOUR APIs PROTECTED IN CYBERSPACE was stenciled across its bubble-shaped helmet.

What to name a company with a mascot like that? Monkey Suit, of course. The name loomed above the doors in garish orange letters.

I was there at nine-thirty the next morning, feeling about as human as I had since I'd arrived in San Francisco—simian motif notwithstanding. I credited my improvement to skipping further in-flask conferences with Old Grand-Dad and my decision to move from the couch to the Murphy bed in the Post Street apartment (after replacing Chris's periwinkle satin sheets with the plainest ones I could find).

I went through the doors and walked up to an orange Formica reception desk. Behind the desk sat a stunning blonde wearing a clingy dress with a deep V-neck. She gave me a smile that landed like a jolt from a cardiac paddle, and I thought—perhaps unfairly—that she would be the more obvious sugar baby for Schlein.

"May I help you?" she asked.

"I sure hope so," I said. "I have some APIs that need protecting."

She looked at me in mock appraisal. "Don't take this the wrong way, but you don't seem like the sort of man who would have APIs."

"Why not?"

"Do you know what API stands for?"

"Well..."

"Application programming interface. So, in order to have an API, you'd need to have a computer program with a defined interface. Do you have a computer program with a defined interface?"

"Not exactly, but—"

"Please. No lines about interfaces, interfacing, or exchanging of phone numbers. I've heard it all before."

I was two for two on underestimating young women. "Of course not." I cleared my throat. "Actually, I'm here to see Mr. Schlein."

"Do you have an appointment?"

She'd been running rings around me up to this point, but the question was a bit of a tactical error on her part. It suggested that Schlein was in the building and possibly unoccupied. "No, but I believe he'll want to see me."

"May I have your name and the company you're with?"

"August Riordan with...August Riordan."

"Fine. I'll ask his admin if he's available."

"Thank you." I hovered over the edge of the desk, expecting her to pick up the phone.

"I'll ask his admin via instant messenger," she said with some asperity. "She may not respond immediately. Why don't you have a seat?"

I traipsed over to a rocket couch situated by a glass coffee table. I sorted my fingers for several minutes, then the receptionist slipped out from behind the desk and strutted over on black pointy-toed pumps.

"I'm sorry, Mr. Riordan. Mr. Schlein is busy. This is his admin's name and number if you'd like to call to schedule an appointment."

She held out a Post-it with the information scribbled on it.

"That's okay. I'll wait until he's available."

"You don't seem to"—she paused—"he's got a full calendar today. It's very unlikely he'll have any time."

"Thirty minutes," I said, smiling as sweetly as I could. "I'll just hang for thirty minutes, and if he doesn't free up, I'll follow your suggestion."

Now she knew I was delusional. "Why, yes, of course. If that's what you prefer." She passed me the Post-it and returned to her desk.

What she didn't realize was that I had a secret dog whistle for calling Schlein. The whole pantomime had been to establish that he was in the office to respond to it. I rolled onto my left hip to extract the prepaid phone Ivy had given me—the one she had used to talk with him. I brought up the messaging app and went to work, feeling inordinately pleased that I remembered to abbreviate "your."

hey daddy, i'm in ur office lobby right now. how about some sugar?

I didn't have long to wait. About five minutes later, a door behind the reception desk cracked open and a man stuck his head through. He was balding with big ears, a big nose, and eyebrows that desperately wanted to come together, thwarted only by some serious plucking. What hair he did have was dark brown with gray tendrils sprouting at the temples. He scowled when he caught sight of me and thrust his athletic frame all the way through the door.

I stood and met him a few feet from the reception desk.

"Who the fuck are you?" he growled, his face inches from mine.

He was my height—about six feet one—but trimmer, and he was dressed exactly the way Ivy had predicted: gray slacks and a mauve shirt with the sleeves carefully rolled up. I put him in his midforties.

"Your conscience?" I suggested.

"Since when does my conscience look like an unemployed strip club bouncer?"

"Since you started raping little girls?"

"Shut up."

I made a point of glancing over at the receptionist, who was staring at us wide-eyed. "Sorry. Should I have said date-raping?"

Schlein gave me a two-handed shove. "Get the hell out of here."

"How about I meet with your wife instead? Let her check out some of these text messages? I'm not a particular connoisseur of dick pics, but you do have a flair for them."

He stared down at the phone in my hands, itching to make a grab for it. "Come back to my office," he said through clenched teeth. "We can talk there."

"There's an idea."

He led me back through the door behind the receptionist's desk and down a short corridor to another closed door. He pulled it open and stepped through, not bothering to hold it for me. I had barely crossed the threshold when he rounded on me, swinging for my head with a right hook.

I was half expecting something like that and managed to partially block the punch with my forearm. He still connected with my left eye, knocking me into the door. We held an awkward tableau for a beat, then I lunged forward to take hold of his shirt and drove him over an ottoman onto the overstuffed leather couch that divided the office. Ivy's phone went flying. We butted foreheads as we landed, my elbows forcing the wind out of him.

It took every ounce of self-restraint I had not to beat him unconscious—or worse. Instead, I concentrated on pummeling his ribs and midsection until my hands were sore.

"Enough, please," he gasped.

I levered myself off the couch and stood tottering over him, sweat and saliva dripping. I was getting too old for this. "Fucker," I spat, and stumbled over to pick up the phone. As I dropped it into my suit coat pocket, I realized the seam in the back had split, leaving the sleeves to dangle well past my wrists. I shrugged them up as best I could.

"What do you want?" asked Schlein.

"Answers to start. Where were you the night before last?"

He said something too soft to hear.

I trudged back to the couch. His face had gone bone white, and fat beads of sweat popped from his forehead and bald pate like warts. His breath came in shallow pants. "Again."

"New York. Business trip."

"Can you prove it?"

"I gave a talk at a conference."

"But you know Chris Duckworth."

He swallowed. "Yeah."

"How?"

"He came here like you, asking about May." May was the fake name Ivy had used on the sugar-daddy site.

"You mean he accused you of sexually assaulting her and told you to leave her alone."

"Something like that."

"You sucker punched him like you did me, didn't you?"

His eyes slid past me to the ceiling. "What May and I did was consensual. I wasn't going to be blackmailed, especially by a little fairy like that."

"Yeah, I heard you are the push-up king. I bet all that training came in handy beating up on someone you outweighed by a hundred pounds."

"Just say your piece and go. I'm not paying, no matter how many guys May sends."

I reached down to take him by the shirt again and pulled him upright. He flinched as the jostling aggravated his bruised ribs.

"Listen carefully, then. It's a three-parter. First and most important, Chris Duckworth was murdered the day before yesterday. If I find that you were not in New York, or that you hired someone to kill him, you won't need to worry about blackmail. Dead men don't pay blackmail. Second, leave May alone. Completely. No more phone calls, emails, text messages, or dick pictures or that phone goes straight to your wife along with a full account of what happened at the Fairmont. Third, before you call someone a fairy, you better learn to take a punch—fairy." I shoved him back down.

I went out of the office, down the short hallway, and out into the lobby. I walked past the receptionist with as much dignity as a man can have with the back of his suit hanging open and pushed through the door out onto Montgomery Street. My phone rang before I made it half a block.

Gretchen's name came up on the display. "I hope you've got good news," I said, "because I sure don't."

"I've got interesting news."

"Let's have it."

"Kittredge called with the preliminary autopsy results. I'll tell you more when I see you, but there's one thing you ought to hear now. It looks like Chris had been in a fight several days before he died. He had an obvious black eye. Kittredge said you couldn't see it at the massage parlor because Chris was lying facedown."

I brought a finger up to my own bruised eye. "Okay, I just reenacted the fight, but I don't think it's related. Anything else?"

"Yes. Chris's last client stopped by."

"You mean Ivy?"

"No, I don't. That's what's interesting."

5
ANGELINA

Gretchen had invited the mysterious "last client" to return at two, so I used the time before the meeting to deal with my wardrobe malfunction. I decided Ivy was right: The suit had to go. I paid a visit to the local Banana Republic where I bought two pairs of gray slacks, six dress shirts in various hues of blue, and a navy blazer. My intuition was that my wing tips were so old that they were back in style again, but intense lobbying from the stick-thin salesman with a whitewall haircut and black square-rimmed glasses convinced me otherwise. I ended up with a pair of pointy ankle boots that looked like standard issue for Robin's Merry Men. The salesman confided that he had a pair just like them at home—which only made it worse.

I made a quick trip to the Post Street apartment to change into my new duds and inhale an All Natural Lemongrass Coconut Tempeh TV dinner I found in the freezer. Then I hoofed it back to the headquarters of Duckworth Investigative Services.

Gretchen was at her desk with another woman when I arrived. Both were smiling, and I'd heard laughter from the hallway before I opened the door. They seemed to be having a grand old time.

"Nice shiner," said Gretchen.

"Thank you, I guess."

The other woman pushed her chair away from the desk to take me in. "Nice shoes," she chimed in.

"Now you're being cruel."

"No, I mean it. They're cool."

I put her in her early thirties. She had large expressive eyes, an impish smile, and dark black hair with blue highlights cut in a layered style with sweeping bangs that I was sure had a name like "Dead Poet Shag." A gleaming silver stud protruded a short way below her lower lip. She was wearing a black leotard beneath a navy zip-up hoodie and a jean skirt. The skirt had a wide leather belt with a skull-and-cross-bones buckle. In spite of the garb and edgy haircut, she was a very attractive woman.

"At the risk of provoking further personal comments, what were you two laughing about?"

"Angelina was just sharing a story about Chris," said Gretchen.

Angelina stood and extended her hand. "A clever, funny story," she emphasized, assuming a more serious expression. "Good to meet you, and I hope you'll accept my condolences for your loss. Chris seemed like a wonderful person."

I took her hand, which was cool and soft to the touch. "He was. August Riordan, by the way."

"Yes, Gretchen told me."

I found myself gawking at her big blue-gray eyes. They were limpid and depthless.

"Don't just stand there," snapped Gretchen. "Pull up a chair and join us."

I wheeled another of the Aeron office chairs from the corner and settled in next to Angelina. "So what's the story?"

"It's actually a story Chris told me," said Angelina. "One day last week after I hired him, he asked to meet at my hotel."

"Sorry to interrupt. You're from out of town, then?"

"Yes, from Vancouver—Vancouver, BC. As I said, we agreed to meet at my hotel. I was sitting at the bar in the lobby, and when Chris came in, I noticed he had a shiner like yours, so I asked him about it. He told me he had gotten it trying to help a female client who was being harassed by a married man. He said talking to the man directly hadn't worked so he'd come up with a different strategy. He reminded me that he sometimes cross-dressed—"

"Oh, no," I said. "He didn't hit on the married guy in drag, did he?" Chris had been eerily convincing as a woman and performed as a torch singer, doing jazz standards and show tunes in clubs. I'd often accompanied him on bass before I moved to Palm Springs.

"No, something more fiendish. He discovered that the guy's wife spends most of her days at the San Francisco Tennis Club. He dressed—to use his terms—as a 'red-hot tennis bimbo,' covered the black eye with a pair of wraparound shades and managed to bump into her at the cabana bar. After a few martinis, he steered the conversation to men and sex. He intimated that he'd been having an affair with a married man and managed to drop enough hints that the wife finally realized that he was talking about her husband. He said she looked like she had swallowed the olive pick from her martini. Then he told her that the husband had passed on an STD, and she just about slapped him."

I let out a little gasp of surprise and looked over at Gretchen. She smiled and shook her head. "Vintage Chris."

"Yes, vintage." But it was vintage for more than one reason: the first, of course, was the clever idea and its execution; the other was the fact that Chris had bragged about it to a near stranger— and client. From what I'd seen of Angelina and her reaction to the story, Chris's confidence seemed to have been well received, but others might regard it as feckless and unprofessional. I was worried that it was an example of the sort of behavior that might have gotten him into trouble.

I brought a finger up to my bruised eye. "Well, judging from to-day's conversation with the gentleman in question, I don't think the missus has tipped her hand regarding her newfound knowledge."

"Probably shopping for divorce lawyers," said Gretchen.

"Let's hope so," I said, and turned back to Angelina. "So you hired Chris—but not through the office, apparently. Gretchen has no record of the case in the files."

"That's right. I have a friend who also cross-dresses, and he met Chris on one of the CD subreddits. Eventually, they exchanged emails and they got to know each other better."

"Okay…"

Gretchen saved me. "Reddit is kind of like a bulletin board for the internet. Discussions on different topics are partitioned into areas called subreddits. There's probably one for just about any interest or hobby you can imagine—and some you can't. We end up using it quite a bit for our investigations."

That made me feel a little bit better about Chris sharing the story about the Schleins. At least Angelina already knew he was a cross-dresser. "All right, I get it. You found out from your friend that Chris was a detective and you contacted him directly. Can you tell us what you hired him for?"

Angelina scooted her chair a little closer. "Of course. I feel terrible about what happened. I hope his death didn't have anything to do with the assignment, but I want to do whatever I can to help. I was trying to find my sister—half sister, actually. She's older than I am and we share the same father, but I hardly had any contact with her growing up. I'd heard she'd moved to San Francisco, but all the obvious things I tried—googling, searching Facebook—came up empty."

"What prompted you to seek her out now?"

Angelina looked down to trace one of the bones on her buckle. "My father—our father—divorced my mother when I was ten. Soon after, he was killed in an automobile accident. My mother died recently of breast cancer. I was her only child, and she never remarried. I guess I felt orphaned. Maybe it's silly at my age, but I thought reconnecting with Corinne would make me feel part of a family again."

"That's not silly at all," said Gretchen.

The building's ancient heating kicked in with a groan and a

muffled bang in the ceiling's ductwork. Dusty air chuffed from the register behind Gretchen's desk. "Not at all," I said, in what sounded like an overly earnest tone.

Angelina looked up, her eyes shining with moisture. "Anyway, I emailed Chris and eventually spoke to him on Skype. I explained I had some vacation coming and that I intended to take it in San Francisco. I asked him to help me look for my sister. He was reluctant at first—he'd already tried a cursory search online after my initial contact—and he felt that it was a job for what he called a 'meat-eating dinosaur PI.'"

Gretchen snorted, covering her mouth as she glanced over at me. Angelina caught the exchange. "Fortunately—or unfortunately," I said, "we are all very *evolved* in this room. But apparently Chris agreed to take your case in the end."

"Yes, he did."

"Give me the full timeline, then. When you arrived, when you met Chris, and what he did."

"I arrived last Tuesday and met with Chris at my hotel that same day. I shared a little file I'd prepared on Corinne and answered all the questions he had for me. We met a second time at the hotel on Thursday—when he told me the cross-dressing story—and he gave me an update."

"Which was?"

"He'd made some progress. One of the few things I knew about Corinne was that she had a degree in architecture. He had gone around to a number of architecture firms and eventually found one where she had worked ten years ago. He learned that she had gotten married and changed her last name, and that she had left the firm when she had gotten pregnant. Unfortunately, no one there knew anything about where she was now."

"But didn't Chris do new searches against her married name?" asked Gretchen.

"He'd started. He found some possible hits but nothing definitive."

"What happened next?" I asked.

"Nothing. I never heard from him again. I tried to contact him, of course, but he didn't respond to my texts or emails. Yesterday I saw an article about his death in the local paper. I found the address for your office, and I came in to see Gretchen this morning."

"So he never said anything about a connection to Golden Fingers, the massage parlor where he was found?"

Angelina bent her lips down, causing the stud beneath her mouth to protrude even more. She shook her head. "No, nothing about that. I'm very open-minded, but I can't imagine my older sister the architect having anything to do with a place like that."

"No, I suppose not." I rubbed the side of my neck. The new shirt, which I hadn't bothered to wash, was chafing like hell. "Look. Gretchen and I want to find out what happened to our friend. It could be completely unrelated, but all we have to go on is the thing he was working on when he died—the search for your sister. If you don't mind, we'd like to pick up the thread again, retracing the steps we know about, and possibly uncovering ones he took after he met with you the final time. Who knows, we may even locate your sister, although I can't promise that."

"Absolutely. Anything I can do to help. As I said earlier, I really hope the search and his murder had nothing to do with each other. I would feel horrible if I knew I was responsible for sending him out on an assignment that led to his death, even indirectly."

"There's no need to feel responsible," said Gretchen. "Even though we're not set up for finding missing persons, there's nothing inherently dangerous in that."

I wasn't sure I agreed, but I didn't want to lay a guilt trip on Angelina. "True. And thank you. We appreciate it. Just a few more questions. What was your sister's maiden name?"

"Evangelista, same as mine. Our father was Italian."

"So you are Angelina Evangelista? Great rapper name."

"Tell me about it. I was teased mercilessly in grade school."

"And your sister's married name—the one Chris discovered at

the architecture firm?"

"Not nearly as hip-hop—White. Corinne White. That may be why Chris was having trouble finding her with the second set of searches."

"Okay. How about the name of the architecture firm?"

"Hillesland, Hillesland, and Cheilek."

"That sounds more like a polka band. And you mentioned a file you gave Chris. Could we get a copy?"

The polka band comment earned me a smothered grin. "I'll email it," she said, nodding herself back to a straight face. "It's not much—old photos, some information on her mother and our father, and a few internet references I found for her in Canada before she moved to the States."

"Did she become a U.S. citizen?"

"At least by the time she worked at the architecture firm, according to Chris."

"Thank you. This is all very helpful."

We exchanged contact information and stood to say good-bye. I walked her to the door. When she was halfway through it, she turned to offer her hand a final time.

"The shoes really *are* cool. And so are you—for a meat-eating dinosaur."

Those big eyes of hers made me feel like a butterfly pinned to a cork board. "You, too," I mumbled.

6
THE LATE SHIFT

After I closed the door and heard the click-clack of her heels fading down the corridor, I returned to stand in front of Gretchen's desk. "What'd you think?"

Gretchen sniggered. "Judging from her last remark, I think she likes you. And judging from your burning red cheeks, I think the feeling is mutual."

Ten years ago, I would've hoped that she'd be jealous—and ten years ago, she might well have been. But Gretchen was more like my long-suffering sister than my ex-fiancée now. "She's nice enough, and she's certainly attractive, but with that hair and those clothes, she's speaking a language I don't understand."

Gretchen laughed outright this time. "She's emo."

"Emo?"

"It comes from the word 'emotional.' Emos are a subculture somewhere between punk rockers and goths. They cultivate the image of being sensitive, self-aware, and occasionally angst ridden."

"Just like me, huh? What I meant was what do you think about this investigation she had Chris doing? Could it be related?"

"I've no idea, but what choice do we have? We have to follow up, don't we?"

"Yeah, we do. I'm going to do a little more digging at Golden

Fingers, then I'll start with the architecture firm. Can you—"

"Yeah, yeah, do an online search for Corinne White."

"Exactly. And don't forget to pester our emo friend for the file she mentioned."

"I won't." She stood and walked out from behind her desk.

"What are you doing?" I asked. "Getting in slapping range?"

"Is this your self-awareness kicking in? Do you realize that you need to be slapped and are bracing for it?"

"Well, no, not exactly."

She shrugged. "I'm tired of sitting, and while I haven't forgotten Angelina's file, I think you've forgotten something I told you earlier on the phone."

I thought back to when she had called me as I was coming out of Schlein's office. "Oh, yeah, you said Kittredge had the preliminary autopsy results. The black eye and something more." I stared into her face for a long moment, trying to read what was there. "The something more's not good, is it?"

"I don't know. I guess you could say it's troubling. Chris had sex shortly before he died."

"He had sex," I repeated robotically. "How do they even know that?"

"August, he was a catcher, not a pitcher."

"Right, of course. Did they find any, ah…"

"No. They found residue of lubricant and latex from a condom."

"And this would be downstairs, not upstairs."

"Correct."

"Can they identify the brand of lubricant?"

"Yep. Astroglide."

"Is that…"

"Popular?"

I nodded.

"Yeah, it's the Coke Classic of personal lubricants among gay men. Nothing for us there."

I thought about it some more. "Was he seeing anyone?"

"Not that I know of. The last guy I heard about moved to Japan."

"Japan?"

"Yeah, to work for Sony. Chris was pretty broken up about it."

"Okay. Was there any indication of sexual assault?"

"Let me put it this way, Kittredge said there was no sign of bruising or other trauma."

"This is not a conversation I would've wanted to have with Kittredge—or vice versa. No wonder he called you instead of me." I looked down at my new shoes and saw a tiny distorted version of my face reflected back in the highly polished toes. "The more we learn, the less we know. Agreeing to take on an investigation that wasn't in his wheelhouse and having sex with a man in a straight massage parlor. What the hell was Chris up to?"

Gretchen reached over to wrap me in a hug. "Somewhere he is looking down at us, smiling at our frustration but absolutely certain we'll figure it out."

"He's definitely smiling about the meat-eating dinosaur comment. It's almost like he arranged for me to hear that."

"Don't be so emo," she said, and pulled me closer.

At eleven-fifty-three that evening, I stood in front of the grimy concrete balustrade guarding the Bush Street overlook to Stockton. Below me, the 30 Stockton trolleybus juddered by, connected to overhead power lines by hinged poles that sprouted from the roof like the antennae of an overgrown insect. A smattering of cars whooshed by behind me on Bush, and a man pushing a woman in a wheelchair gave me a wide berth, almost steering the outside wheel of the chair right off the sidewalk.

The Stockton Street entrance to Golden Fingers was below on my right. Its towering sign, which was nearly at eye-level from where I stood, was still lit, but the parlor had been closed since ten. I was waiting for the janitor to show up in hopes that I could learn more about the discovery of Chris's body. I knew Kittredge would be pissed if he found out, but I didn't entirely credit his version of events and wanted to hear from the horse's mouth.

A white van double-parked in front of Golden Fingers at twelve-ten, and a man and a woman dressed in white uniforms jumped out, leaving the emergency flashers blinking. They hustled to the back of the van, where they decanted a variety of cleaning equipment and supplies to the sidewalk. The man hurried back behind the wheel to move the van while the woman busied herself with transporting the equipment and supplies inside. I loitered at the balustrade until I saw the man round the corner at Sutter and walk back up Stockton toward the massage parlor.

I lumbered down the concrete staircase that led from the overlook to the street. I managed to arrive at the massage parlor door just as the man walked up from the other direction. He was Hispanic, in his late thirties, with a wide, flat face and a full head of unruly black hair. He had just wrapped his hand around the door handle when I said, "Were you the one who found the body here the other night?"

He released the handle and stepped back, clearly nonplussed. "Who are you?"

"I'm a friend of the man who was killed."

That didn't seem to clear up his confusion. He licked his lips and blinked. I remembered that Kittredge had said the janitor who found Chris was from El Salvador and didn't speak much English. I probably spoke even less Spanish, so we would have been at an impasse if the woman who had come with him in the van hadn't picked that moment to poke her head out the door. "What do you want?" she demanded in crisp, unaccented English. There seemed to be a family resemblance in her features, so I guessed she was related to the man, perhaps even his fraternal twin.

"I want to talk with him."

"About what?"

"About the dead man he found here."

She stepped out onto the sidewalk, pressing her butt firmly against the closed door. "Are you a cop?"

"No, a private investigator. I'm a friend of the murdered man. He was also an investigator."

"Mrs. Kongsangchai wouldn't like it."

"What does Mrs. Kong"—I stumbled over the name—"have to do with it?"

"She runs the parlor."

I pulled out the folded stack of twenty dollar bills I had gathered for this purpose. "Look, I've got two hundred bucks here. It's yours—or should I say his—if I can just get some information about what happened on the night my friend's body was found. Like I said, I'm a *private* investigator. Neither the cops nor Mrs. K will ever know about it."

The money prompted a meaningful look between the two of them, then the man launched into some rapid-fire Spanish. It was apparent he had understood more of the conversation than I had assumed. Eventually, the woman shrugged and agreed with a short, "*Si quieres,*" which was one of the few Spanish phrases I recognized.

"Let's go inside," she said to me. "It will give us more of that privacy you've been talking about."

"Great."

I followed her through the door into the dinky reception area. The Sputnik fixture was just as bright as ever, but not being hungover did wonders for my sensitivity to light. The man gestured for me to stay in the reception area, then plunged through the beaded curtain to the hallway beyond. He returned a moment later with three folding chairs, which he arranged in front of the reception desk. He plopped down in the one closest to the curtain and said something in Spanish.

The woman translated. "Have a seat and ask your questions."

I yanked my chair closer and fell into it. "For starters, the police told me there was only one janitor. Were you here that night, too?"

47

"No. Some businesses aren't cleaned every night or they alternate between a light cleaning and a heavy cleaning. I only come with him when he needs help to finish his rounds on time."

"And you are?"

"His wife."

So much for my twin hypothesis and the idea that opposites attract. "That's great."

"If you say so."

"My name is August Riordan, by the way. May I ask yours?"

She puckered her mouth. "First names only. I'm Cristabel and he's Hector."

"Nice to meet you." I gave them a first-names-only smile. "How about if we start by Hector describing how he found the body?"

Hector launched into a response in Spanish without waiting for Cristabel. When she gave me the translation, it was consistent with what Kittredge told me: Hector had arrived around midnight, cleaned the common areas first, then moved on to the individual massage rooms. He found Chris in the second room he cleaned. He called the owner—Mrs. Kongsangchai—and she called the police.

I was disappointed. I'd hoped that the description of finding the body would include some material fact that Kittredge had left out or prompt some other questions. "Have you ever found anything like this before?"

Cristabel snorted and translated the question for Hector. He laughed, too, and answered directly in English. "A dead rat once. In the whirlpool."

"Ever see the man before? At the massage parlor, I mean."

"We're never here when the parlor's open," said Cristabel. "We never see the customers."

"Not even after hours? No private events or special arrangements for good customers?"

Cristabel made a dismissive gesture but put the question to Hector anyway. He gave a two-sentence answer. "Sometimes they stay open later," she translated, "but then they tell us to come later. We are always here alone."

"Did they tell you to come later the night you discovered the body?"

"He already told you," said Cristabel. "He arrived at the regular time—same as tonight."

"Are there any security cameras?"

"No way. The customers would freak."

I looked up at the gilded wainscoting I had noticed on my earlier visit. A faint aroma of chlorine mixed with the nauseating scent of cheap perfume wafted out from the beaded curtain. I hadn't noticed *that* on my earlier visit, but if I had, I probably would have thrown up. "Have there ever been any other crimes here?"

"Come on," said Cristabel. "This place gets raided all the time for prostitution."

"I meant violent crimes."

"You don't call forcing immigrants to have sex against their will violent?"

"All the girls here are victims of sex trafficking?"

"Most of them. There are a few who stayed after they paid off their debt. A few who freelance."

"Who runs them? Mrs. K?"

"No, she's just the mama-san. A Chinatown gang supplies the girls."

There was only one gang in Chinatown with the organization and connections necessary for human trafficking. "Wo Hop To?"

Christabel nodded.

I rested my elbows on my knees and let my head loll. I had killed the former leader of Wo Hop To during the investigation of a fixed mayoral election a few years back. Chris had worked the case with me, helping me to understand how the electronic voting machines had been fiddled with. The possibility that he had been murdered in revenge was downright frightening. I looked back at Cristabel. "Do you know any of the girls here?"

She frowned. "Why?"

"I want to talk to someone who was working that night."

"You think Wo Hop To lets them run around during the day to meet with anybody?"

"One of the freelancers, then. I'll pay."

She looked over at Hector, who said something low and soothing in Spanish. "Write down your phone number," she said to me. "Maybe someone will get in touch."

I took one of my old cards from my wallet and passed it over. She looked down at it, chewing her lip. Something clicked for me. "You used to work here, didn't you?"

"I work here now."

"I mean during the day. You know too much about the operation—and you have too much empathy for the girls."

She thrust her chin out. "Maybe you have too little."

"I didn't—"

"It's not a secret I worked here. Hector knows. It's how we got the contract."

"Okay."

"You have anything else to ask? We're on a schedule. It doesn't do us any good to make an extra two hundred if we don't finish our jobs on time. We'll lose the clients."

"One final question—did Hector notice anything unusual or out of place that night? Apart from the body, of course."

Cristabel translated for Hector, and after thinking a moment, he said something back to her. It wasn't much, but it clearly wasn't "No." Rather than serve up his response, Cristabel said something back to him. He shook his head and gestured toward me.

"What's going on?" I asked.

"Tell him," said Hector.

"My husband is more softhearted than I am," said Cristabel. "He did notice one thing. It's not exactly what you'd call unusual for this sleazy place, but Mrs. Kongsangchai wouldn't want you to know."

"Now you have to tell me."

She sighed and squeezed her temples. I had given her a headache. "There's a room in the basement. It's a place for people to have group sex. It's not used very often, but when it is, we have to clean it, same as the rest of the building. Hector says it was used that evening."

"Is there any particular reason to think my friend might have been there?"

"No" came the relayed answer.

"Was there any blood or other indication that the murder might have taken place in that room instead of the massage room?"

Another no.

"Who exactly has sex in the room?"

Cristabel answered me directly. "Who do you think? Nob Hill society ladies? It's clients of the massage parlor and the girls who work here."

"Does Mrs. K ever rent out the room without supplying the girls?"

Cristabel blew air through her lips. "Who knows? It's possible. It does have a few features you won't find in the typical hotel room."

"Such as?"

"You men are all perverts. How is knowing that going to help your dead friend?"

I looked over at Hector and saw him smiling at me. "Humor me."

"It's mainly a bunch of easily washed, vinyl-covered sofas and ottomans. There are also harnesses that hang from the ceiling and some S&M stuff. Nothing too scary. A few cuffs and clamps and things. Oh, and mirrors, lots of hard-to-clean mirrors."

I don't know what I was expecting, but she was right: The details didn't help. "Did Hector tell the police about the room?"

"No," said Hector emphatically.

"The entrance to it is hidden in the back of a storage area.

We'd be in big trouble if the cops found out. It's one thing to bribe them to turn a blind eye to happy endings, it's another to pay them off for full-service prostitution." Cristabel stood abruptly and held out her hand. "Speaking of payments, I think it's time for you to settle up and go."

I retrieved the folded twenties, supplemented the stack with another hundred's worth and passed them to her. "Thank you. You've been a big help."

"No, we haven't," she said. "We never spoke, and if anyone asks, we don't know you. And don't betray my husband's trust by saying otherwise."

"I won't. We never talked."

Hector stood and unlocked the front door. I slipped through, and he extended his hand for a quick shake.

"Sorry for your friend," he said, and pulled back.

I heard him bolting the door behind me as I trudged up Stockton, a half-dozen improbable theories rattling around in my brain.

7
HISTORIC PRESERVATION

The next morning I resolved to set aside the things I'd learned—or hadn't learned—at Golden Fingers and focus instead on tracing Chris's steps in the search for Angelina's sister. The obvious starting point was the architecture firm that had once employed her: Hillesland, Hillesland, and Cheilek.

Meat-eating dinosaur PIs are not known for their internet skills, but I eventually managed to find the website for the San Francisco chapter of the American Institute of Architects. The only entry in the membership directory that came close to the one I wanted consisted of a single Hillesland with "and Associates" stuck to the end. According to the website, the firm had been established in 1978, employed an architect named Nilsen Hillesland, and focused on projects involving historical preservation. As if to underscore the historical theme, Nilsen listed an AOL email address, which even this dinosaur knew hearkened back to the Precambrian era of screeching dial-up connections.

The firm's office was south of Market on Folsom Street, near the corner of Seventh. It was in a narrow two-story brick building with full-height glass windows. Old-fashioned Venetian blinds covered the windows, and even from the outside, I could see they were caked with dust. Dust also covered the graveyard of dead flies along the sill.

The door opened on a long room with a distressed hardwood floor sprouting massive I-beams at periodic intervals to shore up the equally distressed brick walls. Long tables with rolls of blueprints and other flotsam and jetsam were wedged along the side walls, and a pair of drafting tables sat at right angles to those plunked in the center. The only light in the place came from the windows and a couple of gooseneck lamps bent over the drafting surfaces.

A man on a wheeled stool sat behind one of the tables, reading the *New York Times*. He put his index finger down in the middle of an article as I approached, looked up, and said, "Tattoo parlor is across the street."

That was good because he didn't look like the sort of guy I'd trust with my rainbow unicorn tat. He was pushing seventy or seventy-five, had a rooster comb of white hair, recessed black eyes, crinkly sallow skin, and a hooked nose. He was wearing a brown quilted velour vest over a yellowed dress shirt and probably could have dropped fifty pounds without coming within yodeling distance of his ideal height-to-weight ratio.

"I'm not looking for a tattoo," I said.

He pulled reading glasses from his nose and let them dangle from a cord around his neck. "How about a hundred-floor office building?"

"No, sorry. I'm after information. That is, if this firm used to be called Hillesland, Hillesland, and Cheilek."

"It did. Cheilek died, and the other Hillesland—my son—decided that flogging real estate paid better. He was right."

"Okay, let me ask you this—did a short man with blond hair come by a while ago also looking for information?"

"Yes." He lifted the corner of the newspaper, fished around underneath it, and pulled out a card. He squinted at it from arm's length. "A Chris Duckworth. He also asked about the firm's name, and he also had a black eye. Is this some kind of weird scavenger hunt?"

"I wish it were. I'm a private detective from his office, and he's been murdered. I'm trying to find out if it was related to a case he was working on. Did he ask about Corinne White, formerly Corinne Evangelista?"

He nodded. "Except there was no Evangelista involved. She was plain old Corinne White when she worked here." He put the card back down on the table. "I'm sorry to hear about your associate. He seemed like a nice fellow."

"He was. What else can you tell me?"

"Duckworth said he found Corinne's name in an old *San Francisco Chronicle* article about a project the firm did for Pets.com. That checks out because we hired her in the late 1990s when there was a lot of work refurbishing old South of Market buildings for the dot-coms."

"You were still Hillesland, Hillesland, and Cheilek at that point?"

"Yeah, those were the gold-rush days." He gave a dry chuckle.

"How long did she stay?"

"Six or seven years. She went on maternity leave and never came back. I'm sure she could see the writing on the wall. My son had left by that point, too. But I have to tell you, I can't imagine Corinne being involved in a murder—or any sort of crime. She was good people."

"I'm not saying she was personally involved. Only that looking for her might have gotten Duckworth mixed up in something that went south. Do you have any contact information for her?"

"Duckworth asked for that, too. I told him we shredded the personnel files years ago."

I couldn't stop myself from breaking eye contact to glance around the cluttered office. If Wikipedia needed a photograph to illustrate their article on hoarders, I knew where they could get it.

Hillesland laughed. "I know what you're thinking. Why get religion about the personnel files in particular? My lawyer advised me to get rid of them as soon as the retention laws allowed. To avoid having them subpoenaed for lawsuits."

"Involved in a lot of litigation, are you?"

"No, never sued once. But lawyers are better than architects at finding ways to manufacture billable hours. All is not lost, though."

"Oh yeah?"

"Yeah. After Duckworth left, I got to thinking. When times were good, the firm sent out Christmas cards to clients, partners, and employees. I dug around in back and found our old address file." He waved vaguely behind him, then wheeled over to the other drafting table where he picked up an index card. He pulled on his glasses and read from the card, "Corinne White, 29 Russell Street, San Francisco. It's on Russian Hill."

"Is there a phone number?"

"Yes, but who knows if it's current."

"It's a place to start." I pulled out my smartphone and fumbled open the camera app. "Mind if I photograph it?"

He shrugged. "You kids and your crazy toys."

I managed to capture a decent shot after three shaky attempts, but I knew Chris would have been proud of me for using the camera rather than my notebook. "Did you pass this information to Duckworth?"

"No. I only thought of it yesterday. I was actually planning to call after I finished reading the paper. A busy professional has to plan his schedule, you know."

"Of course." I put out my hand and gave him my name. "Thank you for everything."

Hillesland took it with a surprisingly strong grip. "My pleasure, Mr. Riordan. I hope you find out what happened to your associate. And if you do run across Corrine, tell her Nelly says hello."

I smiled. "Nelly. Got it."

Russell turned out to be a one-block street off Hyde on the south side of Russian Hill. The corner at Hyde was about ten yards from the place I'd seen a twenty-something girl from Argentina get cut down by a machine-gun-wielding gripman. That had been the start of the case that led to my estrangement from Chris and my decision to leave San Francisco. To say the area had bad associations for me was putting it mildly.

The cabbie I flagged to take me here from Hillesland's office stopped by a fire plug on Hyde just as a cable car rumbled down the hill behind us. I pushed too much money at the driver, tumbled out of the cab, and hurried down Russell to avoid seeing the car pass the spot where the girl had been killed.

Odd-numbered houses were on the left side of the street, but when I passed the sawed-off Victorian at number 21, the only thing between it and the two-unit apartment house at 37-39 was the skeleton of a small A-frame. The siding had been stripped to expose weather-stained plywood, and the roof had been replaced by a blue plastic tarp whose edges billowed and snapped in the breeze. I stepped around a porta potty on the sidewalk and climbed up a short brick stair to the front door—or, to be more accurate, the front-door frame. A construction permit was tacked to the side. It had been issued over a month ago to Corrine White and covered "comprehensive" renovation and the addition of an upstairs bathroom.

I stuck my head through the door frame. The interior had been taken down to the studs. There were no workers or any tools or stacked construction materials lying around. I guessed that the demolition crew had finished and the remodeling had yet to begin.

That should have been that. I had confirmed Corrine still owned the property and was presumably living nearby during construction. Heck, she was probably the architect. I had any number of options to locate her. I could speak to the neighbors, I could go to the Department of Building Inspection and pull the permit, or I could even call the number from Hillesland's Christmas-card file. The only problem was the smell: the putrid, licorice-sweet stench that rolled out from the house and fell on me like a pile of compost.

I gagged and stepped back, eying the porta potty on the off chance I was mistaken about the source of the odor. I wasn't. The only thing coming from it was the tang of industrial-strength disinfectant—a veritable spring breeze by comparison.

I pulled a folded handkerchief from my hip pocket and pressed it over my nose and mouth. Then I stepped through the door. If I'd ever done a braver thing, I couldn't remember.

The interior was dim, with shards of light stabbing down from the unglazed windows. Chunks of drywall, wood chips, and pink cotton-candy insulation littered the plywood subfloor. Bent nails and bits of yellowing paper festooned the denuded studs, which had rusting pipes and crumbling wires running between them. I shuffled through the entryway, a bedroom, and a room in back I took for the kitchen, covering my new shoes with a thick gray dust. I was marking time until I worked up the courage to go upstairs to the second floor. Even breathing through the handkerchief, I knew the smell was coming from there.

More gray dust had accumulated against the risers of the staircase like snowdrifts, and that combined with the absence of railings made it hard to climb without slipping. But keeping my feet under me was the least of my worries. With every step I took, the smell increased correspondingly, and it was so bad by the time I reached the landing that I was holding my breath.

At least there was no longer any mystery about the source. Much of the second-story subfloor had been removed, so the only place where the joists were covered was the landing and a square of conspicuously new plywood subflooring beyond it. And lying facedown on that plywood was the flaccid, almost puddled body of a woman.

Her head was twisted to the right, and her arms were bent akimbo at her sides. She was wearing a short-sleeved cotton dress that was blotched with seeping fluids. Her long black hair was matted and snarled. Half-dollar-size circles of decomposition spotted her arms and legs: red, going to black, going to ash farther from her trunk. The skin of each hand was like a melted latex glove, shriveled and deformed, as if the bones underneath had dissolved.

And her face—her face. The features of it sloughed to the floor like houses in a mudslide.

I retched and retreated halfway down the stairs. Between coughing fits and strangled hiccups of breath through the handkerchief, it was several minutes before I summoned the courage to climb back up. But I stayed only long enough to retrieve the red leather shoulder bag I'd seen by her side.

I hurried down the stairs with it, ran out of the house, and walked twenty yards or so up the street where I plunked myself on the curb. The smell of dusty concrete and warm rubber from the rear wheel of the Fiat I was sitting next to was perfume compared to the miasma I'd been breathing. I put away the handkerchief and examined the purse. The strap was gold chain, and ugly gold doodads encrusted the front. In spite of that—or perhaps because of it—it looked expensive. I glanced furtively to my left and right to see if I was being observed, then opened the bag.

Nestled among a key ring, various tubes, a brush, a compact, and ironically—it seemed to me—a bottle of hand sanitizer, was a matching red leather billfold. I unsnapped the catch and rifled the card slots to extract a California driver's license issued to an attractive woman with long straight hair. She was named Corrine E. White, born a little more than forty-four years ago and residing at 29 Russell Street, San Francisco.

I shoved everything back in the purse, hid it under my arm as best I could, and levered myself up. I jogged back to the intersection with Hyde, turned right, and commenced a forced march down the hill toward my old neighborhood. A few blocks from the Post Street apartment, I diverted to a nondescript building that served as headquarters for a local union. There, in the reception area with a chipped green linoleum floor, was one of the two-hundred-odd payphones that remained in San Francisco. I knew that because I'd had occasion to use it several times after missing payments on my phone bill.

I picked up the receiver and dialed 911. When the operator asked me what my emergency was, I responded, "Dead body," and gave the Russian Hill address. I hung up before she could ask for my name or any other details and hurried out the door.

Fifteen minutes later, I was standing under the shower in the Post Street apartment, sanding my skin with one of Chris's loofah sponges.

8
PRISON COUTURE

When she answered the door to her hotel room later that afternoon, Angelina Evangelista was wearing stripes: jailbird stripes like the man on Monopoly's Get Out of Jail Free card. Only her garment was a dress and it was short. Very short. She'd accessorized with a belt slung low on her hips that served no real purpose except to emphasize the shortness of the dress and telegraph an insolent sexuality. Black stockings and a crazy pair of knee-high Chuck Taylors with laces three yards long completed the ensemble.

She was staying at the venerable Huntington Hotel on California Street, and after a considerable amount of temporizing on my part, I had made an appointment to meet her there to give her a progress report on the case. The "progress" being anything but that, of course.

The high-wattage smile on her face dimmed as she noticed the red leather bag clutched under my arm. "Is that a man purse?"

"Ah, no. Not my thing."

"Looks like Gucci."

"I'll have to take your word for that."

"Trust me, it is. Expensive, too. Come in—and pull up a chair."

I took a chair from the black lacquer desk along the near wall, and since there was nowhere else to sit, Angelina plopped herself on the corner of the overstuffed bed. She turned her knees to one side and tugged at her skirt with both hands. It didn't make any discernible progress down her legs. I had the feeling she'd dressed in a way she hoped I'd find attractive but realized too late that the meeting wasn't going to be a social occasion.

"Is it my sister's?" she asked.

"Pretty obvious, huh?"

She gave a small shrug. "If it's not yours, why else would you have brought it?"

"I'm ninety-nine percent certain it's hers." I unsnapped the clasp and extracted the driver's license I'd examined earlier. I stood and handed it to her, then feeling uncomfortable hovering over her, I returned to the chair.

She looked at the photo for a long moment, nodding her head slightly at first, then with more emphasis. "Definitely. She looks older, of course, but it's definitely her. Besides, it's got her name on it, including the E for Evangelista. Why the uncertainty? Were you worried someone stole her identity?"

"Not really. I was just hoping..."

"Hoping what?"

I hesitated, then spat it out, "Look, it's like this. I found the purse next to a body—the body of a dead woman."

Angelina's eyes flashed, and her voice lost its usual teasing lilt. "Did the woman look like this picture?"

I cleared my throat and leaned forward to rest my elbows on my knees. "I can't be sure. The body was badly decomposed—"

"Jesus."

"But—but I found it at the address on the license. The house is empty. It's being renovated. The body was on the second floor, and it was clear it had been there a while. Two weeks at least."

Angelina closed her eyes as if she were bracing for a physical jolt or shock, then fell back on the bed.

I jumped up, thinking that she had fainted or worse. I sat beside her and reached to take her pulse, but I realized that unless it was missing entirely I wouldn't learn anything from it. I settled for placing my hand on her forehead, which was pale and cool to the touch. "Are you okay?"

"Define okay," she said, as tears leaked from the corners of her eyes.

"Are you physically okay?"

"I didn't pass out if that's what you're worried about. What did you do after you found her?"

"What do you mean?"

"You didn't just leave her there, did you?"

I pulled my hand away from her forehead, but she clasped it to her midsection. "I phoned the police. I didn't want them to be the ones to tell you, so I called from a pay phone without giving my name. They'll have picked up the body and taken it to the morgue by now. We'll need to go down and make a formal identification."

She turned her head away from me and the bad news. Tears rolled off the bridge of her nose to the bedspread, staining the white material with bits of mascara. "Will you be in trouble?" she asked after a long moment.

"For calling it in anonymously? A little, maybe. But Kittredge, the police lieutenant investigating Chris's murder, will probably settle for a dressing-down if we go in soon."

Angelina sniffed and squinched her eyes tighter. "You think she was murdered? Like Chris?"

The last thing I wanted to get into was an extended discussion of the condition of her sister's body. "I didn't see any obvious wounds. It could have been a heart attack or even an accident. The house is pretty torn up, and the footing is treacherous in places. Maybe she tripped going up the stairs."

"But you don't think so?"

"No, not really. It seems like too much of a coincidence. From what I've learned by retracing Chris's steps, I wouldn't be surprised if he also discovered her address—perhaps even found her body as well. I think their deaths are linked. The autopsy could tell us more."

She sniffed again and released my hand to push herself up. "Oh, yes, the autopsy," she said, wiping her tears away.

I rolled over on my hip to extract a fresh handkerchief. I had already dropped the one I had used at the Russell Street house— and all the clothes I'd worn there—at the cleaners on the first floor of my building. "Here," I said. "Try this."

She gave a wan smile and took the handkerchief, dabbing at her eyes and nose. "Who carries handkerchiefs these days?"

"Older men without man purses."

"I knew you guys were good for something."

I nodded. "Ready to sop up tears or mucus at a moment's notice."

"Hold me."

"What?"

"I have something to ask, and I can't look at you while I do it."

I frowned, then leaned over to take her in an awkward side-by-side hug. She felt tiny, delicate, but I also noticed a stiffness from some sort of elaborate undergarment beneath her clothes. "How's this?" I said to the far wall.

"It's nice. Tell me the truth, am I to blame for Chris's death?"

I started to pull away, but she tensed and pulled me closer.

"Be honest."

"No. There's no way you could have known. In fact, we don't know for certain that there *is* a connection. It's just a gut feeling."

"You're not just saying what I want to hear? You and Gretchen won't secretly blame me later?"

"We've all lost someone close to us. There's no point in blaming one another. We need to find the people who are actually responsible."

A beat went by. "Thank you."

"Don't thank me. There's nothing to thank me for." I gave her a little squeeze. "Can we break the clinch now?"

She nodded and released me. She looked down in her lap as she wound the cloth of the handkerchief around a finger. With nearly all of the garish eye makeup rubbed off, she looked child-like and innocent. Strangely, or maybe not so strangely, I found myself drawn to her more when she wasn't trying so hard.

"What do we do next?" she asked.

"Well, we need to go down to the station."

"But after? I want to find the people responsible, too, but there doesn't seem to be anything to go on."

"There may be. I found a key ring in your sister's purse. It has an obvious car key, but a couple of keys look like door keys. Your sister had to live somewhere while she renovated her house. I'm thinking the door keys go to an apartment or a house she was renting."

"Where?"

"I don't know. But her neighbors on Russell Street might."

"Hmm. So your idea is to withhold the information about the keys from the police and search her rental before they find out about it? Isn't that going to get you in even more hot water?"

"Not if they don't know. I've already removed the keys from her bag. But speaking of the police—"

"Yes, yes, we need to go down to the station. Just give me a moment to fix my face."

I reached over to take her hand. "Don't. Go as you are."

We took a cab from the Huntington to the new San Francisco Police Headquarters in the Mission Bay neighborhood. I foolishly called Kittredge to tell him we were coming, wanting both to confirm that he was available and defuse the impact of an in-person bombshell.

It was a big mistake. It only gave him more time to research the 911 call and the associated police report, and find more reasons to yell at me. Two things particularly stuck in his craw: that I'd discovered who Chris's last client was without informing him—something he had specifically cautioned me against—and that I'd removed the purse from the house on Russell Street.

He separated Angelina and me early on, and I ended up cooling my heels in an interrogation room while he confirmed my version of the story. After I stared at the walls for nearly two hours wondering if I was going to be locked up, Kittredge barged in, shooting his French cuffs and wafting a citrusy cologne that made me want to gag. He was dressed, as he often was, in an expensive suit.

"Nobody wears suits these days," I taunted, channeling Ivy.

"Oh, yeah? Then what were you wearing the night I dragged your drunken ass down to the massage parlor? Sure looked like a number off the Kmart rack to me."

"Not everyone can afford the Trump signature collection."

"Fuck you. This is Brioni."

"I can never tell them apart."

Kittredge stepped forward, gripping the back of the chair across the table like he wanted to grab my throat. "Cut the crap, Riordan. I'm giving you one last warning. You find out anything else relevant to this investigation, you let me know immediately."

"Or?"

"Or the state is going to be picking your suits, and you know what color they'll be. Orange."

I waved him off, trying not to think about the keys I'd taken from Corrine White's purse. "Did you find out what Duckworth was doing at the massage parlor?"

"Were you not listening? We were talking about *you* keeping *me* informed."

"The question stands."

Kittredge ran his hand through his hair and muttered under his breath. "He didn't go there during business hours. No one on the staff claims to recognize him, and there's no record of him or anyone like him booking an appointment."

"How did he get inside?"

"If I had to guess, I'd say a rogue employee let him in after hours."

"Which begs the obvious question—who has keys to the place?"

Kittredge reddened. "Only the manager and the janitor."

"The janitor from El Salvador with a limited command of English who discovered and reported the body?"

"Yes, damn it."

"Then either he's a criminal mastermind or it sounds like you should be talking to the manager."

"We did, you moron. She has a solid alibi for the evening and had possession of the keys the whole time. But it's possible duplicates were made without her knowledge."

"What do her friends from Wo Hop To have to say?"

"Congratulations. You learned the place has gang connections. They would be the last people to bring this kind of attention to their business. If Wo Hop To had murdered Duckworth, they would have dumped his body in the Bay."

He had a point. "Okay, thank you. I appreciate it. One last question. Do you have the final autopsy results on Chris?"

"I gave Sabatini most everything we've learned."

"Most everything?"

Kittredge sighed. "We've identified the slug. It's a .22 long rifle. Probably shot from a handgun."

"You mean one of those target pistols?"

"Yeah. They can tell from the marks the barrel rifling makes."

"Who uses a target pistol to kill somebody?"

"I don't know. They've got no stopping power it's true, but put a round in the back of the head and the slug will ricochet around inside the skull. It can do a hell of a lot of damage."

"Christ." I watched as Kittredge slipped a finger under his collar and tugged. The knot of his already loose tie loosened more. "There's something you're not telling me."

He glanced beseechingly at the ceiling, then leveled a hard stare at me. "You probably didn't spend enough quality time with her to notice, but there was also a hole in the base of Corrine White's skull. It looks like it's from a .22. When they recover the slug in the autopsy, they can check to see if the rifling matches."

"It was the same shooter?"

"Yes. Probably. Now you've wrung me dry. Get the hell out of here and remember what I said about keeping me informed. Your jailbait girlfriend is waiting in the lobby."

"She's over twenty-one—and she's not my girlfriend," I said, but he had already turned away.

I found Angelina lying on a vinyl couch in front of a plaque listing police officers who had died in the line of duty. It was clear she had been crying again, and she looked tired and dispirited.

"Oh, August," she said, and stood to wrap me in a hug. I found myself hugging her back with more ardor than I had intended.

"They didn't"—I hesitated—"How are you holding up?"

She knew what I had started to ask. "No, they didn't make me look at the body. They said they could use dental records."

"When—"

"I don't want to talk anymore. Please take me home."

We cabbed it back to the Huntington. I planned to say good-bye in the lobby, but she pulled me wordlessly into the elevator. I didn't leave until the next morning.

9
CARLOS G'S

The elaborate undergarment beneath Angelina's dress proved to be a black satin corset. It was draped over the headboard like discarded armor when I slipped from the room at 7 a.m., Angelina acknowledging my departure with a drowsy two-finger wave.

Rain persuaded me to loiter under the hotel awning before starting the walk home, and loitering gave me time to notice the figure leaning against a lamppost directly across the street in Huntington Park. He or she was slight and wearing a hoodie zipped tightly around the face, and in spite of standing unsheltered in a city park at seven-thirty in the morning, the person did not give the impression of being homeless.

I ducked back into the hotel to "borrow" an umbrella from the reception desk. When I returned, the figure was gone, but caution, intuition, or barometric pressure made me turn right onto California Street to head away from the Post Street apartment.

I walked past the Crocker Garage, the Mark Hopkins hotel, and the Stanford Court hotel—which together with the Huntington Hotel provided namesakes for all the "Big Four" robber barons who built the transcontinental railroad—and pulled up short at Powell Street. A groaning charter bus full of gamblers heading to Reno was attempting to negotiate the sharp right turn onto Powell in spite of the sign prohibiting commercial vehicles over three tons. As it wallowed in the intersection, partway on the Powell Street cable-car tracks and partway on the sidewalk, I got a clear look at my reflection in its tinted windows. Behind that reflection, ambling splay-footed up the sidewalk, was my friend in the hoodie.

I was fairly certain now that he was male, and for a heart-stopping moment, I was seized with the irrational notion that he was Chris come back to life. He had the same delicate features and the same slender build, but he was taller and lacked Chris's quicksilver movements. Chris's doppelgänger or not, I couldn't help but wonder why he was following me around San Francisco.

I dodged past the nose of the still-struggling bus and hurried down Powell toward Union Square. The rain came harder now, and the slick pavement combined with the steep grade of the street made the footing tricky. A clanging cable car passed me, a smell of scorched pine trailing in its wake as the car's wooden brakes worked to find purchase on the rain-soaked track. A red light stopped me at Bush Street, and as I stood waiting next to an art student carrying an outsize portfolio, I resisted the temptation to look behind me.

Just past Sutter, I darted across the roadway and hurried past a doorman in Beefeater livery at the door of the Sir Francis Drake Hotel. I went up the entrance steps and ducked behind one of the marble columns in front of the lobby bar. A moment later, my pursuer jogged up the same steps and stood dripping and bewildered on the rococo carpet, one hand resting on the back of an overstuffed love seat.

I tossed the umbrella aside and stepped out from behind the column to grab the sleeve of his hoodie. "It's really pissing down, isn't it?" I said genially.

He flinched and tried to pull away, but I reeled him back in. Seeing him up close, my earlier impression of androgyny was confirmed—even amplified. The skin of his face was smooth and soft, and I was pretty sure he was wearing eyeliner.

"What do you want?" he said, straining to keep his voice under control.

"If you're granting wishes, I'll take a bottle of Glenlivet."

"That's not funny."

"Neither is following me around. Why are you doing it?"

He looked down at his shoes—a pair of slip-on sneakers—and pursed his lips.

"Let's try a different question. Why were you watching the hotel?"

That got his attention. He snapped his gaze up. "Just leave her the fuck alone, old man."

I was sifting through my vast catalog of clever rejoinders when he yanked down the zipper to his hoodie. He shucked off the garment; half dove, half rolled over the back of the love seat; and lurched toward the bank of superannuated elevators on the far side of the lobby. I gave chase, but he slid through the closing doors of an ascending car before I could nab him. I watched as the arrow on the floor indicator paused at five, then continued upward. There didn't seem to be any point in going after him. I wouldn't know what floor he got out on or how he would come down.

At least I'd learned one thing: He knew Angelina and he didn't appreciate this "old man" spending the night with her.

I checked the pockets of his hoodie, found nothing, and draped it on the back of the love seat. I retrieved the umbrella and covered the half mile back to my old apartment in less than ten minutes. There I learned yet another thing: Someone had searched it. Nothing had been terribly disturbed, but no one could replicate Chris's precise alignment. Even his alphabetized collection of Broadway playbills had been rifled. But who was doing the searching, what they were looking for, and whether they had found it were not part of my newfound knowledge.

* * *

By ten-thirty the rain had stopped, and I was once again standing at the mouth of Russell Street. I had gotten there via a zigzag route involving a bus, a cab, and plain old shoe leather, and I was confident that no one had followed me. In my pocket was Corrine White's key ring, and my plan was to canvass her neighborhood to determine if anyone knew the address of the place she was staying while she remodeled her house.

In my experience, people home during the day were more likely to have useful information and were more likely to come to the door to receive packages. In spite of that, it didn't go well. Only two answered my ring. The first slammed the door shut before I'd even introduced myself. The second was a young dude in flannel and a woolen cap who sported an extravagantly oiled beard that smelled like cedar from three feet away. He was happy to talk. He was happy to talk about the apps on his iPhone, craft beer, and his latest post on something called Medium, but he didn't know Corrine White—didn't even realize a house on the street was being renovated.

My next idea was to ask some of the local shopkeepers. The obvious place to begin was the Searchlight Market, the small grocery store half a block away at the corner of Union and Hyde. I waited in line behind three customers to talk to the checker only to be told that she had started last week and didn't know any of the regulars.

I was losing steam fast, but I decided to make one last push with the shopkeeper idea. The only problem was deciding which shops to target. If I went west on Union, I'd run into North Beach's vast assortment of cafes, restaurants, delis, and clothing boutiques. If I went east, I'd find myself in the smaller retail district along Polk Street. In the end I chose Polk because it was closer and easier.

I half walked, half jogged down the steep two-block grade to

Polk. When I reached the retail district, I realized that fewer shops didn't necessarily mean few shops. A hardware store, a dry cleaner, a hairdresser, a coffee shop, and a United Nations of ethnic restaurants were all within steps of where I was standing.

I had just about determined to make my selection by spinning the empty bottle of MD 20/20 lying in the gutter beside me when it struck me that there might be a way to apply a little method to my madness. I was looking for a shopkeeper who'd become friendly with Corrine, who knew her well enough that Corrine had told him or her about the house remodel and the fact that she was living somewhere else temporarily. And come to think of it, if she *was* living in another neighborhood, why would she even come back to this one to shop? She would only do so if she had an ongoing relationship with a store.

The dry cleaners might fit the bill, but it wasn't exactly the sort of place where you made friends and shared confidences with the staff. I decided the only business that might engender loyalty and shared confidences was the hairdresser: Carlos G's.

It was a tiny place sandwiched between the coffee shop and a Vietnamese restaurant. Inside were two chairs, a sink for washing hair, and a closet with a sliding curtain across it. The floor was concrete, but someone had painted an elaborate compass design on it, and that and the rusty iron sconces gave off a shabby-chic vibe. Standing on the east compass point was a chubby fifty-something man with slicked-back hair going gray at the temples. He looked a little like an aging Clark Gable sans the big ears.

"May I help you?" he asked a bit standoffishly.

I probably didn't fit his usual customer profile.

"I sure hope so," I said. "My friend Corrine recommended someone on Polk to get my hair cut. I don't remember the name of the place, though. Are you the only shop in the neighborhood?"

He laughed. "Corrine White? She better recommend me. I've been doing her hair for years."

"Yes, Corrine White," I said, then hesitated. That was my

undoing.

He didn't miss a beat. Grabbing a sort of flimsy half-robe from a hanger, he said, "I can take you right now. My first scheduled appointment isn't until noon. Use the dressing room to change into this smock."

I'd never worn a smock in my life, much less changed into one behind a curtain while another man waited on the other side, but I did it. He'd called my bluff, and I doubted that admitting Corrine was dead would earn his cooperation now.

After he washed my hair and got me situated in the chair, he leaned down to tug at the tufts on either side of my head. "Ah, if you don't mind my asking, who cut your hair last?"

"My neighbor Ray." My retired eighty-three-year-old neighbor who had used a pair of dime-store scissors.

"I see. And how are you wanting it cut today?"

"Oh, just the same." I watched him grimace in the mirror. "Kidding. However you think is best. Something that's in style."

"I know just the cut. Shorter on the sides—and most especially, *even* on the sides—with some weight on top. About four inches over the crown and the front. It's the new look Brad Pitt is rocking since he broke up with Angelina."

"If there's anyone whose look I'd like to rock, it's Brad Pitt's."

He nodded and began snipping away. He was a regular chatterbox. He raved about what a stunning woman Angelina Jolie was, he enthused over an exhibition of Cartier jewelry he'd seen at the Legion of Honor, and he gave me tips on restaurants and current movies. He finished the main assault with the scissors and began mopping up with an electric trimmer, and I still hadn't managed to reintroduce Corrine White to the conversation. But he saved me the trouble.

"And how do you know Corrine?" he asked.

I decided the truth—or at least a half-truth—was best. "I met her through her sister."

"Is she from Canada?"

"That's right."

"Corrine said she was from there originally."

"Angelina—that's the sister's name—came down to visit."

"Wonderful. I gather she's not staying with Corrine because of the remodel."

"No, Angelina is at a hotel. I did hear something about a remodel. Corrine is redoing her house?"

He set the clippers down and combed his fingers through my hair. "I think that's about it."

"Very nice."

"A little product to hold it in place?"

Normally "product" would have been the last thing in the world I would want on my hair, but I didn't want to break the spell. "If it's good enough for Brad..."

"Absolutely." Carlos reached for a jar of gooey stuff and got a big glob on his fingers. "Yes, Corrine is doing a complete remodel," he said, as he massaged in the goop. "She took the house all the way down to the studs. But she used to be an architect, so she knows what she's doing."

"And she had to move out while the construction is underway?"

"Right. She's subletting a one-bedroom apartment in Lower Pacific Heights. It's in a big old Victorian. She told me she always wanted to live in a real Victorian. This is her chance—for a little while, at least."

He finished slicking back my hair and wiped his hands on a towel. Then he picked up a hand mirror and passed it to me. "Have a look in back."

I held the mirror to check my neckline while he rotated the chair. "Perfect. Much better than my neighbor's work."

He chuckled. "That was a *low* bar, I'm afraid."

"You said Corrine's Victorian is in Lower Pacific Heights? Whereabouts? I used to live around there."

"It's near the corner of Clay and Broderick. It even has a garage, which is unusual for a Victorian. She says the driveway is scary steep, though."

I nodded while he removed the cloth he'd draped over my shoulders, then I went back to the dressing room to ditch the smock. When I got out, I paid him a sum three times higher than I'd ever paid for a haircut—with a healthy tip. He'd earned it.

I was halfway out the door when he called me back. He had one more surprise up his sleeve. "Say, you don't know Corrine's friend Chris, do you? She also sent him here for a haircut."

There were only four Victorians in the immediate vicinity of Clay and Broderick. One didn't have a garage, one was clearly a duplex with a separate entrance for each flat, and one had a driveway with hardly any slope at all. The remaining one had a frighteningly steep driveway leading to a garage below the living space. I went up an equally steep brick stair to get to the front door.

White was written on a small piece of paper taped to the mailbox for apartment number three. The other mailboxes had embossed labels, suggesting more permanence. All doubt vanished when the first key on Corrine's ring turned the lock easily.

The interior was dim despite the canary-yellow walls and the ornate chandelier in the entryway. I paused, listening for sounds of tenants, but heard only the rumble of a passing delivery truck. I crept down a spongy hallway runner to confirm that neither of the apartments on the first floor was the one I wanted, then doubled back to climb the baroque walnut stair to the next floor. Apartment number three was to the left behind the landing. I used the other house key on the ring to open the door and slipped inside.

If the signs that Chris's apartment had been searched were subtle, the same could not be said for Corrine White's. It looked like an airplane crash site.

10
THE BEAT-HIVE

The door opened on a short hallway. Immediately to the right was an alcove with a niche in the wall for an old candlestick phone—or at least a replica of one. The phone lay in pieces on the floor.

The bedroom was farther to the right, and whoever tossed it had used the frappé setting. The bed was completely destroyed. The frame was upended, the slats dumped on the floor, and the mattress and box spring flung to the side and crisscrossed with knife slashes. Sheets and covers were strewn across the room, and the pillows—also slashed—had vomited feathers everywhere. There was no closet or dresser, but a mirrored wardrobe had been pitched on its side. Clothing on hangers, shoes, socks, underwear, and even a vibrator were piled in front like guts from a disemboweling. Shards from the broken mirror glittered in a halo around the pile.

The rest of the apartment had been treated much the same way, from the ransacked medicine cabinet, whose contents had been clawed out as if someone were scooping candy from a piñata, to the Salvador Dalí meets Jackson Pollock installation in the kitchen, complete with bent utensils, broken crockery, and skid marks of sour-smelling condiments in three different shades.

I had no idea what was being searched for, how big it was, or if it had been found. But there was no doubt in my mind that a lot of anger had been involved. There didn't seem to be any percentage in sifting further through the detritus, so I backed out the way I came, being careful not to touch anything as I went. At the door, I wiped the knob to remove any prints, pulled it shut, and snicked the deadbolt back into place with the key.

I peered over the banister to make sure the coast was clear, then made my way down the staircase to the entryway below. I paused beneath the chandelier. After all the effort I'd put into finding the house, it was disappointing to leave empty-handed. I thought back to my conversation with the hairdresser and his description of the Victorian and its garage. I flipped through the keys on Corrine White's ring and found one that belonged to a car, a late-model Lexus by the look of it.

The garage was one floor down, and as I didn't remember seeing a lock or a handle on the exterior door, I assumed there had to be a way to get to it from inside. I walked behind the main staircase and found a door that opened on a plunging stair with a splintery unvarnished railing.

A dull yellow light came from below, and as I descended, the air got cooler and mustier. At the bottom, I stepped onto a rough concrete pad that had just enough space for three cars if you didn't mind maneuvering around the metal poles shoring up the ceiling. The only vehicle in the place was a bronze Lexus SC 430 shoehorned into a spot between a moldering brick wall and one of the poles.

I pressed the lock button on the fat end of the key and was rewarded with the sound of the doors clicking open. The car's interior was nearly spotless. The only things inside that weren't factory original were a small bottle of hand sanitizer in the glove box and a couple of reusable grocery bags from Whole Foods in the back seat. The trunk was my last chance. I walked to the rear of the car, patted the lid for good luck, and pressed the button.

The lid yawned open to reveal several rolled blueprints and another grocery bag with a can of olive oil in it. Each of the blueprints was labeled with the address of the Russell Street house, and once I got them unspooled, I determined that they were the drawings for the remodel. This couldn't have been what all the fuss was about, especially since the plans would also have been filed with the Department of Building Inspection. The olive oil seemed even less promising.

On closer inspection, however, I realized that the can was not new and it didn't contain oil. It was a half-gallon tin decorated with a lithograph of two grizzly bears frolicking under an olive tree. From the style of the lettering, the fading of the paint, and the discoloration on the tin, I guessed it had been manufactured in the '40s or '50s.

Someone had fabricated a homemade lid from a scrap of tin, and once I pried that off, I found yet another roll of paper inside. I didn't know what it was exactly, but it wasn't a blueprint. The roll, a series of eight-and-one-half-inch strips of paper scotch-taped together, must have been more than a hundred feet long. Covering the paper was manually typed single-spaced text without margins or paragraph breaks. It was titled, "The Beat-hive," and it was wild. Really wild. Like this:

Sunday morning in the Beat-hive and wherever you look there is wax & pollen & ciggy butts but no honey. Honey to make jelly, honey to make jelly. Jelly, jelly, jelly, the fag queen wants royal jelly. Yes, we got no jelly today. But that's OK—and every-thing will be OK because the new Beat awakening is nigh and the goddamn Buddha Beat—not the queen, not the queen, you see— will take her place at the front of the conga line. Cha, cha, cha we will go. Cha, cha, cha out the hive we will go, into the golden light. "What?" you inquire, "the goddamn Buddha Beat is a she?" Yes, she's a she and he and a me when he/she/me wants to be. In the hive gender is fluid. Gender is fluid as a melted milkshake from a moo-cow. We've got drones & workers & droney-workers & workery-drones. All for the good of the colony. We swarm together and we screw together and everyone feels good. Everyone feels good and if they don't they can change. Change like they want. Being a droney-worker doesn't boat your float? Doesn't job the get done? Spin the big wheel & try again. Everyone wins new plumbing or new ways to use their old.

And so on for another ninety-nine feet. I still had no idea if this was what had prompted the search of the apartment—and the murders of Corrine White and Chris—but there was no disputing the fact that it was unusual. And maybe unusual meant valuable or desirable to some. To me, it seemed like so much drivel.

I rolled up the scroll, intending to return it to its jerry-rigged container. It was then that I noticed a card at the bottom of the tin. Thomas A. Fingerhut Rare Books was embossed above an address on Third Street. That didn't ring any immediate bells, but I knew as much about rare books as I did quantum mechanics. I shoved the card in my hip pocket and replaced the scroll.

I put the tin and the blueprints in the grocery bag, slung the bag over my shoulder, and closed the trunk of the Lexus. Then I crept up the garage stairs into the first-floor hallway, which was still as quiet as a convent. I padded up to the front door and hurried down the brick stairs to Clay Street.

I was congratulating myself on making a clean getaway when I spotted a Nissan with two men inside parked across the street. They weren't looking *at* me, but they were definitely looking in my direction. Trying to act unconcerned, I went up the block toward Divisadero, and when I was several car lengths in front of their vehicle, I jogged across to their side of the street.

Farther up the block, I ducked into a narrow alley between apartment buildings that led to Sacramento Street. When I was out of their line of sight, I began running to the corner market I'd seen earlier. If the men in the car were following me, I could hide there long enough to call a cab. If they weren't, I could toast my paranoia with a cold beer.

Turns out, I had no reason to celebrate. The Nissan materialized at the mouth of the alley, and the driver stumbled out. I looked back, intending to reverse direction, but the other man was pounding up the asphalt behind me. That meant I had to dodge or rush the driver—until I realized he was holding a gun.

I stopped on the sidewalk as the gunman ambled around the car to meet me. He had a big lima-bean head with a high forehead topped by a chunk of Brillo-pad hair. His mouth was small, moist, and puckered, and he was wearing tiny rimless glasses that had slipped too far down his nose. His eyes were squeezed into narrow slits, and beneath a nub of a chin, his bullfrog throat had reddened from exertion or excitement. All in all, he looked like a B-movie Nazi scientist.

"Have you been shopping?" he asked.

"Not for you," I said.

"You never know what I might like."

I heard footsteps behind me and felt the bag being pulled from my shoulder. Childishly, I gripped it tighter.

Lima Bean raised the gun and aimed it at my midsection. It had a suppressor screwed onto the barrel and some sort of space-age sighting system attached to the slide, but all the gizmos couldn't hide the fact that it was a .22 target pistol. "Nice gun," I said.

"Yes, it is. And I won't be disturbing any neighbors if I fire. It makes even less noise than a BB gun."

I let the bag slip from my hand. "Very considerate of you, I'm sure." I glanced back at the other man. He was taller, thinner, and younger. He had a foxy-looking face with something of a Slavic cast to it.

"Eyes and hands front," chided Lima Bean. "You can walk away from here in good health if you cooperate."

"Curing my bursitis, are you?"

"Shut up."

"Blueprints for the house," said the man behind me. His accent was European—possibly German. "And a can of olive oil."

"Olive oil?" said Lima Bean. "What did you want with that?"

"I eat a lot of salad."

"Wait a minute," continued the man behind me. "The can is just a container. It looks…it's what we want."

The man with the gun formed his mouth into a prissy little smile that made me want to slap him. "Where did you find it?" he asked.

"Find what?'"

"Don't play stupid. The manuscript."

"What exactly *is* the manuscript?"

"You are even dumber than I was led to believe. Never mind, just tell me where you found it."

"It was behind a false back in one the kitchen cabinets." It made me feel the tiniest bit better to make them think they'd missed out on something.

"Impossible," said the taller man, coming around to stand next to Lima Bean. He had the oil tin tucked under his arm.

Lima Bean shrugged. "Even a blind pig finds an acorn. You'd better drive."

The other man nodded and hurried around to the driver's door. He opened it, gingerly laid the can on the passenger seat, and got behind the wheel.

Lima Bean backed around to the far side of the car, keeping me in his sights the whole time. He unlatched the rear door and stood with the gun aimed over the roof, smirking away. "Well, this is good-bye." He leaned farther over the roof, and I realized with a jolt that he was going to shoot me.

I dove to the ground, rolling into a bed of succulents planted in front of an apartment house. I heard a pop, followed by the louder *whock* of a bullet ricocheting off the concrete.

"Hey—what's going on here?" came a shout from farther up Sacramento.

The door to the Nissan slammed, and I watched as the rear tire spun out of view.

I had gotten to my feet and was dusting off my knees when a mailman in a pith helmet and navy-blue shorts came up the sidewalk pushing a little cart with a satchel full of mail.

"Was that what I think it was?" he asked.

"Yeah. Damn Jehovah's Witnesses."

11
SMASHED FINGER

I had lost the scroll, or the manuscript, or whatever it was, but I still had the card for Fingerhut, the rare-book dealer. I decided to pay him a visit.

As I should have realized from the low street number in the address, his office was on the corner of Market and Third Street in the Hearst Building. Originally built by William Randolph Hearst of *Citizen Kane* "Rosebud" fame to house the offices of his newspaper, the building was now home to thirteen stories of small businesses.

I'd read somewhere that Julia Morgan, the architect who designed Hearst Castle, had also done the exterior entryway and the lobby. You could discern her handiwork in the crest with the capital letter *H* above the front entry, the bronze medallions with fanciful unicorn-like animals above the door, and the heavy ornamentation of the lobby.

I went up to the front desk to sign in. The guy behind the desk barely glanced at me as I put pen to paper, but when he saw the name of the tenant I was visiting, he said, "You got any business with them or you one of those lookie-loos?"

I set the pen down and straightened to face him. He was a big guy with a shaved head, and he had a yellow *H* like the one over the front entry embroidered on his blazer.

"What's that supposed to mean?"

He gave me a dead stare and cleared his throat. "Never mind."

"Okay, be that way," I said, and wandered over to the elevators.

Fingerhut was on the fifth floor in number 530. He was in a small suite sandwiched next to a stairwell around the corner from the elevator bank. I hoped he was getting a discount because there had to be a lot of noise.

I tried the door to the suite and found it locked, so I tapped lightly under Fingerhut's name in gold letters and waited. I heard a cough, a shuffling of feet, then the door pulled open a few inches and someone on the other side said, "Who is it?"

"What do you mean—who is it? A customer."

The door retracted to the point where it was almost closed. "You didn't call first."

"No, I didn't. Aren't you open to the public?"

"Not really. Most of our sales are by appointment."

I was beginning to notice a slight accent in the voice: Chicago devolving to West Coast maybe. There was something about the way he pronounced his *a*'s.

"Look, I'm here now and I want to talk about a manuscript. I won't bite."

The door seemed to hover for a long moment, then slowly, ever so slowly, it pulled back. Standing behind it was a balding guy in his fifties. He wore a green cardigan sweater over a checked shirt and had a pair of thick tortoiseshell glasses with a gray tint balanced on his nose. He was nearly as tall as I was, but he would have beat me by several inches if he didn't stoop.

"Hello," he said tentatively.

I held out my hand and tried to look innocuous. "Mr. Fingerhut? My name is Riordan. August Riordan."

"I'm not Fingerhut," he said, not taking my hand.

"I see. Is he on vacation?"

He turned without answering and walked to a table at the

back of the office where he eased himself into a chair. Eight-foot-high bookshelves towered around him, covering nearly all the wall space. Several other tables with display cases were positioned in front of the shelves, and two doorways—one to the left and another at the back—led into rooms full of still more books. The floor was covered in green linoleum tiles and tumbleweed-size dust bunnies. Although it was bigger than I expected, the whole place felt gloomy and claustrophobic.

Not knowing what else to do, I closed the door and came forward to stand by his desk. There was no customer chair. "Are you Fingerhut's associate?"

"No, his employee."

"What's going on? Why are you so jittery?"

"He was murdered."

"Where? In the office?"

"Yes, in the room behind me."

As if on cue, a small dog with a gray muzzle limped out from the room. The man behind the desk saw me staring at it and turned to look himself. "That's Bibi," he said, turning back to me. "Tom's dog. He keeps wandering around the office hoping to find him. I've been taking care of him, but my wife doesn't like animals. I don't know what I'm going to do with him."

"Mr. Fingerhut didn't have any family?"

"No, he lived alone."

There's nothing sadder than a sad dog—and Bibi was pretty damn sad. "I'm sorry. Was Fingerhut shot by any chance?"

"Yes."

"Was it a small-caliber weapon?"

He frowned. "I don't know anything about guns."

"Do the police like anyone for the murder?"

"*Like* is a funny way to put it. They have no suspects and no obvious motive."

"I take it there was no robbery."

"This isn't a business where you keep a lot of cash. And no

books were taken."

"Did you discover the body?"

He hugged himself and shivered. "Yes, the following morning. Why are you asking all these questions? Are you a reporter or something?"

"Or something. I'm a private investigator."

"Are you investigating Tom's—the murder here?"

"This is the first I've heard of it. I'm on another case that involves a manuscript." I didn't want to tell him about the business card, so I said, "Is that something you would deal in? Manuscripts, I mean?"

He seemed to relax now that he was on familiar ground. "Not exactly. It's rare to have a whole manuscript. Those are usually held with an author's papers at a museum or library. Occasionally, though, we'll get a few pages of a handwritten or typescript draft. We deal in letters of well-known authors or historical figures more often. For instance, we have a letter from Mark Twain in our current catalog."

"Do people ever bring material to you to have it appraised?"

"Sure. All the time. Collectors hire us to appraise or reappraise established collections. Sometimes we appraise books or papers from an estate during probate."

"Do you keep a record of customers?"

"For appraisals?"

"Yeah, and in general."

"We keep a list of all of our buyers, certainly. We mail quarterly catalogs to the serious collectors and send emails to the casual customers. We would have a record of any appraisal we did. But a customer like that wouldn't necessarily end up on our catalog list. Often they are lawyers or people who contact us after inheriting books or papers from a relative."

"Can you check a name against your customer list for me?"

He tilted his head and treated me to some side-eye. "We don't normally share information about customers. Would it be someone with a manuscript? Who wanted it appraised?"

"Theoretically."

"There's been no one like that in here for a long while—ever, in fact, as far as I know. As I said, a whole manuscript from a collected author would be extremely rare. Most are already accounted for in big institutions."

"And you would know? I mean, Fingerhut couldn't have dealt with the customer himself?"

"No, I may not initiate much business, but I end up touching every transaction if only for the bookkeeping."

I shifted my feet and tried to look deserving. "Corrine White. Can you just check if she appears in any of your records? I can't promise it, but it's just possible what I'm looking into has some bearing on the murder of your boss."

For no reason I could tell, he toughened up. "You sound just like the dolts who come in convinced they have a signed first edition of Joyce's *Ulysses*. It's too far-fetched."

Bibi picked up on something in his voice. The old hound took a couple of doddering steps forward and barked at me.

"What's the harm?" I insisted. "I just need to know if she's there. No details, no specifics, just a yes or no."

He sighed and reached across the desk for a laptop. He flipped open the lid and punched a few keys. "She's not on our mailing list." He did some hunting and pecking on the touch pad, then made more clickety-clack noises. "And she's not in our accounts receivable file. We've not had contact with her. There—are you satisfied?"

"Satisfied, no. But I will stop pestering you."

He pulled off his glasses and looked at me through weak, myopic orbs. He seemed strangely deflated. "Well, okay. If you do find anything that bears on Tom's murder, I'd appreciate hearing about it."

"Absolutely. I'll let you know, Mr.—"

"Bloom. Leo Bloom."

"Thanks."

Bibi whined at me as I turned to go out the door. On Market Street, away from the dusty catacomb of rare books, the city suddenly seemed vivid and bright.

12
BEAT EPIPHANY

"So who is he, exactly?" I was sitting across the table from Angelina in a small coffee shop on Pine. After the twin debacles at her sister's apartment and the rare-book-dealer's office, I'd arranged to meet her and was now trying to learn more about the mystery man who'd followed me from the hotel.

"Like I said, he's a friend." She was wearing a sleeveless T-shirt and a pair of distressed jeans. The T-shirt had the image of a skeletal hand stenciled on the front—its bony fingers arching over her breasts nearly to her throat—and she'd accessorized with a wide-brimmed hat worn far back on her head. "Are you jealous?" she said with a smirk.

"I'll take the Fifth on that. But to clarify, he's a friend—*from Canada*?"

"Yep."

"He followed you here?"

"Apparently."

"Did you know he was coming?"

"No, I had no idea. Look, August, I'm not trying to hide anything. I actually mentioned him to you before."

"You did?"

She nodded. "At the office. When I described how I found

Chris. Jeff is the one who introduced me."

I leaned back in my chair. "You mean he's the other cross-dresser Chris got to know through the internet. On Ribbit."

Angelina smiled. "Reddit. It's called Reddit. But, yes, he's the one."

"Then he's gay?"

"If you have to categorize him, it would be best if you thought of him as bisexual."

"He seemed pretty upset with the idea of our spending the night. Are you in a relationship with him?"

She picked up her cup of coffee and took a sip. "Hmm...this is good."

"I'll take that as a yes."

"Just winding you up. I lived with him and several other roommates in a big house in Vancouver. We may have hooked up once or twice, but I definitely wouldn't call it a relationship."

"But he might? Or he might wish it were?"

"Maybe."

"Even though he dresses in girl's clothes?" I said more loudly than I had intended. An older woman sitting to the left of us lowered her newspaper to glare.

"Boy, August, you need to get out of your cisgender box. And what does all this have to do with my sister's murder?"

I let my eyes wander to the wall behind her. It was decorated with a display of skateboards plastered with colorful stickers. One sticker showed a rabbit with Xs for eyes injecting purple liquid into a carrot with a hypodermic. I wasn't sure exactly what that signified—and I wasn't exactly sure why I was asking so many questions about Jeff. Maybe I *was* jealous.

I shook my head. "Possibly nothing. Did you tell him you were coming to San Francisco to look for her?"

"Not that I recall."

"You still have his phone number?"

"Sure."

"Then call him up and ask him what the heck he's doing here and when he arrived and how he knew you were traveling here. And one more thing. Ask him if he knows the two jokers who dry-gulched me outside your sister's apartment."

"I can't imagine he would. Who *are* they?"

"I haven't the foggiest. And you're absolutely certain you don't?"

She lifted her hat to push a strand of hair farther back on her forehead, then set it back down at a rakish angle. "A Nazi scientist and a foxy-faced guy who speaks with a German accent? They sure don't sound like anyone I know."

"What about the manuscript I found in the car? Do you think your sister might have written it?"

"It's possible, I guess. I didn't spend much time with her growing up, but when I knew her, she was more interested in drawing and painting than writing. I wasn't surprised when Chris told me she'd become an architect because it seemed like a natural choice for her. But given the card you found for the book dealer, isn't it more likely that it was someone else's work? In school we studied a Spanish novel called *La Colmena. The Hive.* Maybe it was a copy of that."

"Unless it was written in English, it would have to be a translated copy. I suppose I could check. Do you remember what the author's name is?"

"Sure. It's Cela. He won the Nobel Prize for Literature. He was kind of a weird dude. He offered to demonstrate how much water he could suck up his asshole during a TV interview."

The older woman to the left stood abruptly and hurried past us to the door. At the threshold, she paused and gave us a look that would have frozen magma.

"Made ourselves a new friend there," I said. "Weird would definitely describe what I read. But there's still the English problem and the fact that it seems to be typewritten."

Angelina nodded and looked down at her lap. "Just a thought.

But what do we do now, August? If Chris and my sister were killed for this manuscript, those men have it now. They apparently got what they wanted. And if they aren't from here, they may be on their way back to Germany—or wherever they're from. How would you or the police ever go about finding them?"

I looked back at the wall of stickered skateboards. "I don't know."

After I walked Angelina back to her hotel and kissed her good-bye, I drifted down California to the intersection with Powell where I'd encountered the tour bus the day before. I made a right on Powell and stayed on it until it dead-ended at Market where the cable cars are turned around for the trip up Nob Hill. I waded through a horde of tourists queuing for their seven-dollar ride, brushed past a shirtless tap dancer in parachute pants, maneuvered around a Chinese woman with a large sign reading, THE CHINESE COMMUNIST PARTY IS SATAN, and walked up to the entrance of the Flood Building.

Lacking any better ideas, I was heading back to the office to pick Gretchen's brain. I also owed her an update as we hadn't spoken since the evening I discovered Corrine White's body.

I found her at her desk, brow furrowed, clicking away on her computer mouse. She was wearing black again—a slim body-hugging dress with sleeves that ended just below her elbows in French cuffs. And, like always, she wore it well.

"You look like you dropped your lollipop in the cat box," she said.

I slumped into the Aeron chair across from her. "Your analogy, while overly graphic, is apt." I proceeded to give her a rundown on everything that had happened during the last forty-eight hours.

She listened carefully until the end.

"Did you sleep with her?"

"Come on. With everything I told you, you ask that?"

"I ask because you have a stylish new haircut, and unless I'm mistaken, you actually put some gel in it. It's almost as if you were attempting to appeal to a younger woman."

"I told you I found Corrine's apartment by talking to the owner of a neighborhood business. The business was a hair salon."

"*You* went to a *hair salon*? Did they make you wear a smock and wash your hair in a bowl? Did you take pictures?"

"I'm not getting into the details. Suffice it to say that it was all done in the line of duty."

She smiled at me in a manner that made me think of us in the old way. "Well, this is the only time I'm going to say this, but it looks good. You look good."

"Thank you."

"You didn't answer my question, though."

"No, and I don't intend to. Have you got anything else more relevant to ask or, more to the point, something to tell me?"

"Kittredge called. He confirmed the bullet that killed Corrine was a .22 and that the rifling marks on it match the marks on the bullet that killed Chris."

"And both sets were probably made by the gun of the guy I ran into today."

"Your Nazi scientist?"

"Yes, I'm thinking of him as *Herr Doktor* until I learn his real name."

"Well, are you planning to tell Kittredge about *Herr Doktor*?"

"I'm not sure. I'll have to own up to a lot more hanky-panky with Corrine White's house keys before I can bring *Herr Doktor* and his friend into the picture. This time, Kittredge might not let it slide."

Gretchen pursed her lips. "I figured you were going to say that. But Kittredge could bring a lot of resources to bear."

"I don't think so. At least not until I learn more. All I really have is a general description of two weirdos. I might not even be able to convince Kittredge to look for them. And I don't have any real proof that they did anything. I could confess to pocketing the keys and searching the apartment and the car, and accomplish nothing more than an all-expense-paid trip to the county jail."

She wagged her finger. "You've a bad case of LWS and always have."

"LWS?"

"Lone Wolf Syndrome. But you are not working alone and I have done some clever research that will help correct a major misapprehension that you are operating under."

"Do tell."

"You are way off base about the manuscript. It has nothing to do with this Spanish writer Angelina mentioned."

"Then what does it have to do with?"

"Give me the title again."

"The Beat-hive."

"And what—or who—are the Beats?"

"You're asking a jazz bassist about beats?"

"Not musical beats. The Beat Generation—Ginsberg, Burroughs, and Kerouac. That's the sort of Beat we're talking about. The manuscript you found was a Beat composition."

I let my jaw hinge open. She was right. I didn't know much about Beat writing, but I did know they favored a manic stream-of-consciousness style with a lot of repetition. That certainly fit with what I'd read. And then there was the title, which was an obvious pun—or obvious once Gretchen pointed it out. "How did you know?"

"Chris's internet search history. I've been going through his computer files, and that was one of the things I checked. He must have come back to the office after hours while he was on vacation because there were a number of recent searches about Beat writers, the history of the Beats in San Francisco, and Beat experts."

I was impressed. For the first time I understood that she and Chris had been real partners in the business. It was exactly the sort of thing Chris would have unearthed for me in our investigations. "That's tremendous, Gretchen. You definitely earned your gold star for today."

She cocked her head to look at me, and the faintest of smiles played on her lips. "There's more. I found a Beat expert Chris talked to, an old guy who actually knew some of them."

"Then I need to talk to him, too."

"You do. That's why I set up an appointment for you tomorrow morning." She peeled a Post-it off a pad on her desk and handed it to me. "All the details."

"Thank you." I looked down at the note. It struck me again how much Chris had figured out. There was hardly anything we'd discovered that he didn't already seem to know.

"I bet I can guess what you're thinking," said Gretchen.

"What?"

"You're thinking that we've been eating Chris's dust this whole time."

"Exactly. In fact, I'm surprised *he* didn't find the manuscript."

Gretchen reached her hand across the desk to take mine. "It's fine for us to be following him—that's how we find his killer. Just don't follow him to the end."

13
ARNIE JEWEL

The next morning I unlatched the security gate at the entrance to the Post Street apartment and stepped outside. Almost immediately, a divot materialized in the building facade just inches from my nose. There was no audible crack or report, so it took me a moment to realize I was being shot at. I crouched behind the gate as more shots whanged off its steel bars. I managed to fumble open the building's door and dive inside.

There wasn't much doubt about who was flinging the rounds since the gunman was obviously using a suppressor. I supposed *Herr Doktor* and his buddy were looking to eliminate the final witness, and I decided—belatedly—that it was time for some countermeasures. I walked well back from the door, parked myself on a lobby bench, and yanked out my cell phone. I didn't call the police—I was pretty sure *Herr Doktor* was long gone and the only thing I'd have to show the cops was chips in a brick wall— so I called Ray, my neighbor in Palm Springs. He picked up on the third ring.

"I've been meaning to call you," he said in lieu of hello. His voice, like always, was high and reedy.

"You have?" My voice, unlike always, was warbly. Near-death experiences have that effect on me.

"Yeah, but you first. What's on your mind?"

"I need you to ship my Luger and holster to me here in San Francisco."

There was a long pause. "Is that legal?"

"Shipping guns? Sort of. If you are a dealer or—"

"Don't tell me. I'd rather plead ignorance than operate with full knowledge of my crime."

"That's the spirit. I need it overnighted. Fastest delivery."

"Okay, but you're paying for it."

"Of course. Put it on my tab. And when you fill out the forms—"

"August, I'm not an idiot. I'm not going to list the contents as an illegal gun shipment."

Ray certainly wasn't an idiot. He was a retired aerospace engineer—and a damn good one at that. He was, however, a little lacking in common sense. "Of course not. Let me give you the coordinates." I dictated the address of the Flood Building office.

"I take it the gun is in its usual secure location?"

"Yeah, under the bed."

"I'll get it out today." He paused to clear his throat. "You going to tell me what's going on?"

"My old partner—he was definitely murdered." It was surprising how hard it was to say that out loud.

"Do you know who did it?"

"I've identified a person or two of interest, but it's complicated."

"And dangerous, apparently."

"Yeah."

"You need me to come up and help?"

Although Ray was well into his eighth decade, it wasn't a question I took lightly. He and his electronic gizmos had saved my bacon several times before. "Thanks, Ray. I appreciate the offer. It's not your sort of thing. If circumstances change, I'll let you know."

"You do that."

"What did you have for me?"

"You got a letter."

I'd asked him to take in my mail, so the news wasn't exactly unexpected. "Ray, I may not be the most popular guy in the world, but even I get the occasional utility bill."

"It's not a bill, and it's postmarked from San Francisco."

"Who sent it?"

"It doesn't say, exactly. The only thing written in the space for the return address is *CD*."

I didn't have to think very long to figure out who that was. "Open it up," I commanded.

"I will, but I already know what's in it." I heard the receiver being put down, then paper being torn. The clatter of metal followed. Ray picked up the phone. "It's a key."

"Just a key? No paper, no note?"

"Nope."

"Can you tell what kind of key?"

"It's a little small for a house key. Maybe a padlock?"

"How about a safe deposit box?"

Ray grunted. "No, there's no number stamped on it. And those are usually thinner and longer. No, it's a padlock key—or maybe a locker key."

"When was it sent?"

"Four days ago. Like I said, I didn't call you about it right away."

I let my head loll forward. "Jesus."

"It's from your old partner, isn't it?"

"It has to be. But hell if I know what it's for."

I hung up after asking him to include the key in the shipment and went upstairs to scope out the street from the fire escape. If there was anyone still waiting to ambush me, I couldn't spot them. I eventually felt confident enough to slink out the front door again—and no bullets punctuated my arrival on the sidewalk.

I hurried up Post Street until I got close enough to Union Square to find an honest-to-goodness taxicab and waved it down.

I gave the driver an address on Broadway near Jones, a Russian Hill destination less than half a mile from Corrine White's house. I was heading to an appointment with Arnie Jewel, the Beat expert Gretchen had located via Chris's internet search history.

He lived in a blocky Victorian that had been chopped into several apartments. His was on the second floor, and when he greeted me at the door, it was clear he was even older than Ray. He had a laurel of white hair, a wispy white beard, and thin parchment skin marked with liver spots and spider veins. He wore a baggy gray cambric shirt and a pair of equally loose-fitting dress pants cinched tightly at the waist.

After I introduced myself, he said, "You've got some schmutz on your face if you care."

I brushed at my cheek and came away with pulverized brick grit, residue from my close ballistic encounter. Even though he had to be pushing ninety and peered through thick owlish glasses, Mr. Jewel had not lost his powers of observation.

"Thanks," I mumbled.

He led me down a corridor covered with paintings, posters, and photographs to a messy office lined with shelves that bowed under the weight of hundreds of books. On the top shelf, they were piled horizontally in layers that looked like sedimentary rock. In the corner of the room was an L-shape desk with more piles of books and papers strewn across it. A manual typewriter sat on a desk pullout, and on the far side of that, a bamboo cane chair with a ratty cushion. Jewel eased himself into the cane chair and waved at a rocker gathering dust in the far corner.

I pulled the rocker closer to him and sat down in it with a creak that was probably heard in Oakland. "Thanks for taking time to see me."

"So your friend is dead?" Jewel said without preamble.

"Yes, but...Gretchen told you that?"

"I wouldn't have agreed to see you if there wasn't a compelling reason. I'm tired of talking about the Beats. That's all anyone wants to discuss these days. My own work is ignored completely."

"You're a writer, too?"

He waved vaguely behind him, then placed a mottled hand on top of a stack of books near the typewriter. All the books in the stack had his name on them. "No. I just have a fetish for wood pulp."

"Sorry. If it makes any difference, the Beats have been dropped on my head. I don't have an intrinsic interest."

"Ask your questions."

"When did my friend come to see you?"

"A little less than a week ago. He was smart enough to position the visit as an opportunity to get a book signed. Only after we discussed my novel—which he'd actually read and appreciated—did he slip in some questions about the Beats."

"What did he ask?"

"I could tell he already had a good general knowledge. He was focused on the time in late 1951 when Jack Kerouac came to San Francisco to live with Neal Cassady and his wife Carolyn."

"I see."

It must have sounded to Jewel like I didn't see much of anything. "You don't know who Neal Cassady is, do you?"

"On a scale of yes or no, no."

"He's a major Beat figure. And he was also associated with the sixties counterculture—Ken Kesey and the Merry Pranksters in particular. He had aspirations to be a writer, but he is best known as a sort of muse to Kerouac and Ginsberg. He encouraged Kerouac to adopt a more spontaneous writing style and served as the model for several of Kerouac's characters, including Dean Moriarty in Kerouac's most popular novel, *On the Road*."

"Did you know him?"

"I knew most all these characters. I went to school with Kerouac and Ginsberg at Columbia, and I met Cassady in San Francisco through Ginsberg. He was crazy. He was always on—like one big twitching human nerve. It's no wonder he's remembered for encouraging spontaneity."

"You said he had aspirations to be a writer. Did he actually produce anything?"

"He worked sporadically on an autobiographical novel called *The First Third*, but it wasn't published until after his death. The piece of prose he is best known for is a long letter he wrote to Kerouac during a three-day Benzedrine high. It's been dubbed the Joan Anderson Letter because it mentions a lover of his by that name. It's this letter that Kerouac credited as the inspiration for the style he used in *On the Road* and later books."

I fidgeted in the rocker, producing another discordant creak. Cassady seemed like a bit of a sideline. I couldn't quite believe all this hoopla had been about him. "What about Kerouac?" I asked. "What was he working on during the time of this visit—late 1951, you said?"

Jewel nodded. "Late '51 through the spring of '52. Your friend asked the same thing. It was a very productive time for Kerouac. He was basically being supported by the Cassadys—by Carolyn, actually, who was the only one of the three who had a paying job. Kerouac worked every day in the loft bedroom of the cottage the Cassadys were renting. He was still polishing *On the Road*, which wouldn't be published until 1957, and he also finished a draft of *Visions of Cody*, which was sort of a recapitulation and expansion of *Road* in an even more experimental style. Some of it is actually based on rap sessions with Cassady he taped in the Russell Street house."

It almost slid by me like another widget on an assembly line. "Wait a minute. Russell Street?"

"Yes, not far from here—on Russian Hill."

"29 Russell Street?"

"That's right, why?"

"The fickle finger of fate is trying its damnedest to get up my nose." Without mentioning her name, I gave him a brief summary of the search for Corrine White and my discovery of her body on the second floor of the house.

"That can't be a coincidence," said Jewel, finally seeming to develop an interest in the conversation. "That's right where Kerouac would have been working."

"Is it possible he worked on something else besides *On the Road* and this *Cody* book?"

"Of course. His habit was to work on multiple projects simultaneously. Some of them were eventually abandoned, some weren't published until he became more popular, and a few of them didn't see print until he died. *Visions of Cody*, for instance, was published posthumously. Which book are you thinking about?"

I ignored the question. "I assume he wrote on a typewriter. Did he ever use long strips of paper taped together in a sort of continuous scroll?"

Jewel gave a strangled cough that managed to sound dismissive. "You really are a babe in the woods, aren't you?"

"What's that supposed to mean?"

He pushed the carriage of his typewriter to the left until the bell rang. "Yes, he often used a typewriter. Many of the writers of my generation did—and do. But Kerouac is famous for writing a draft of *On the Road* on a scroll of paper he scotch-taped together. He used rolls of architectural tracing paper—sometimes called bumwad because it's thin like toilet paper. You'll often hear that he used teletype paper since Kerouac mentioned it on *The Steve Allen Show*, but he didn't. It was bumwad. He made the scroll so he could type continuously without having to change sheets. By the time he finished, it was one hundred and twenty feet long."

"Does the scroll version of *On the Road* still exist?"

"It does. A collector owns it."

"What's it worth?"

"The auction price in 2001 was two-point-four million dollars. I'm sure it would fetch more than five today."

"Wow." I looked past Jewel to the layers of tattered books along the wall. It was hard to imagine that a book—let alone a rough manuscript—could be worth that much. "Then let me ask you this. What if an unknown and previously unpublished Kerouac scroll were to be discovered. How much would it fetch?"

Jewel made a harrumphing noise and took off his glasses. After several false starts, he yanked out a shirttail to wipe the lenses, then set the glasses back on his face with a trembling hand. "Is that what this is about? You think you found a lost manuscript?"

"I think the woman I mentioned earlier discovered a manuscript while remodeling the Russell Street house. Maybe in a wall of the bedroom Kerouac was using."

"Why would he put it there?"

"I don't know. Maybe as a sort of time capsule. Maybe it was something he didn't want to come out when he was alive. Something controversial, something too hot to handle."

"I can't imagine anything being too hot to handle for Kerouac. That's what he was about—shaking up the establishment. Too hot to handle was all in a day's work for him. But if it is a legitimate manuscript, I'll wager it's a draft of an existing book. Does the work have a title?"

"The Beat-hive."

"Hmm…And how would you describe the content?"

"Honestly? As a bunch of mumbo jumbo."

He chuckled dryly. "You wouldn't be alone in that assessment of Kerouac's oeuvre. Truman Capote famously dismissed it as 'not writing, just typing.' But Kerouac definitely has a place in the American literary pantheon. *On the Road* is consistently listed in the top one hundred novels of the twentieth century. Can you give me a more specific impression? Like a lot of writers, Kerouac frequently changed titles of works in progress. While I confess I've never heard of 'The Beat-hive,' it may be a jettisoned title for another book."

"All right, but I only saw a few sentences." I described the stew of allegory, sex, gender-bending, collective living, and bee's wax in the excerpt I read.

Jewel combed his chin hair with his fingers. "Interesting," he said at last. "You might be on to something after all. Kerouac and Cassady were bisexual. Ginsberg was gay, as was Burroughs. They all slept with one another, and a number of them were involved in what we might now call polyamorous triads. For instance, Cassady encouraged Carolyn to sleep with Kerouac. In fact, Cassady tried to get them all into bed together, but Kerouac was too squeamish. That squeamishness didn't prevent LuAnne, Cassady's first wife, from jacking both men off simultaneously while they were on one of their famous road trips."

He stared over at me like he was expecting some sort of reaction.

"Okay."

"Furthermore, the Beats often lived together in communal quarters. They shared crash pads in New York, Denver, Berkeley, San Francisco, and even Paris. And there was constant rivalry and jealousy between them. Ginsberg and Kerouac were jealous of each other's relationship with Cassady and both of them were critical of the other's work at times. Ginsberg could be the fag queen mentioned dismissively in the manuscript. All of them—with the notable exception of Cassady—were distressed and tormented by their sexuality at some point in their lives, Kerouac most of all."

"So you're saying the writing I saw could have been inspired by real-life themes and events."

"Without a doubt. If there was ever a writer to grind up his experiences to make a product, it was Kerouac. And more to the point, I *have* seen a reference to something like this. Not by this title, and not as something to be buried in the wall in a time capsule, but as Kerouac's Utopian prescription for a better world. A better world where he would no longer be ashamed and tormented by his sexuality."

"You say 'reference.' Are there any known copies of the book itself?"

"No. The only mention I'm aware of is in a fragment of a letter from Kerouac to Cassady. Most of the letter was lost, but

Carolyn—who lived the longest—retained a page. Kerouac describes a novel of his that will show the world that the true meaning of Beat is beatific. And, as you suggested, he makes clear that it's something for posterity, for future generations. Most Beat scholars assumed it was a project that Kerouac never started or abandoned early on. He had plenty of those in his career."

I thought of Fingerhut. "Would someone like a rare-book dealer be aware of the book—or the possibility of a book on this topic from Kerouac?"

"Maybe. It would depend on how much the dealer specialized in Beat literature. This is pretty inside baseball."

"If it existed, would this thing be as valuable as the *On the Road* scroll?"

"You're really stuck on this value question, aren't you?"

"Humor me."

Jewel turned to the typewriter and repeatedly pressed the space bar. The carriage bumped along with a staccato vibration. "If it were finished," he said without glancing up, "and if it were written during the late '40s, early '50s when Kerouac did his best work, it would be quite valuable—both as a collector's item and as a new work to be published. No doubt many current-day Beats would see it as a sort of holy text, a prescription for living."

He took his finger off the space bar and looked me in the eye. "But if you're wondering if someone would kill for it, the answer is yes, decidedly yes. To the right sort of person—or the wrong sort—murder would be a small price to pay."

14
NUMBER ONE WITH A BULLET

Standing on the sidewalk in front of Jewel's apartment, I took out my phone to call a cab, then thought better of it. The walk home was mostly downhill, and I figured I could use the time to mull over what I'd learned. I dialed Angelina instead. I was eager to give her the news about the manuscript and find out if her sister had ever expressed an interest in the Beats—at least that's what I told myself.

The call went to voice mail almost immediately, and Angelina's flip greeting—"Think fast!"—caught me flat-footed. I hemmed and hawed but eventually managed to leave a message about the scroll and ended by asking her to dinner.

I pocketed the phone and trekked west on Broadway, then south on Jones. The going *was* downhill at first, but I'd underestimated the amount of altitude I had to claw back to traverse Nob Hill. I'd peeled off my jacket and was blotting sweat from my forehead by the time I reached the 1930s art deco tower that marked the summit. A techie type struggling with a folding commuter bike nodded at me from under the canopied awning of the building as I wheezed by.

Picking up steam on the downhill side, I found myself thinking about my encounter with *Herr Doktor* earlier that morning. I'd told Gretchen that I didn't have anything to link him and his side-kick to the murders, but I realized that the potshots he took at me might have changed that. As I approached the Post Street apartment, I scoped the surrounding area to make sure no one was lying in ambush—and once I assured myself that the coast was clear—I got down on my haunches by the building's entrance.

I worked out from the gate in concentric semicircles, looking for one of the slugs from this morning's ambush. I found pigeon crap, dried bubblegum, cigarette butts, and even a hypodermic needle, but no bullets. Then, in a groove in the sidewalk near the red-painted curb, an oblong peanut of metal winked up at me. It was flattened on one side from the impact with the gate or the building's facade but it was otherwise intact. I picked it up in a fold of my handkerchief, wadded everything into a tight little bundle, and shoved it into my hip pocket.

I stood up and was pressing my fists into the small of my back to unravel my spine when my phone buzzed with an incoming text from Angelina.

sounds like progress, daddy-o! spoke to jeff & will update you this evening, a harmonic convergence which will hopefully involve more than dinner. missed you last nite! :)

I supposed "daddy-o" was a nod to my discovery of the Beat connection, but given the difference in our ages, I was a little sensitive about any mention of daddies. Still, I had to admit to a considerable thrill at the suggestion of a return engagement in the bedroom. The evening I took her home from the police station was so fraught that I wasn't sure how much she appreciated my presence—to say nothing of my rusty efforts at lovemaking.

I thumbed a response.

I missed you, too, and will do my best to make our convergence extra harmonic!

Then I used the phone to call Kittredge, who elicited no thrill in me at all. After our usual exchange of snarls, he agreed to meet me for lunch at the Farm Club, a sports bar in the Tenderloin. His selection of the venue, which was only a couple of blocks from the Post Street apartment, halfway convinced me that he was already in the area.

The Farm Club was in a shotgun building on Mason with exposed brick walls and a necklace of eighteen flat-screen TVs strung around the circumference that showed everything from football to poker to mixed martial arts. An oak bar ran the length of the left side, and a splattering of high-top tables occupied the right. Kittredge was already sitting at one of the tables with his back against the wall. A couple of hot dogs in paper trays were sitting on the table, and the one closest to Kittredge had a big bite taken out of it.

"What if I don't want a hot dog?" I asked as I sat down.

"There are only two things on the menu, hot dogs and nachos. The hot dogs are here, and the nachos are coming. You're paying for everything."

"Swell."

Kittredge took another bite of his dog and chewed it leisurely. "Well, it's your party. What did you want?"

"You got one of those evidence bags you guys carry around?"

"Maybe."

"Give it here."

Kittredge grunted, leaned to one side, and reached into the pocket of his fancy suit. He extracted a plastic evidence bag—which was nothing more than a Ziplock with a chain-of-custody label printed on it—and passed it over. I retrieved my wadded handkerchief, thrust it into the mouth of the bag, then shook it until the bullet fell out. I sealed the bag and set it on the table with a flourish.

"What the fuck is that?"

In lieu of an answer, I took a bite of my own hot dog.

Kittredge picked up the bag reluctantly. "A .22 slug, huh? Did the tooth fairy leave it under your pillow?"

"No. More like it missed my nose by two inches."

"When?"

"This morning." I gave a bare-bones account of being shot at as I left the Post Street apartment, then described how I had searched the sidewalk in front of the entrance to find the slug. I didn't mention that there had been several hours between the two events. I didn't want Kittredge objecting that the bullet could have come from a *different* shooting.

"You think the bullet was fired from the gun that killed Duckworth and White?"

"There's only one way to find out."

"Hmm. Did you see the shooter?"

I nodded as I inhaled the majority of my dog. "In a car across the street," I said when I came up for air.

"And?"

I gave an abbreviated description of *Herr Doktor*, referencing his sidekick only as a shadowy figure in the front seat. As I hadn't actually seen either of them this morning, I didn't want to lay it on too thick. It was still too thick for Kittredge.

"So you step out on the sidewalk, immediately come under fire, dive back behind the gate, retract into the building like a chilled testicle—and *still* have the presence of mind to make your assailant."

I shrugged. "Some of us show more grace under fire than others."

"Had you seen this guy before this morning?"

"No."

"Had any inkling someone was following you?"

"No."

"Been poking your nose in places that might prompt retaliation—places, I might add, that you heretofore have neglected to mention?"

"No." And then I thought that I should throw him a bone. "I spent yesterday canvassing Corrine White's neighborhood trying to find someone who could tell me more about her or why she might have been killed. I struck out."

Kittredge growled. "We already interviewed all the neighbors—thoroughly. You were wasting your time."

"Agreed. But the point is I was wasting it in a way that wouldn't have prompted retaliation. Especially if you'd already done the same thing."

A waitress came up with a basket of nachos and two mugs of beer. I started to complain about not having a say in the choice of beer, but Kittredge cut me off. "You'll drink it and like it."

"And pay for it, too?"

"Exactly."

There was a truce while we finished the hot dogs and worked our way through the nachos and Stella Artois. When we were done, Kittredge leaned back against the wall and belched. "I don't believe half of what you're saying, Riordan. But I'll test the bullet. If it matches, then you are going to have to do a much better job of explaining how it came into your possession and how you were able to describe the alleged shooter."

"Are you saying I made the whole thing up?"

"I'm saying it wouldn't surprise me if you put your foot in some other crime scene and took the slug away as a souvenir. Now you're trying to get me to bite on this phony shooting story without explaining what you were really up to."

"You can check the Post Street apartment. The facade is chipped and there must be other slugs in the area."

"Whatever."

"Are you at least going to put out a description of my guy? Maybe have a police artist work up a sketch?"

"If and when we match the bullet."

A group at the bar let out a loud whoop as a Japanese woman

with braided hair dropped her opponent in a mixed martial arts match. My conversation with Kittredge seemed to have run its course. I expected him to slide off his stool and go, leaving me to pick up the check as promised—but he lingered.

"Something else on your mind?" I asked.

"Mrs. Kongsangchai has gone missing."

"Who's Mrs. Kong—"

"Don't play dumb, Riordan. We already established you've been sniffing around Golden Fingers."

"I guess we have. She's the manager, right? I thought you said you already talked to her."

"We did. I went back to the massage parlor this morning to do a follow-up, and they told me she hasn't come into work for two days. Hasn't called to explain why."

"You check her house?"

"Yeah, I sent a squad car to her building. Got the apartment manager to open her unit—no dice. Neighbors say they haven't seen her either."

I pulled a toothpick from the dispenser on the table, stabbed the last jalapeño from our nachogeddon, and popped it in my mouth. "It doesn't have to be tied to Duckworth. Not directly, at least. You said yourself that Wo Hop To wouldn't want a body discovered at their business. Maybe they decided it was time to rid themselves of the mama-san who let it happen on her watch."

"I thought of that. But I got to believe they would have handled it differently. For one, they wouldn't have left everyone at the business dangling. They would have sent someone to manage it."

"Maybe that's why they didn't. So you wouldn't think they were involved."

"Possibly, but I also think they would have cleaned out her apartment to make it look like she skipped town. Too many loose ends otherwise."

"Can you talk to them?"

"Wo Hop To? Apart from the fact that they are *criminals* and

I represent *law enforcement*, the chain of command is a little murky since you just about chopped the top guy's head off several mayoral elections ago."

"Sorry, not sorry."

"Doesn't matter. Wo Hop To is not the answer."

"Meaning the manager's disappearance is tied to Duckworth's murder?"

"Meaning someone might be going around trying to eliminate people involved in the case, including you—if your cock-and-bull story about being shot at is to be believed."

15
HAND FINISH

Kittredge left and I settled the tab to the tune of $53.45 plus tip. I exited the sports bar and hadn't gone three steps up the sidewalk when my phone made more noise. This time it was an incoming call from a San Francisco number I didn't recognize.

"August Riordan," I intoned, trying hard not to burp nachos into the receiver.

"I heard you wanted to talk to me."

"Heard how, exactly?" The person on the other end of the line was female and spoke with a slight accent. Precisely what sort of accent I couldn't place.

"From Cristabel."

"Cristabel?" I repeated, then I remembered—the wife from the cleaning team at Golden Fingers. "Oh, yeah, I remember. You work there? At Golden Fingers?"

"No, I'm a shift manager at Burger King. I got all your flame-broiling secrets right here."

"Funny. When can we meet?"

"First things first. How much are you paying?"

"I don't know what you're going to tell me yet. It depends—"

"Two hundred—in cash."

I mashed the phone to my shoulder while I reached for my

wallet. I barely had enough even with all the rumpled singles. I didn't think it was a coincidence my caller had asked for the same amount I had offered Cristabel and her husband. "Okay. Two hundred."

"Plus the price of a manicure."

"I'm going to pay for you to get a manicure?"

"No, you're going to pay me to give you one. That's my day job. We can talk while I work."

First some new clothes, then a new haircut, and now a manicure. I was going to be a completely new man. "Okay, where and when?"

"Nailed It."

"What?"

"That's the name of the salon. Come over now if you're free."

"Who do I ask for?"

"Kim."

Nailed It was conveniently located in the Polk Gulch neighborhood between an SRO hotel and a dry cleaner's. At the entrance was a reception desk done in black lacquer, and on the wall opposite, a chromatic display of at least a hundred different shades of nail polish. Padded vinyl chairs for the clients lined the walls on either side, and squatting at the back, surrounded by lit candles, river rocks, and offerings of food and drink, was a green soapstone Buddha. An Asian woman with hair dyed a Day-Glo shade of fuchsia nodded at me from behind the desk. She wore yoga pants and a black cotton T-shirt over a lithe figure. Her face was an oval with full pouty lips and a flat nose.

"Mr. Riordan?"

"Don't get many male clients, huh?"

She grinned. "We don't. It's a shame, really. Men don't take good care of their hands."

I was tempted to make a crack about men taking care of other parts of their anatomy at Golden Fingers but thought better of it. I held up my mitts. "You've got your work cut out for you—Kim, you said?"

"Yes, Kim. No worries, I like a challenge. Follow me."

She led me to a chair about halfway down on the left side. The only other customers in the place were two older women getting the full treatment—manicure, pedicure, and some sort of facial waxing operation—in chairs at the back, so it appeared that we'd have some privacy to talk.

She got me seated and put a bolster on my lap and covered that with a clean towel. Then she wheeled up a caddy holding chrome instruments and a variety of bottled potions, and took a seat in a low stool beside me. "Don't think I didn't know you were about to make a joke about hand jobs when I mentioned male clients," she said in an undertone.

"It never crossed my mind."

"Right. Put your hands on the towel, please."

I put them down as directed, and she immediately took hold of my fingers, pulling, bending, and twisting them to position them under a bright fluorescent light. Her own nails were varnished in a high-gloss fuchsia that matched her hair.

"Jesus. You weren't kidding. You look like you break rocks for a living."

"Metaphorically speaking."

"Maybe you should go with metaphorical rocks, too. Let's start by softening the cuticles with some oil." She reached for a bottle with green liquid and began massaging it into my nail beds. "Here's where you ask your questions."

"Were you at Golden Fingers the night the man—Chris Duckworth—was murdered?"

"I worked a shift that evening, but I didn't see him."

"Had you ever seen him?"

"No."

"Do you know if any of the other girls saw him?"

"We talked about it, of course. No one remembers him. We think he must have come in after hours or…"

"Or what?"

"Cristabel told you about the secret room?" Kim looked up to gauge my response, her big brown eyes bright and inquisitive. I noticed a beauty mark on the side of her chin for the first time.

"She told me."

"There was a private party that used the room that night. Mrs. Kongsangchai hustled them down to the basement when they arrived, so no one got a good look at any of them."

"Had they been there before?"

"That's hard to tell since—"

"Since no one got a good look at them. I get it. How about other times? Have you ever seen people who've used the room?"

Kim set down the bottle of green glop and picked up a pair of nail clippers. She looked at me with a smug expression. "I've seen just about all you can see of them."

"You've been in the room with them?"

"Yep. It's mainly booked by swingers' clubs. As you might expect, there tend to be fewer women than men in the clubs, so sometimes they ask Mrs. Kongsangchai to supply a girl or two to spice things up."

"And that's where you come in."

She took hold of my pinkie finger and began clipping. "I'm pretty spicy."

"You'd have my vote. What sort of people are in these—these swingers' clubs?"

"It's not what you think. It's not a bunch of people who look like porn stars. There's the occasional beautiful person, but it's mainly people who look like your aunt or uncle."

I didn't have any aunts or uncles, but the mental image she conjured up wasn't exactly one I wanted to linger over. "And the sex they have—it's all, ah, straight?"

She looked up at me again. "Aren't you the curious one."

"The man who was killed—he was gay. I've been trying to figure out what he would have been doing at Golden Fingers. If he was with the group in the basement, it would make more sense if—"

"Got it. I've only done the swingers' gig a couple of times. Both with the same group, and they were pretty conventional. They were more than happy to have the women put on a show with a little girl-on-girl action, but I'm pretty sure they'd freak if two men started to get it on."

"Are other groups more adventurous?"

She nodded. "This is San Francisco, after all. I heard about a different group from another girl who works at Golden Fingers. She said it wasn't so much a club as a kind of fucked-up family. They were polyamorous and polysexual, and there were power relationships between the members."

"Whoa, you're going to have to break that down a little for me. What's with all the polys—and the power for that matter."

"Polyamorous in that each member has sexual relations with more than one person."

"Aren't all swingers polyamorous by definition?"

"Yeah, it's just a newfangled word for screwing around with other people. For not being monogamous. Polysexual, on the other hand, means that you are up for having sex with multiple genders."

"You mean you're up for having sex with the *same* gender in addition to the opposite one."

"You need to expand your worldview. You're assuming there are only two genders. Polysexuals may also be attracted to non-binary gendered people, too."

"Okay, okay, I'm not even going to open the gender can of worms. What about the power part?"

She finished with the clippers and picked up an emery board. "That's where the family stuff kicks in. There's a kind of hierarchy. There's one older dude at the top. He has penetrative sex with everybody."

I looked around the salon to make sure no one was listening. "You mean he fucks everybody?"

"Well, at least nobody fucks him. He can receive oral, but he wouldn't give it, in general."

"And?"

"And it all rolls down from there. Each member has a place in the family, and their attraction to other genders and level of sub-missiveness determines who does what to whom."

"Jesus. This older guy at the top, he's the father figure, isn't he?"

"Yeah, he's the daddy, why?"

"Again with the daddies. I'm running into them wherever I go. But for all the fancy new terms, this doesn't sound very enlight-ened. It just sounds like the Manson cult."

She shrugged. "To be fair, there's no coercion or brainwashing involved, including the power part. Some people like being domi-nated, and some like to dominate, and some like to do both."

I watched as she picked up a bottle of clear liquid and began squeezing a dollop of it onto each of my nails. "What are you doing now?"

"Cuticle dissolver. It helps to lift off dead skin—of which you have plenty."

She reached back to her caddy to pick up a chrome instrument with a blunt tip. She used it on each nail to push the skin back. As proficient as she was at the task, I couldn't help but think about the juxtaposition with her nighttime gig. "Why do you do it?"

"Dead cuticle, especially dead, *split* cuticle is ugly."

"No, I meant why do you work at Golden Fingers? Cristabel told me you're a freelancer, so it can't be because Wo Hop To is forcing you. I don't know where you're from, but your accent is barely noticeable and you're very articulate. You—"

She pointed the chrome instrument at me. "Don't say it. Don't say, 'You speak English very well.'"

"Well you do."

"What were you expecting, 'Me so horny, me love you long

time?'"

"No, I—"

"Look, I'm a U.S. citizen—second generation. My family is from Vietnam, but I grew up here."

"Okay, but that just begs the question."

She shoved the chrome instrument right under my nose. "Know what you call this?" she hissed.

I pulled back. "Ah, no."

"A pusher. I had a relationship with the other sort of pusher that was costing a lot of money. I started working there to get more money for drugs."

"And now?"

She went back to working on my nails. "Now I'm clean. And now I'm not long for that place, especially since Mrs. Kongsangchai disappeared."

"Why *did* she disappear?"

"No one knows. She simply didn't show up for work. It's clear Wo Hop To doesn't know either. They sent their bag man to collect the earnings for the week and he was as surprised as anyone to find she wasn't there."

"Do the girls have any theories?"

"Dozens of them. Most of them bullshit. But it has to be related to the dead man. She went missing the day after the police questioned her."

"You think she killed him?"

"No, I don't. She wouldn't have been at the club when he died."

I looked over at the pair of women in the back corner. The one closest to me had her hands under a machine that was giving off a blue light. Her upper lip was glowing bright red from the wax job. "Wait a minute. You told me Mrs. K hustled a group of swingers down to the basement. Wouldn't she stay to lock up after them? She wouldn't just leave them the key and say, 'Have a good time, kids,' would she?"

Kim gave me a thin smile, set aside the pusher, and reached for a small towel that she soaked with a liquid from yet another bottle. She used the towel to rub away the detritus from her battle with my dead cuticles. "You're not quite as dumb as you look. You remember I mentioned another girl had told me about being with a poly-poly family in the basement?"

"Yes."

"She was with the group that used the basement the night the man was killed."

"You said no one saw anything."

"You didn't let me finish—no one saw anything who's talking. This girl has gone missing, too."

"How could she go missing? Wo Hop To is supposed to keep close tabs on all them."

"She's another freelancer. This basement room was all on the side. Mrs. Kongsangchai only used freelancers there."

"Do the cops know this girl is missing?"

"How would they? To be honest, I wouldn't have talked to you at all if it weren't for the fact that she's gone. I'm leaving Golden Fingers, and I don't want to get involved with the police, but it didn't feel right to abandon her. She was a friend—she *is* a friend, I mean."

"What's her name?"

Kim finished with the towel and reached down to a lower shelf on the caddy. She came up with a business card, which she placed beside my outstretched hands. A name and address were printed on the back.

"That's her, Tuyen."

"Have you tried her place?"

"Yes, several times. There's no answer."

"How can you be so sure Wo Hop To isn't involved in this? Maybe they found out that Mrs. K was running the basement room on the side, and they decided to disappear both her and Tuyen. Maybe the murdered man got caught in the crossfire."

"Don't think I haven't considered it. They can be ruthless. It doesn't jibe with the bag man not knowing Mrs. Kongsangchai was gone, though."

We were essentially replaying the argument I'd had about Wo Hop To with Kittredge—and I still wasn't convinced. "It's a big organization. One hand might not know what the other is doing."

"Maybe. You want polish? A nice clear finish?"

I almost jerked my hands off the towel. "Pass."

She laughed aloud. It was a pleasant, cheerful laugh. "I didn't think so. You're never going to make it in the polysexual business." She picked up a small block of pumice and began passing it over my nails. "I'll just give them a light buffing to smooth down the ridges. There won't be a shine."

"Thank you."

"You know, I googled you before I called."

"You did?"

"Yeah, I did. I'm taking a risk here, and I didn't want someone who would make things worse or drag me into the middle." She paused. "And if something did happen to Tuyen, I wanted someone who could help make it right—or as right as it can be."

"And what did you conclude based on your research?"

"I concluded that you were a meat cleaver and you think everything looks like a rooster neck...but maybe there *are* a lot of rooster necks."

16
EL SOBRARBE SURPRISE

Kim's friend Tuyen lived in a residence hotel on Turk Street called the Sobrarbe Residence. It sounded Spanish to me, so maybe it should have been called El Sobrarbe. Two men sat with their backs to the wall by the entrance sharing swigs from a jumbo bottle of Country Club malt liquor. In the parlance of the Tenderloin neighborhood where the hotel was located, they were pulling a "forty-ounce holiday."

"How's it going?" I said as I went past them to the door.

"Fuck you," said the one closest to me, a young guy in a baseball cap covered by a hoodie.

"Yeah, fuck you," added his friend, whose over-the-ear headphones didn't prevent him from hearing—and participating in—the exchange.

"We should do this more often," I said as I opened the front door. The lobby was surprisingly large, but most of the cracked mosaic floor was given over to bits of orange peel, peanut shells, and flattened cigarette butts. The only furnishings were three wobbly aluminum tables surrounded by equally wobbly lawn chairs whose turquoise webbing dangled off their frames like streamers. Sprinkler pipes crisscrossed the ceiling, crowding superannuated ceiling fans whose blades barely cleared the plumbing.

Three pendant lamps with chipped glass shades illuminated the reception counter along the back wall. The guy behind the counter was big and bald, and had a monstrous goatee the size and shape of a whisk broom. He was hunched in a chair, a game controller clutched to his ample belly while he battled the Zytrons from Zytor—or whatever the aliens in the game were called—on a computer that was out of my view. What wasn't obscured were the grating ping-ping-zips emanating from the titanic struggle.

I considered sneaking past him to the stairwell I had spotted to the left, but there was a sign on the wall stating, ALL GUESTS MUST SIGN IN.

"Excuse me. I'm here to see Tuyen Do."

He gave me the briefest of glances. "Knock yourself out."

"Don't I need to sign in?"

He looked up again, clearly annoyed. "Consider yourself signed."

I gave him a nod he didn't see and walked toward the stairwell. Halfway there, I heard an explosion from the computer followed by a curse. "Now look what you made me do."

The stairwell smelled of bleach with an undertone of puke trying very hard to become an overtone. The stair treads were covered with the same cracked mosaic from the lobby—and were festooned with the same potpourri of trash—but the risers, balusters, and grimy metal hand railings were painted fire-engine red. For variety, I guessed.

Tuyen's room, I knew from the card Kim had given me, was on the third floor, number 303. It didn't take long to establish that the door was locked and no one was answering. While the building was old and poorly maintained, its bones were good. The door was solid core, and there was both a knob and a deadbolt lock. I wouldn't be kicking my way in, and with my lockpicks sitting in the glovebox of my Galaxie 500 in Palm Springs, I wouldn't be flimflamming my way in either.

I briefly considered quizzing neighbors about Tuyen's comings and goings but decided that was just nibbling around the edges. I needed to pry the game controller out of the desk clerk's hands and get him to unlock the door.

I drifted down the vomity staircase and planted myself in front of the reception counter. The incessant laser cannon noises from the computer told me the battle for Zytor was still in full swing.

"Tuyen's not answering."

This time he didn't even bother looking up. "What do you want me to do—lay an egg?"

"Interesting. I hear it's correlated with excessive screen time."

"What?"

"Your egg problem. Comes from computer games."

He slammed the controller down and stood, ejecting the wheeled chair behind him. "If she's not in, then you'll need to come back later. That's how it works."

"Her parents are worried about her."

He gave me an oily grin, and I realized for the first time he had braces. If he was concerned about his appearance, I had several makeover tips that should have had a higher priority. "Let me guess," he said. "They're worried their little girl is a cock holster?"

"That's not nice."

"I'm not paid to be nice. I'm paid to run the front desk at this lowlife Hilton, and she is one of the lowest. I'm always getting complaints about johns in her room."

"What if one of those johns hurt her? We should go up and see if she's all right."

"What if *you* are one of those johns?"

"I already told you—her parents hired me. I'm a private investigator."

"Yeah, right."

California requires private investigators to carry a copy of their license and a special photo ID. I fished both cards out of my wallet and passed them over. "See for yourself."

He glanced at them briefly, then passed them back. "So what?

That doesn't prove you're working for her parents. You probably have some other hustle going. Collecting on a loan or chasing her for a bail bond. That's fine, but I'm under no obligation to help you."

"When's the last time you saw her?"

He shrugged. "It's been a while. But I work the day shift. She's a nightcrawler. I wouldn't expect to see her each and every day."

"Look, all I'm asking is that you go up with me and scope out her room. If she's not there—fine—I'm out of your hair. If she is there, I won't make it difficult. I'll just give her my card and ask her to get in touch on her own time."

"You left out the possibility you seemed so worried about."

"If she's there but can't answer? Then the sooner we find that out the better."

"Fuck me," he said, and reached to pull a rolling metal shutter down across the counter opening. He emerged from a side door a moment later carrying a big ring of keys. "I bet you a fiver we walk in on her giving some dude a blow job."

"Don't sell yourself short. No way anyone could sneak past you to her room."

"You should do open mic at the Elks Lodge."

We trudged back up to the third floor, the keys on his ring jangling with each galumphing step he took. At Tuyen's room, he pounded on the door and called her name. When no one answered, he rattled the knob and shouted into the door jam, "It's Dave. I'm coming in. If you've got a client in there, you better tell him to pull up his pants."

When there was still no answer, he shoved a key into the deadbolt and snicked it back. Then he used the key on the knob lock and pushed the door open. It swung in a creaking arc to the interior wall where it banged against the plaster.

I could tell immediately something was wrong. There was a smell in the air. It wasn't as strong as the smell at the Russell Street house, but the odor still screamed death and decay to my lizard brain. Dave noticed it, too, and he produced a rasping noise halfway between a grunt and a throat clearing. No amount of that was going to make a difference, though.

I pushed past him into the main room. A double bed took up most of the space, and a small table and a TV on a trolley cart consumed nearly all the rest. The bed was neatly made, and a stuffed panda in a bow tie slouched against the headboard. His constipated eyes looked vaguely sad.

There was nothing for us here, so I pulled open one of two doors that led off the room. Behind it was a shoe box of a kitchen with a dinky four-burner range and a half-pint refrigerator. As I stepped onto the buckled linoleum floor, the compressor on the refrigerator kicked in, prompting Dave to gasp behind me.

"Jesus. This is creeping me out."

"Stay tuned, Dave, stay tuned."

I maneuvered around him to get to the second door, which opened on a bathroom straight from the 1940s. There was a cracked pedestal sink, a toilet with a warped wooden lid, and aquamarine tiling on every vertical surface. In contrast to the dazzling walls, the floor tiles were a sterile black-and-white honeycomb—which made the single drop of blood in the middle of the floor stand out all the more dramatically. Dave made a new noise—a strangled gurgle.

The only place left to look was behind the vinyl curtain that encircled the bathtub. I swept it aside and peered into the tub. There, like sardines in a can, were two dead Asian women. The older was dressed in a red cheongsam dress with a Mandarin collar. Her hair was styled in a severe bob with long bangs shellacked to her head like a 1920s football helmet. Her makeup was almost operatic in its extravagance.

The younger woman was curvy, attractive, and dressed in a cotton T-shirt and shorts, possibly something she slept in. Her feet were bare, and her head was turned to the side. I could see that she had been shot at the base of the skull. It had to be Tuyen

Do. I wasn't quite as certain about the identity of the older woman, but I had a pretty good idea.

Dave had been silent while I took all this in, but now he called attention to himself with a bang when his head hit the tiled wall as he slumped to the ground. He had fainted. I laid him out on the floor, propping his feet on the tub to get the blood flowing in the right direction—then pulled out my phone to dial Kittredge.

The lieutenant didn't waste time with a greeting, assuming I was calling to pester him about the ballistics test. "Cool your jets, Riordan. I just turned in the slug. With the current backlog, it's going to take at least two days."

"That's what I figured. But I got a couple more to add to the order."

He hesitated. For all his other faults, Kittredge wasn't stupid. "You're not talking about more from the sidewalk in front of your apartment, are you?"

"No, I'm not. These are in the brainpans of Mrs. Kongsangchai and an employee of hers from Golden Fingers."

17
CHECK OUT TIME

When Kittredge walked through the hotel room door twenty minutes later, Dave was stretched out on the bed in the front room, his forearm covering his eyes. The stuffed panda peered over the mound of his stomach.

"Who's that?" asked Kittredge.

"I'm surprised at you, lieutenant. That's Bao Bao, the giant panda."

"Of course. And her walrus friend?"

"Dave, the desk clerk. He experienced a sudden drop in cabin pressure when we discovered the bodies." Dave did look like a walrus, come to think of it.

"Fuck you guys," he said.

"And where exactly are these bodies?"

"In the bathtub."

Two obvious lab ghoulies hovered outside in the hallway. One set a case down and pulled out some crime scene booties. He passed a pair across the threshold to Kittredge, who pulled them on with a sigh.

"Too late for this. I'm sure Riordan has tromped all over the damn place."

"Pretty much," I admitted.

"We can photograph his soles to distinguish their imprints from the suspect's," said the lab guy. He had a crew cut and a sparse salt-and-pepper beard.

"If there are any," snorted the lieutenant as he strode into the bathroom. The bearded guy joined him, followed by a skinny fellow with a camera.

"Oh, they're already getting ripe," announced Kittredge, his voice echoing off the tile walls. "How long has it been?"

"Hard to know until we get them back to the morgue," said the guy with the beard. His voice sounded softer, almost inaudible.

"Yeah, yeah, just give me your best guess."

"Well, rigor has passed. That makes it over forty-eight hours. Based on that and the initial signs of putrefaction, I'd say three or four days."

"Fine. Do your thing. I'm going to question these jokers."

Kittredge came back into the main room, but I beat him to the punch on the questioning. "Three to four days," I said. "That would match up pretty well with the timing of Chris's murder."

"Maybe. You are jumping to all kinds of conclusions, though."

"That *is* Mrs. Kongsangchai, isn't it?"

He sniffed fiercely and shot his cuffs. "Yeah," he admitted, fingering a cuff link. "That's Mrs. Kongsangchai."

"And both women were shot execution style in the back of the head with a small-caliber round."

"So it appears."

"Then—"

"Then nothing. You've got some explaining to do. Who's the other girl in the tub?"

"Tuyen Do. This is her room."

"And Ms. Do does what for a living?"

"Sucks cocks," Dave said from the bed.

"Shut up, walrus boy. I'll talk to you later. You were saying, Riordan?"

"She works at Golden Fingers. She hasn't been seen since the night of Chris's murder."

"Says who?"

That was the question I'd been dreading. I didn't want to break my promise to Kim to keep her out of the investigation so I had a cover ready. "Says a customer."

"A customer?"

"Yeah, a regular who heard it from another girl."

"Gee, that's interesting. We questioned all the employees at Golden Fingers and none of them mentioned a missing girl."

"Would you talk to the police if you were under the thumb of Wo Hop To?"

"So she blabs it to a client instead?"

I shrugged. "Pillow talk, I guess."

Kittredge laughed. "More like table talk. How'd you find this client?"

A series of flashes reflected off the bathroom walls as the skinny dude worked his camera.

"I staked out Golden Fingers and followed a businessman after his lunchtime pick-me-up."

"You told me you were working for her parents," said Dave.

"I said shut up," snapped Kittredge, not even glancing toward the bed. "Okay, give. Who is this businessman?"

"He's not going to be happy I told you."

"You think I care? You are not going to be happy if I bring you in on obstruction of justice."

"Nate Schlein. He runs a startup called Monkey Suit over on Montgomery."

Kittredge narrowed his eyes. "This better check out."

"It will. He'll probably deny talking to me, but I was seen at the office. Ask the receptionist. She'll remember me since the conversation got, ah, a little heated."

He slipped a notebook and a pen from the breast pocket of his suit coat and made some notes. "Let me guess. You threatened to tell Mr. Schlein's wife what he does on his lunch break?"

I cleared my throat. "Something like that."

"Did he say who at Golden Fingers told him?"

"No, he didn't. He said he'd been a customer of Tuyen's before. Maybe he asked for her when he went in and was curious about why she wasn't available." I was really laying it on thick now.

"And how'd you find Tuyen's address?"

"Schlein knew it. I had the impression he'd visited after hours. Dave told me there were complaints about her having johns in her room."

"That right, Dave?"

"Yeah," said Dave grudgingly.

"Okay, now maybe you can explain why you didn't mention this lead during our lunch at the Farm Club?"

"You mean the all-expenses-paid feast I sprung for?"

"That one."

"I didn't think it would check out. I figured Schlein was probably lying to get me off his back."

Kittredge looked at me with an ironic expression. "I hate when that happens."

I waved my hands. "If we are done with the third-degree, can we get back to the important stuff? If the slugs match the one you got from Chris, then what you said at lunch was right. Someone is going around trying to eliminate witnesses."

Kittredge flipped his little notebook closed. He opened his mouth to speak, but before he could get anything out, the forensic technician with the beard appeared at the door of the bathroom.

"The younger girl," he said softly. "She was tortured."

I stepped out of the residence hotel onto Turk Street about twenty minutes later. The comedy team by the entrance was gone, and I was actually disappointed. I could have used the distraction.

Tuyen had been tortured with a heated blade applied to sensitive areas—sensitive areas beneath her shorts and top. We found the knife encrusted with cauterized flesh in the kitchen sink next to an oven mitt that the torturer must have used to hold it. A burner on the dinky range was almost certainly the source of heat.

I was due to meet Angelina in the lobby of her hotel at six-thirty. I really should have taken a taxi to get there on time, but I decided to walk so I could clear my head. Dave had passed out again when the forensic tech started to describe the particulars of the torture, and even Kittredge looked green around the gills. Neither he nor I could come up with a theory that would explain the torturer's motivation. Eliminating witnesses was one thing, but what knowledge would a girl working at a massage parlor have—and apparently fight to retain—that would lead to this level of cruelty? The idea that the torture had nothing to do with gaining information was even more appalling.

I arrived at the Huntington winded and perspiring from the hike up Nob Hill, still unsettled and perplexed by the discoveries at the residence hotel. Angelina wasn't in the lobby, so I parked myself on the tufted red sofa in the middle of the room and tried to think pleasant thoughts while I waited. I was eager to see her but didn't want my bleak mood to spoil our reunion.

I watched businessmen, tourists, and the occasional gaggle of uniformed airline employees stream into the hotel for fifteen minutes and still no Angelina. I took out my phone and texted her. She didn't respond. A few minutes later, I called and went straight to voice mail.

Panic tightened my chest. I hurried to the elevator and rode up to her floor. I bolted from the car past a startled maid juggling a tray of room-service dishes and stopped at her door. Tapping followed by outright pounding and shouts brought no response. I realized with a start that I was in exactly the same boat as I had been when I stood outside Tuyen's door.

I retraced my steps to the lobby and went up to the imposing granite reception desk. I knew I had to sound calm and levelheaded to have any chance of convincing the clerk to let me into Angelina's room, but my tachometer was redlining and it was hard not to let it show. I got off on the wrong foot immediately with a phony smile that felt stiff to me and probably looked serial-killer manic to her.

"Good evening, sir," said the clerk. "Checking in?" She was tall and thin and had stringy blonde hair pulled back in a ponytail.

"Ah, no. A friend of mine is staying at the hotel, and I have reason to believe she may be sick or injured."

She held her face still, not giving me anything to work with.

"I was hoping you could let me into her room so we could check on her."

"I can call her."

"No, I've already tried. She's not answering. I'm worried she may not be able to answer."

"May I ask her name?"

"Angelina Evangelista."

She took her upper lip between her teeth as she typed something into a computer. She glanced at the display, then back up at me. "Would you wait here a moment?"

She went into an alcove behind the desk and returned a moment later with a tall black man with a buzz cut. He came around the desk, took me firmly by the elbow, and led me to a quiet corner by an oversize torchiere. A badge pinned to the lapel of his blazer read, Walter Ellis, Assistant Manager.

"My name's Ellis," he said. "And you are?"

"Riordan, August Riordan."

"Bethany tells me you have a concern about one of our guests."

"I'm worried she's injured—or worse."

"May I ask why?"

I started to explain about her being late for our appointment but realized that sounded lame and—now that I thought about it—paranoid. "I just came from an apartment with two dead women," I blurted out. "I'm worried she'll be next."

Ellis glanced around the lobby to see if anyone had heard my outburst, then looked back at me. He ran his thumb and forefinger around the edges of his goatee before speaking. "That sounds a little fantastic, Mr. Riordan. Are you with the police?"

"No."

"Here in any official capacity?"

"I'm a private investigator. I'm working for Ms. Evangelista."

He took a deep breath and let it out through his nose. "It's against hotel policy to let outsiders into guests' room. But I can send someone up to knock on her—"

"Never mind. If you want police, I'll get you police." I took out my phone and punched the number for Kittredge from my call history.

He came on almost immediately, road noise in the background making it clear he was answering from his car. "Riordan," he shouted over some sort of speaker gizmo. "What? What the fuck is it now? Haven't you done enough for one day?"

I pulled the phone away from my ear to protect my hearing and watched as Ellis did another of his searching glances around the lobby. "I'm at the Huntington Hotel," I told Kittredge, then explained the situation with Angelina and the difficulty with the hotel staff.

"Put him on."

I passed the phone to Ellis, who took it reluctantly. He stiffened as Kittredge gave him the full benefit of his personality. I didn't hear everything that was said, but "Just pretend it's a fucking turndown service" came through loud and clear. A sick look came over Ellis's face, and eventually he passed the phone back to me.

"He wants to talk to you again."

"Me," I said into the receiver.

"I'll be there in five. I hope to hell you're wrong about this."

"No kidding."

Ellis jerked his head toward the elevator bank and set off in that direction. I followed him into a waiting car, and he punched the number for Angelina's floor. "I'm going along with this," he said, "but that doesn't mean I have to like it. Let me do all the talking."

"Fine. I just hope there's talking to do."

Ellis strode out of the elevator when it stopped, hurrying to get to Angelina's room before I did. He tapped lightly on her door, then said, "Ms. Evangelista? Hotel staff."

When there was no response, he tapped some more and repeated his spiel. Finally, he pulled out a card key, pushed it into the slot, and turned to me. "Wait here."

I let him poke his head through the door and call Angelina's name again. When there was still no answer, I pushed past him and barged into the room. No one was in the bedroom, but it looked far from normal. The chair in front of the lacquer desk was flipped over, and the closet door yawned open with a dress wadded on the floor. The dresser drawers were also open with underwear and socks dribbling out.

I didn't waste any time puzzling over those developments and pushed straight into the bathroom, where I found a glass shower stall. It was empty.

I stepped back into the bedroom and stood with my hands laced over my head. "Christ," I said to the ceiling.

Ellis was leaning down to pick up the dress in front of the closet.

"Don't," I snapped.

"Why? What does it mean?"

"It means she left in a hurry. Or someone made her leave in a hurry. She hadn't checked out, had she?"

"No, she was still registered. We have her credit card on file. She had just notified the front desk she intended to stay another week."

I nodded.

"What do we do now?" asked Ellis.

"Wait."

I used the time to make a more thorough search of the room,

noticing only that Angelina's suitcase was gone and that many—but not all—of her cosmetics and toiletries had been scooped up from the bathroom. I was squatting down to look under the bed when another tap sounded on the door. Ellis pulled it open to reveal Kittredge looming in the hallway with the blonde desk clerk standing anxiously behind him.

Kittredge elbowed his way in, holding his badge up for Ellis to see. He pushed the door closed on the clerk's worried face.

"Give," he said to me.

"She's not here, but a lot of her things are gone and it looks like she left in a hurry."

Kittredge nodded and made a quick sweep of the room. He zoomed in on the desk chair and used a handkerchief to pull it upright. I noticed for the first time that there was a small length of duct tape stuck to one of the front legs.

"Not good," he said.

"What?"

"After you left the residence hotel, we found a bunch of tape wadded up in the trash can. We think it was used to restrain Tuyen while they—"

I thrust out my hand. "I know what they did."

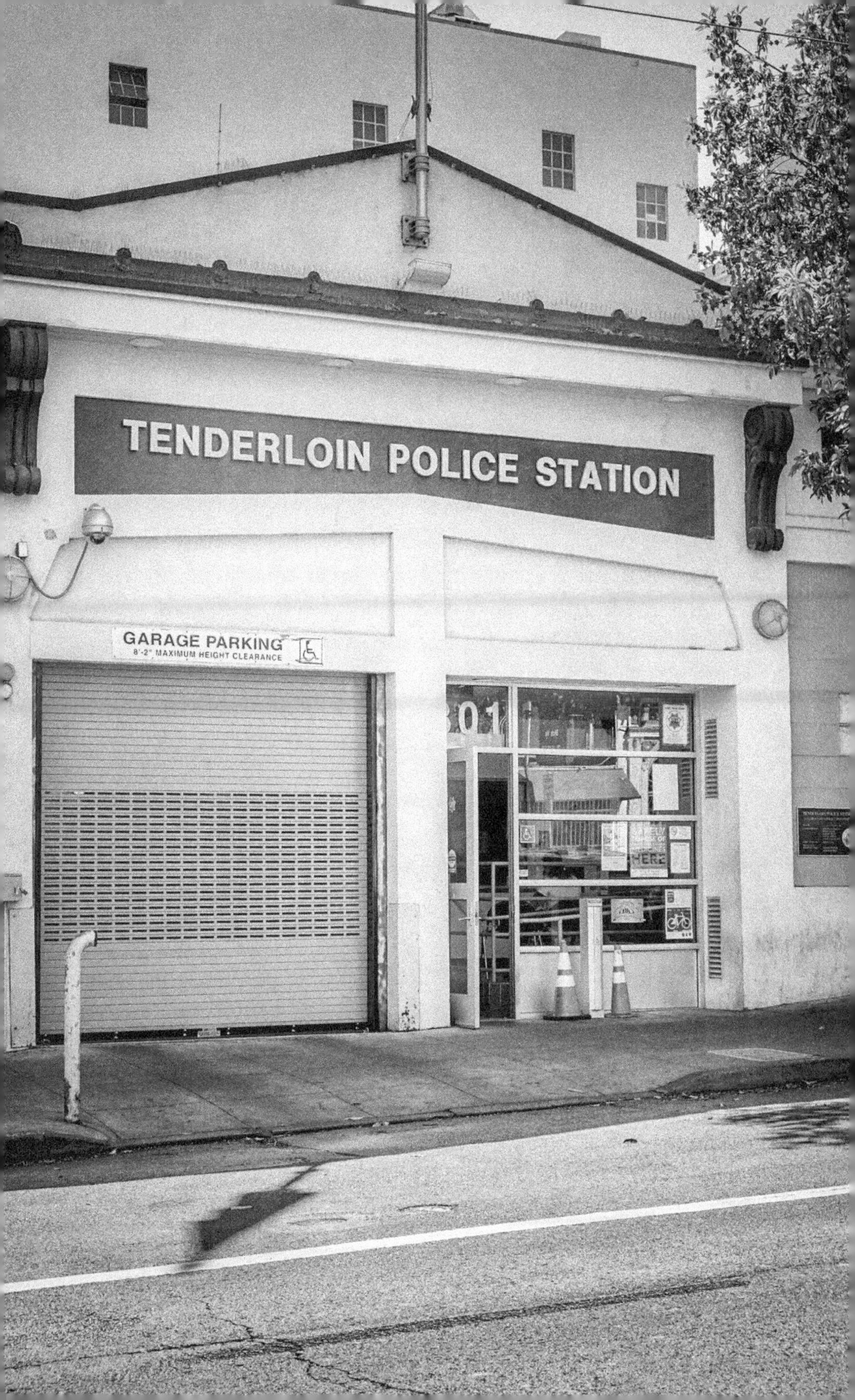
TENDERLOIN POLICE STATION
GARAGE PARKING
8'-2" MAXIMUM HEIGHT CLEARANCE
301

18
SING A TONG OF SIX GENTS

I was very careful leaving the Post Street apartment the next morning. I made it all the way to the intersection with Levenworth without being shot at—but I let my guard down too soon. As I stepped off the curb, a stretch Hummer with tinted windows appeared out of nowhere and blocked my path. The door closest to me burst open and two Asian light heavyweights tumbled out.

If I hadn't spent an anxious night imagining worst-case scenarios for Angelina, I might have had the energy and presence of mind to avoid being scooped up. As it was, each man grabbed an arm and shoved me headfirst into the Hummer. I landed on one of the bench seats next to a cool customer with swept-back hair and oversize black-rimmed glasses. He looked to be in his midforties. The first of my kidnappers piled in next to me, and the other took a spot by two guys in front. A sixth guy behind me touched the back of my neck with something pointy and metallic that I had to assume was a knife.

The cool cat with the glasses murmured an order in Chinese, and we pulled away from the curb.

"This is nice," I said, "but I didn't call an Uber."

"You don't call an Uber," said the guy with the glasses. "You use an app."

"I knew that."

"But speaking of transport, perhaps you'll recognize the car."

"It's been a long time since my senior prom."

"Very funny, Riordan. This is Squid Boy's old limo."

I had known they were Wo Hop To the moment they pulled up. I vaguely remembered that Squid Boy, the former leader of the gang I had killed in a one-on-one fight, had his gigantic ass ferried around in a Hummer. "Mr. Squid never gave me a ride."

"That is fortunate. They tended to be one way."

"I imagine. Are you here to give me the ride I never had?"

He looked away from me and smoothed the lapel of his charcoal worsted suit. "No, I'm not. As it happens, I—and the rest of our organization—benefited greatly from Squid Boy's removal."

"And you are?"

"You can call me Mr. Wong."

"From what I understand about Chinese names, that's like calling you Mr. Smith. You took over the gang from Squid Boy?"

"We are not a gang. We are a benevolent association."

"But you took over?"

"Yes, I have the honor of leading the association. And one of the changes I made was to put us on a more business-like footing and avoid some of the unnecessary flash and attention Squid Boy generated."

"This limo is about as subtle as an open casket."

Wong shrugged. "It's a sunk cost that has several more years to amortize."

"But you've had some other write-downs recently, haven't you?"

"Ah, now we get to it. And, you, you've lost a friend and associate, I believe."

I watched as the limo crossed California and kept climbing Nob Hill. "I have—a very good friend and associate. One who played an important role in bringing down Squid Boy. I couldn't help but wonder if the, ah, *association* killed him to even the score."

"No. I've already told you that we have no interest in avenging Squid Boy. Had you been a business competitor, it would have been a different story. But as it was, you were just a—"

"Civilian who got in over his head?"

Wong smiled primly. "I'm not sure I would have used the world 'civilian,' but let's go with that. There is also the matter of the body being discovered on our property. If we wanted to eliminate your friend, you can be sure that it would never have been found. Having the police set up a crime scene and interfere with our business runs completely counter to what I told you about avoiding unwanted attention."

"You may or may not be pleased to hear a certain police lieutenant told me the same thing."

"I only care what the police think when they investigate Kongsangchai's killing."

"Then you heard how she was found?"

"We have our sources."

"And who she was found with?"

"Yes, in the room of a girl who worked at the massage parlor. This is the purpose of our meeting. I need you to tell me everything you know about the investigation. Uncle Yuen, who is sitting in the seat behind you, is here to ensure your cooperation."

I glanced back to take in a fierce-looking individual with a hammerhead shark tattoo swimming up his neck. He looked anything but avuncular. He smiled to reveal teeth that had been filed to points and brought the tip of a gleaming knife an inch from my eye. I flinched and scooted forward in the seat. The thug to my right shot a restraining arm across my chest. I wasn't going anywhere.

Any belief I had that Wo Hop To had been involved in Chris's murder had faded when I found Mrs. Kongsangchai's and Tuyen's bodies. It had disappeared completely with Angelina's kidnapping. I didn't have a problem sharing information with Wong—to a point. "I get it," I mumbled.

"Excuse me."

"I understand," I said more clearly.

"Good. Now spill."

"That won't take long. The police don't have a clue."

"That sounds too pat. They must have discovered something."

"They—or we, to be more accurate—have, but the discoveries have only added to the list of crimes, they haven't explained them." I launched into an abbreviated summary of the investigation to date, starting with our realization that Angelina was Chris's last client. I told Wong about finding her sister's body, the fact that the sister had been killed by the same weapon as Chris, and the possibility that Kongsangchai and Tuyen had also been killed by the same gun. And the torture—I also told him about the torture. I didn't mention any of my encounters with *Herr Doktor* and his sidekick, the link to Beats, and the lost Kerouac manuscript, and I certainly didn't mention my conversations with Kim and the cleaning team at Golden Fingers. I finished with Angelina's apparent kidnapping by the same people who had killed Kongsangchai and Tuyen.

Providing Wong with the details about the torture and Angelina's kidnapping sent my pulse into overdrive again.

The tong leader was silent for a long moment. He leaned back in his seat and patted the sides of his lacquered hair with his palms. "This is madness. I assumed that the murder of your friend was unrelated to our business. That at most some fool had committed the act at Golden Fingers without understanding what he was dropping himself into. But with Mrs. Kongsangchai—and the torture of the girl—that makes it..."

"Personal?"

"No. Everything I do is strictly business. 'Intentional' is the word. It makes the killers' motives *intentional*."

His prep-school-mobster act was beginning to grate. "Well, Wong, or whatever your name is, you can be sure that it isn't business to me. It's swell that we appear to be on the same side, but when I find out who's responsible, you can be sure that it's going to be strictly *personal*."

I wasn't sure the guy to my right completely understood what I had said, but he picked up on the tone and again reached an arm across my chest. Wong just laughed. "Yes, I believe Squid Boy was the recipient of some of your personal animus. I'm glad to hear that you are once again personally motivated to achieve an outcome that is good for both of us. But getting back to motivation, I have a question—several, in fact. You've found no reason for all of this? What do the killers hope to achieve?"

"I don't know," I lied. But only partially. The Kerouac manuscript was the only thing I had to go on. "What I particularly don't know is how Chris, Chris's client, and her sister overlap with your world."

"Yes, exactly. Is it true that your friend was a homosexual?"

"Yes," I said evenly.

"Then he would have no reason to go to Golden Fingers that you're aware of."

"None at all. Apart from, you know, the desire to get an actual massage like you advertise on the door."

"Ha-ha. And how did the police know to go to this girl Tuyen's apartment?"

It was the same question Kittredge had asked, and I gave a variant of the same cover story. "From a Golden Fingers' customer. The customer apparently had an appointment with Tuyen but was told she was AWOL."

"Hmm. This is exactly what I feared. The police are harassing our customers and are going to continue to harass them until this is resolved. Unacceptable."

Wong was silent again. The limo driver muscled the Hummer right onto Pacific, then right again onto Jones to begin the descent down Nob Hill. Ironically, we had come within a block of Arnie Jewel's apartment and turned away—much as my story to Wong had almost but not quite touched on the Beat connection.

The atmosphere in the car was getting hot and smelly. Wong was wearing a woody cologne, but the scents coming off the other men—cigarette smoke, BO, garlic, and a piquant spice I couldn't identify—were turning me into a mouth-breather.

"All right," Wong said as we crossed Sacramento. "I have two things for you. The first is this." He pulled a card from his breast pocket and passed it over. "If you need to reach me, call that number, identify yourself, and leave a number where I can call you back. Don't try to leave a message and expect it will take some time for me to respond. Can I rely on you knowing *when* to reach me?"

I turned to look back at Uncle Yuen, who sneered to reveal a sharpened incisor. "When I learn something relevant about the investigation?"

"Exactly. Here is the second thing." He passed over a note card with a name and two addresses written in a spidery hand. "Those are the home and work addresses of Mrs. Kongsangchai's son."

"Her son?" I looked down at the card. The name on it was Danny Thompson. "The last names aren't the same."

"Yes, in point of fact, Mrs. Kongsangchai never married. The Mrs. is a sort of honorific she assumed to better fit the role of mama-san. She did have a son, though."

"Who decided to take his father's name?"

"No, he never knew his father. He picked Thompson because his father was white and he didn't want to be a Kongsangchai. Didn't want to be associated with his mother and her line of work once he finished high school."

"Let me guess—she started as a working girl herself, got pregnant from a customer, and raised the son on her own."

"That's right. It almost goes without saying that you can't be a mama-san unless you've spent the requisite number of years on your back learning the trade."

I decided to withhold comment on his management-training

system. "What's the point of giving me the son's address if he was estranged from her?"

"They weren't entirely estranged. They still saw each other periodically, and if there was anyone that Mrs. Kongsangchai trusted—really trusted—it would be him. I'd like to believe that she wasn't hustling any business behind my back that precipitated this incident, but if she was, the son would know."

I looked down at the card again. Danny's employer was a major cloud-computing company headquartered in San Francisco. He had certainly fallen far from the tree. "He won't talk to you, huh?"

"There's no point in trying. As I said, he doesn't want to be associated with his mother's line of work, and furthermore, he doesn't even want to acknowledge his Asian heritage. His eyes don't have the epicanthic fold and he is trying to pass as a *gwailou*."

I knew that *gwailou* was Cantonese slang for white person—literally "white ghost"—and didn't exactly have the most positive connotation. "Okay, I'll talk to him. Does he know his mother's dead?"

Wong shrugged. "I've no idea." He said something in Chinese to the driver, who promptly wrestled the car over to the curb. We were smack dab in the middle of the Tenderloin near Eddy. The Tenderloin Police Station was just across the way.

The guy next to me jumped out and reached back to tug at my sleeve. I slithered out of the car and stood on the sidewalk. He humped back to the car and slammed the door shut. Just when I thought they were going to pull away, the window opened and Wong leaned over to look at me.

"Don't fuck up," he said, and the Hummer drove off.

I put the cards Wong had given me in my coat pocket, took a deep breath to clear my head, and started walking toward my old office. Not half a block into my journey, my phone rang. It was Gretchen.

"You've got a package," she said without preamble.

"Good. I was expecting one."

"There's just one problem. I can't get rid of the delivery boy."

"Is he waiting for a tip or something?"

"No, he's about eighty years old and he claims he knows you. Says his name is Ray."

19
THE GREY EARL

I was less than ten paces from the elevator on the twelfth floor of the Flood Building when the door to Duckworth Investigative Solutions opened and Gretchen stepped out. She hurried down the corridor but stopped short when she caught sight of me.

"I didn't think you'd get here this fast."

"What part of 'I'll be there in five minutes' wasn't clear?"

"The part where I triple any time estimate you give me. It's known as the Riordan factor." She was wearing chiffon harem pants with a form-fitting blouse—all black, naturally.

"You didn't leave Ray alone in the office, did you?"

"Yes, he wanted Earl Grey tea and we didn't have any. I was going to borrow some from a neighbor. Why? You worried he'll steal the paper clips?"

"Steal them? No. Solder them together maybe."

She peered into my face. "There's something wrong, isn't there?"

"Just about everything." I tried to give a coherent, levelheaded description of the last thirty-six hours, beginning with my visit to Arnie Jewel and ending with my conversation with Wong, but when I got to the part about discovering Tuyen, my narration jumped track. "They tortured her before they killed her. And then they kidnapped Angelina—and they may have tortured her, too."

Gretchen's face became pale behind her makeup. "August, no. Are you certain?"

"Dead certain."

She pulled me close. "What is going on? What do they want?"

I drew in a ragged breath. "No idea."

"Why didn't you call me?"

"I wanted to, but I didn't think I should bother you at home."

"Okay." We both knew that "bother you at home" was code for "antagonize your urologist husband." He had just about forbidden her to see me by the time I left San Francisco.

She gave me a squeeze and took a step back. "But this doesn't add up. If they've recovered this fabulous unpublished Kerouac manuscript, why would they take her? Why wouldn't they just leave town?"

"There's a certain irony in your observation. The last time I spoke to Angelina she was also worried they had already left town. That we would never catch them."

"There's something we're missing. Something we don't understand. Have you told me everything?"

"Nearly everything." I fleshed out the story of searching Angelina's hotel room and finished with my tête-à-tête with Wong.

She shook her head. "That doesn't help. But maybe there's hope. If there's something else they want, maybe they took Angelina for leverage. Maybe they'll contact us to trade."

"The only 'contact' I've had is potshots taken at me from across the street."

"I agree that shooting at you isn't a great way to start negotiations, but things might have changed between when they ambushed you and when they took Angelina."

"It's possible. Any developments on your side?"

The door to Duckworth Investigative Solutions opened before Gretchen could respond. A teacup crossed the threshold, followed by a spindly arm attached to a stooped old man with thinning gray hair and a Santa Claus beard. He was wearing khaki pants rubbed thin from many washings and a ratty cardigan sweater. My neighbor Ray.

"I thought I heard voices," he said. "I was wondering about the Earl Grey."

"Give your damn tea a rest," I snapped. "And what are you doing here anyway?"

"Yes, I had a pleasant trip. Thank you for asking."

I let my chin drop to my chest. "Sorry. Things are not going well. We just lost our client—the one who originally hired my partner."

"Lost her how?"

"She's been kidnapped."

He nodded and combed his beard with bony fingers. "Did you get involved with her, too?'

"Ray!"

Gretchen struggled mightily to suppress a smile and failed just as mightily. "Even from this short acquaintance, I can see Ray has a keen insight into human nature." She pointed at the office door. "Let's take this show inside. And I do have instant cocoa. Would that be okay?"

"Of course," said Ray.

Ray and I filed through the door and took seats in front of Gretchen's desk while she took Ray's cup over to an electric tea kettle on a small table along the back wall and doctored it up. She passed the cup to Ray when she was finished, then slipped into her chair. "Well, boys, let's try to have a constructive conversation, shall we?"

"Where's the Luger?" I asked.

Ray pointed behind him. "In the other office—with your holster. And I brought your knife and the ankle sheath, too."

"Thank you, I appreciate it. But I have to ask—why did you bring yourself as well? I told you this wasn't your sort of thing."

"Nonsense. I can help. Have already helped, in fact."

"How exactly?"

He leaned onto a hip and pulled a folded envelope from his back pocket. "This is the letter you received—and this is the key it contained." He dumped the key onto the desk with a clatter.

I took the envelope from him, examined it, then passed it to Gretchen. It was definitely Chris's writing. The key didn't mean anything to me. As Ray had suggested on the phone, it was smaller than a house key and looked like it went to a padlock, but what padlock and why it was important, I didn't have a clue. "I'm guessing there's a punchline."

Ray grunted and hoisted himself to his feet. He reached into a bulging front pocket and pulled out a shiny new padlock, which he placed on the desk in front of me.

"*Voilà*," he said, and fell into his seat.

"If that's the padlock the key fits, I don't see the point in Chris's mailing it to us."

"It's not the very padlock, but it is the same brand and model. I went to a big-box hardware store and looked at every padlock they had in the place until I found one that matched the key. It's a top-of-the-line number with a solid body and case-hardened shank."

Something in the back of my brain squirmed. I didn't exactly recognize the brand of the lock or know what Chris might have used it for, but I felt I should. "Okay, I'm getting a bit of déjà vu, but I'm not sure why."

"Ahem," said Gretchen. "You asked me in the hallway if there were any developments from my side."

"That's right," I agreed, thankful not to have the two of them staring at me while I tried to place the lock.

"I've been making the arrangements for Chris's funeral."

It hadn't even occurred to me, and I felt terrible for not assisting. "Thank you, Gretchen."

"The first thing I did was call Chris's lawyer to see if he had left funeral instructions in his will. He had. They are quite involved.

The lawyer also told me that we are both beneficiaries—"

"That's not—"

Gretchen held up a hand. "And we can learn about the terms when it's convenient and appropriate. But he also said that Chris had recently sent him an envelope to be delivered to you in the event of his death."

"Do you have it?"

She reached into her desk drawer and extracted a smallish square envelope. My name in Chris's writing was the only thing written on the front.

"How come the lawyer didn't tell me before now?"

"He tried, but he didn't have any luck reaching you in Palm Springs and he didn't want to trust it to the mail."

I took the envelope with a shaking hand and greedily ripped it open. The only thing inside was a card with ticking time bomb written on one side.

I slumped back into my chair and pressed my hands into the sides of my head.

"What?" Gretchen and Ray asked in unison.

"I know where the padlock is. It's on a storage unit in China Basin. Chris rented it for us when we had the trouble with"—I groped for the right euphemism—"with the people from Argentina."

Gretchen's eyes met mine in a knowing look, but Ray said, "What people from Argentina?"

"It's a long story, Ray, and not a pretty one. It's the reason I came to Palm Springs and the reason Chris and I fell out."

"But if this, ah, incident is associated with such bad memories, why would Duckworth keep the storage unit?"

"Because he had to." I flipped the card onto the desk so Ray could read it. "The storage unit was a crime scene. A crime that we committed. No matter how well we cleaned it, we were worried a determined forensic team would still uncover evidence. We decided that we couldn't afford to let another tenant get ahold of the unit for a while. So Chris agreed to keep it, but on the night we all went our separate ways—he called it a 'ticking time bomb' because of the lingering risk."

"Okay," said Gretchen. "I get that he was trying to communicate in a way that only you would understand, but why did he send the key and the card by separate means?"

"He was being extra careful," said Ray. "If one or the other thing was intercepted, it wouldn't mean anything—even to Riordan, apparently."

"But what could be in the storage unit?" asked Gretchen. "Nothing to do with the Argentines?"

"No. We disposed of everything we could dispose of. We were worried about a forensic team finding microscopic amounts of blood with a luminol test. If there's anything in there now, it's something to do with *this* case that Chris wanted us to see."

Gretchen and I watched as Ray hoisted himself to his feet again and walked into Chris's office. When he returned, he was carrying my holstered Luger and my knife in its sheath. He held them out to me. "There's only one way to find out."

WARNING!

California Mini Storage
Has Installed
Infrared Lazer Security Beams

**DO NOT TAILGATE!
ONE CAR AT A TIME.**

ACCESS HOURS:
MON-FRI   7:00 am to 8:45 pm
SATURDAY 8:00 am to 4:45 pm
SUNDAY   10:00 am to 4:45 pm

WARNING

20
CHRIS'S PLAY

Ray was staying at the Hotel Union Square on Powell Street less than a block from the Flood Building. That was just as well since there wasn't room for him to bunk with me at the Post Street apartment. I was less pleased to discover that he'd driven up from Palm Springs in his 1987 Dodge Aries—the Chrysler K-car he'd bought when he retired from McDonnell Douglas—and the front-wheel drive rattletrap was now parked in the lot behind the hotel. Worse, he insisted on taking it to the storage unit. Worse still, he refused to let me drive.

"Ray," I asked while we waited on the sidewalk for the parking-lot attendant to retrieve his car, "why didn't you fly?"

"I was worried about carrying the gun on the plane."

"It's perfectly legal to take them in checked baggage."

"Never check my luggage. You can't trust the airlines."

"What I don't trust is you behind the wheel. The last time you just about drove us off a cliff."

He tugged at the hem of his cardigan sweater. "Hills make me nervous."

"Good thing San Francisco is so flat."

The attendant rumbled up in the Aries, jumped out, and held open the driver's door. "Here you go, chief," he said. "Your car's leaking oil, by the way. Left a big puddle on the lot."

"Just marking its territory." Ray handed the attendant a rumpled single and eased himself into the car.

I piled in next to him, belted up, and looked over at him, trying my damnedest not to smirk.

"Don't say a word," Ray muttered. "Your car is even older."

As luck would have it, China Basin was one of the flattest parts of town. I directed Ray south of Market, then onto Sixth Street so we could jump on Highway 280. While we were stopped at an intersection on Sixth, Ray looked over at a futuristic, steam-iron-shaped car in the right lane. The millennial male driver had a man bun and a doodad made of multicolored threads dangling from his rearview mirror.

"You should never hang *anything* from your rearview mirror," Ray pronounced.

"How about fuzzy dice?"

"No."

"Graduation tassel?"

"No."

"Religious symbol—cross, Buddha, Satanic pentagram?"

"Definitely not."

"Parking sticker?"

"That would be the one exception," he said, and floored it as the light turned green. The Aries lurched forward in a crescendo of knocks and pings.

We went south on 280 for a couple of miles, then I directed Ray to exit at Cesar Chavez. He meandered his way through a confusing intersection involving the off-ramp, Chavez, and Pennsylvania Avenue, and finally managed to steer north onto Pennsylvania. The storage-unit facility was on the left, nestled among a mix of vacant lots, warehouses, and industrial yards.

A rolling gate controlled by a push-button security console protected the entrance, and Ray rolled down the driver's side window to reach the keypad, and I realized then that I had no idea what the code might be.

"What numbers should I push?" Ray asked.

"You got me. Each customer is assigned his own code. I'm sure I knew at one point, but I don't remember. It's been years."

Ray chewed the mustache hairs at the corner of his mouth. "Maybe Duckworth changed it to something significant. Something you'd know."

A horn beeped behind us, and I turned to look at the grill of a U-Haul idling right on our butt. "Try oh-seven-two-oh."

"What's that?"

"Gretchen's birthday."

Ray reached a crooked finger across to punch in the numbers. Something buzzed inside the little metal box, and the gate began to bump open.

"July twentieth," Ray said. "That's also the date of the moon landing."

"Yeah, I know."

"McDonnell Douglas built the Saturn V's third stage. I did some of the design work for the telemetry transmitters."

"Yeah, I know."

"One of the privileges of being an old man is you're allowed to retell favorite stories."

"Believe me, I know that, too."

Ray grunted and pulled the car into the facility. I directed him past the office, then down the row where the unit was located. I remembered that we had specifically requested the last unit in the row right up against the property fence to keep as far away from other customers as possible.

Ray beached the Aries in front of the unit and we got out. He handed me the key Chris had sent us, and I slipped it into the padlock on the roller door. The lock fell open as I turned it.

"Score one for you, Ray."

He nodded as if there had never been any doubt and helped me push up the door. Inside was a ten-foot-by-ten-foot space with corrugated aluminum walls and a bare concrete floor. A cord for a single light bulb dangled from the ceiling, but Chris had removed the bulb and replaced it with a screw-in adapter that provided two power outlets. One he used for a light and the other for an extension cord that led to a folding table with a laptop computer and printer on it. The laptop looked like a run-of-the-mill laptop, but the printer was funky. For one thing, it had a keyboard. For another, it was made of steel and heavy plastic painted an industrial beige. It was connected to the laptop via a cable that had been spliced open to expose individual wires, which in turn were soldered to a small circuit board that had wires for another cable soldered to it, which led to a USB connector on the laptop.

The only other thing in the room was a lacquered Chinese box lying in a cardboard box beneath the table.

"What the hell?" I said.

Ray laughed. "I haven't seen one of those in thirty years."

"One of what?"

Ray pointed to the printer. "That's a Model 38 Teletype. It's a variant of the Model 33, which was introduced in 1963. We used them all the time at McDonnell Douglas."

"Used them how?"

"As a computer terminal. Before there were video monitors, you interacted with computers on a teletype, typing in commands, getting results back. There was a continuous scroll of paper to record the session, and you could tear off portions if you wanted to save it." Ray pointed at a cleft-shaped gizmo on the side of the teletype keyboard. "That's a paper-tape reader. If you wanted to input lots of commands at once, you could encode them on a paper tape and run it through the reader. It was an early form of nonvolatile memory."

After Ray said the world "scroll," I only half paid attention to his explanation. I touched the paper fed around the platen of the teletype. It was thin like that from the Kerouac manuscript.

"That's not standard teletype paper," said Ray. "Teletype paper is cheap, pulpy stuff."

"You're right. This is architectural tracing paper." I looked up at Ray. "Can the teletype be used as a printer? Just for output?"

"Sure. It looks like your partner did exactly that. He had to jerry-rig the interface because the old teletypes used a serial ASCII connection. That's what the circuit board is for, converting the USB protocol to seven-bit serial so the teletype can understand it. The throughput would be very low, however, compared to something like a modern laser printer."

"But unlike a laser printer, the output would be typewritten."

"Sure, it's basically just a motorized typewriter. As a matter of fact, the only difference between the Model 38 and the Model 33 was that the Model 38 could do upper and lowercase. So anything printed on the Model 38 would look pretty close to something typed on a typewriter."

"Where would he have found one of these things?"

"Oh, hundreds of thousands of them were manufactured. You can get them from collectors and enthusiasts on the Internet."

Until this point, I hadn't had the opportunity to explain the Kerouac connection to Ray. "Okay, listen to this." I launched into a summary of my adventures leading to the discovery of the scroll in Corrine White's trunk and a replay of the conversation I'd had with Arnie Jewel about the significance of the find.

Ray used one hand to lean on the table and the other to stroke his beard. "You think Duckworth made a *duplicate* of the scroll?"

"Is it possible?"

"The only practical way to do it would be to scan the text from the original and use optical character recognition software to digitize it. Then he could have loaded the digital file on the laptop and printed it out." Ray shook his head. "I don't know. That's a lot of text to digitize if the scroll is as long as you say. And OCR isn't perfect. There would be a lot of typos to correct before you printed it out."

"What if he didn't scan the whole thing and used filler text or simply repeated the portion he'd scanned? It wouldn't hold up if someone had the time to read through the whole manuscript, but it would pass muster on a casual examination."

Ray pushed off from the table. "Easy enough to find out." He powered on the laptop, and when prompted for a password, typed in 0720 without missing a beat. The password screen cleared to reveal the desktop, which had the icon for a single word processing file on it. Ray double-clicked on the icon, and it opened on a single-spaced document titled "The Beat-hive."

I read the first few sentences and immediately recognized the text from the manuscript in Corrine White's car. "That's it."

"That's some weird shit," said Ray. "Let's see how much of it Duckworth actually scanned." He began paging through the file, and it wasn't long before I saw the opening line with the reference to ciggy butts again.

"There," I said, pointing at the screen. "That's the beginning section."

Ray nodded and made a desultory pass through the remainder of the document. "And it's turtles all the way down," he concluded.

"But where's the real scroll?" I asked.

Ray nudged the box under the table with the toe of his Velcro sneaker. "I don't think that's a big mystery, do you?"

I squatted to retrieve the lacquered box and set it on the table next to the laptop. The lid was fastened by a metal latch, but there was no lock. I undid the latch and flipped up the lid. Inside was another roll of tracing paper dimpled with type. And next to that was an envelope with my name on it, just like the one Chris had left with his attorney.

I lifted the manuscript out and gingerly unspooled the first three feet or so. It was older than the stuff in the teletype, dotted here and there with brown spots, and the typing on it was less even and uniformly spaced than the teletype output. I continued until I got to the first seam in the roll—held together by yellowed Scotch tape—scanning enough of the text along the way to assure myself that it didn't repeat.

"What do you think?" I said.

"I think you've yourself got a legitimate dead Beat scroll. Give it here. You better open the envelope."

I passed the scroll over to Ray for him to rewind and picked up the envelope. Inside was a final message from Chris.

Dear August,

The chances of your seeing this are almost zero—I feel silly for even writing it. I'm planning to trick the polys into skipping town with a phony Kerouac they "recover" on their own. But if things do go south, Brendan, the father of the family, and Andreas, his number one son, are the ones you want. No time or space for more details, but if you are reading this, you shouldn't need them.

Love, Chris

P.S. Yes, this is the real Kerouac.

P.P.S. I'm sorry for what happened between us. You were not to blame.

21
SON OF A MAMA-SAN

I rested a forearm on the roof of Ray's car. He was back behind the wheel, but this time his only passenger was the lacquered Chinese box containing the Kerouac scroll. I motioned for him to roll the window down.

He pressed the button and the electric motor answered the call with a herky-jerky plunge. "Are you sure you don't want to leave it in the storage unit?" he asked. "After all, they haven't found it so far."

"No. The unit is registered in Chris's name. I know they've searched his apartment, and they might well have found a bill or something linking it him to it."

"Okay, I'll check it at the hotel like you said."

"Yeah, but now that I think about it, we better not use your hotel. Take it to the Pickwick on Fifth Street. It's just across Market about three blocks from your dump. The place was built in the '20s, and they've got a proper locked storage room with shelves."

"All right. What do I do with the claim check? Eat it?"

"I like your initiative, but no." I fished out a pen and an old receipt from my pocket and scribbled a P.O. box number on it. "Put it in an envelope and mail it here. That's a box we have for the agency."

He shook his head. "You can never be too rich, too thin—or too paranoid."

I patted the side of the Aries. "Godspeed, John Glenn."

"That's the Mercury project, not the Apollo."

"Whatever."

He lifted off, a trail of blue smoke wafting behind.

I went after him, careful to select a route well away from the noxious exhaust. While I walked, I took out the card Chris had left with the box and examined it again. It was clear that I didn't know nearly as much as Chris thought I would. It seemed safe to assume that the person I thought of as *Herr Doktor* was Chris's Brendan, and *Herr Doktor's* sidekick was the person Chris called Andreas. And from what Chris had written, they were apparently part of a polysexual family of the sort Kim had described to me.

The other thing that seemed clear—as Gretchen predicted—was that Chris's love of adventure had clouded his judgment. He must have found Corrine White's body, discovered the Kerouac manuscript, had a run-in with Brendan and Andreas, and tried to fob off a fake scroll—all without involving the police.

I lingered over the second postscript where Chris absolved me of blame for our split. I felt a tremendous relief from a burden I hadn't been fully conscious I was carrying—and would have felt even better if Angelina's kidnapping wasn't weighing on me even more. I hoped having the real scroll would give me a bargaining chip to trade for her return—assuming, that is, that I found a way to contact Brendan without getting shot.

When I got to the entrance of the storage facility, I slipped out the pedestrian gate and went down Pennsylvania until I got to Twenty-second Street, where there was a Caltrain station under Highway 280. I knew there would be taxis waiting for disembarking passengers, and I planned to take one downtown. As Ray had pointed out, I could have just as easily ridden back with him, but I didn't think he would be particularly helpful for the interview I planned next, and I didn't want to expose him to danger from Brendan and his clan.

I found a cabbie drowsing in the driver's seat with a newspaper spread over his stomach and tapped on the window to wake him up. For $22.01 plus tip he delivered me to 415 Mission Street, the address of the tallest building in San Francisco. The 1,070-foot-high tower has been compared to everything from a dildo to a robot's middle finger, but I thought the most apt comparison had come from the female architecture critic who said it looked like a giant tampon applicator.

Danny Thompson worked for a company that had a reception desk on the thirty-fifth floor. The vast space was flooded with light from the floor-to-ceiling windows, and the view across fog-covered San Francisco Bay to the protruding suspension towers of the Golden Gate Bridge and the foothills of Marin County was spectacular. I traipsed across a couple of acres of exotic hard-wood flooring to a strange reception desk made of white plastic in the shape of a flattened marshmallow. There I was greeted by a bearded dude with his hair pulled back into a minuscule pony tail with just enough fuzz for a calligraphy brush.

"Welcome to Steam Power. How can I help you?"

I told him I wanted to talk with Danny Thompson, but it soon became clear that that by itself wasn't going to cut it.

"Is he expecting you?"

"Yes."

"May I have your name and what this is regarding?"

I gave him my real name but was momentarily flummoxed for a cover story. My eyes fell on one of those yellow signs janitors leave behind after they've mopped. The Spanish phrase for wet floor—*piso mojado*—was printed below the English. "It's about the Mojado project."

"Okay," he said a little uncertainly. He got Thompson on the line almost immediately. "August Riordan is here to see you about the Mohair project."

He listened to Thompson for a moment, then covered the line. "How do you say the name of the project again?"

I gave him a sympathetic smile. "It's a little tricky. *Mo* like motorcycle, *ha* like ha-ha, and *doe*, like the baby deer."

"Got it," he said, and uncovered the receiver. "The mojito project," he pronounced with confidence.

This time I heard Thompson's voice barking out of the receiver. "Never mind. I'm coming down."

The receptionist reddened and replaced the phone with exaggerated care before looking back at me. "He says he'll be right down."

"Great."

He nodded and led me through the process of using a touch-screen kiosk to print a visitor's badge complete with a bar code. I had just clipped the badge on my lapel when the elevator doors opened and a smallish guy with thick jet-black hair blew out of them. As Wong had told me, his eyes didn't have an epicanthic fold, and his skin tone was rather light. If you didn't know his background, you might have guessed that he was Spanish or Greek, but being Irish-English myself, I wasn't sure if a Brit name like Thompson was the best choice for his new identity.

He moved like a bigger man, marching right up and planting himself not a foot away with his arms held akimbo. "What is this about?"

"It can't be about the Mojado project?"

"There is no Mojado project and I don't know any August Riordan."

"Maybe not, Mr. Kongsangchai, but I bet you know a character who calls himself Wong and owns a business on Stockton Street."

He pivoted without saying a word, heading back toward the elevator.

"Wait," I called after him. "You're going to want to hear this." I was banking on the idea that he wasn't aware of his mother's death—or at least would want to know more details if he was.

He paused and half turned in my direction. "What do I want to hear?"

"It's not a shakedown. I'm not trying to get anything over on you, but it *is* important. And it's not something to talk about in the lobby."

He gestured to a glassed-in conference room along the far wall. "I'll give you five minutes."

I followed him over to the conference room where he made a point of seating me in one of the interior chairs around the big glass table while he kept the one closest to the door for himself. He thrust his hands into the pockets of his sport coat and leaned back in his chair. "Clock's ticking."

It was clear he didn't know what was coming, and I was starting to feel bad about the way I'd maneuvered him into the meeting. "Look, Mr. Thompson, this isn't good news."

"Oh, it's Thompson now, is it?"

"I only mentioned your mother's name to get you to the table. The thing is...she's dead. She's been killed."

His facade cracked a little, but he still thought he saw a way clear. "I read the newspaper articles about the murder at Golden Fingers. But that was a customer, not my mother. And no one from the police got in touch."

"No one from the police even knows you exist. And you're right—the person killed at Golden Fingers wasn't your mother. It was a good friend of mine named Chris Duckworth. That's how I'm involved."

"So?"

"So what you missed was another article, a more recent one about two women being found in a Tenderloin hotel."

He yanked his hand out of his jacket pocket and fumbled out his smartphone. He unlocked it and began typing furiously. After a moment, he quoted a headline, "Two women shot, killed in San Francisco Tenderloin."

"Yes."

He read more of the article, then looked up at me, tears already welling in his eyes. "I told her this is how it would end. She never listened." After staring at the screen again, he said, "Wait. How do I know this is really her? They don't give any names."

"Call Wong. I know you don't like him, but he's got no reason to lie about it."

"Of course he does! He caused her death—or had her killed."

I didn't want to point out to him that he'd jumped from not believing that she was dead to being convinced Wong was personally responsible. "No, that's the thing. He doesn't know how or why she died. He doesn't think it has anything to do with him or the association—"

"It's a fucking *tong*."

"Okay, he doesn't think it has anything to do with the tong."

Thompson sniffed and wiped at his eyes roughly with the back of his hand. "How do you know him?"

I explained to him about being scooped off the street by Wong because of my connection to Chris and my discovery of his mother and Tuyen in the Tenderloin apartment.

He sniffed again. "My mother's death—was it a bad one?"

I pulled out the last of my clean handkerchiefs and underhanded it across to him. He looked down at it like I'd thrown my liver on the table, but he eventually picked it up to blot his eyes.

"I don't think she suffered. I think they were eliminating witnesses."

"Witnesses to what?"

"I don't know, exactly. My friend is gay, so there was no obvious reason for him to be at the massage parlor. He was shot after hours, and there are no known witnesses to his killing. What he was doing there and who else was with him are complete blanks."

I saw something flicker behind his eyes, but he covered the reaction by dabbing again with the handkerchief. "Why did Wong put you onto me?"

"He knew you'd never talk to him."

"He got that right, but Wong doesn't give two shits for me or my mother. He wouldn't have cared whether I knew she was dead."

I shrugged. "For what it's worth, I had the impression he respected her...managerial skills. But, no, he didn't send me to deliver a sympathy card. And strictly speaking, he didn't send me to do anything. I'm not in his pocket, and as a matter of fact, Wo Hop To and I have a history. I initially thought they'd killed my friend for revenge."

He blinked at me. "I do remember your name now. You're the one who did in Squid Boy."

I nodded.

"That still doesn't explain why you're here."

"I think you know. If anyone could give me the inside scoop about operations at Golden Fingers, it would be you. You'd be helping to get justice for both your mother and my friend."

"I want nothing to do with my mother's world. I left home at eighteen, changed my name, and never looked back."

"But you were still in touch with her. And she must have been proud"—I waved my hand at the magnificent view out the window—"of all this. There was still a connection between the two of you. I think you know something that could help—that could explain what my friend was doing there after hours." I considered telling him I knew about the hidden room, but I was hoping he'd be more forthcoming if I didn't use it as a lever.

He dropped back in his chair and looked at me across the table. "She did have one thing going on the side that could explain your friend's presence."

"Okay."

"She cleared out a room in the basement and set it up as a kind of sex lounge. She'd rent it out to individuals and groups after hours."

"And Wo Hop To didn't know about it?"

"No. She wanted to keep the income for herself. Her retirement fund, she called it."

"Is there any sort of log or calendar that would tell us who rented it the night of the shooting?"

"No. When she told me what she was planning, I tried to talk her out of it. And when I couldn't do that, I made her agree not to keep any records. That would have been asking for trouble from Wong and his minions."

"What's your job here, by the way?"

"I'm in finance, why?"

"Just curious. So you can't think of any way to find out who was there that evening?"

He blew his nose loudly into the handkerchief. "There might be one thing. She told me recently that renting the room out on a one-off basis wasn't generating enough income. She said she was talking to some sort of swingers' club about leasing it out long-term. I tried to discourage her. I told her it would disrupt the regular operations of the massage parlor and eventually Wo Hop To would catch on."

"Did she go ahead anyway?"

"I've no idea."

"Did she say if the club had a name?"

"She did. I remember it because it seemed so odd. She said they were called the Hive's Dream."

That landed like a shot to my solar plexus. "Jesus. You sure it was the Hive's Dream and not the Beat-hive?"

"No, there was no beating involved. In the name, I mean. Who knows what kind of kinky shit they get up to."

"You remember any details about how she found them or who she negotiated with? Anything that would give me a handle on them."

He shook his head. "No. You're on your own as far as that. I don't know anything about them." He stood. "Look, you better go. I still don't entirely believe you about my mother being dead, and if it is true, I've—I've got a lot to process."

There didn't seem to be any point in tormenting him further. He realized his mother was dead, and while he wasn't going to shoot the messenger, he was finished collaborating with him. I got out of the chair and walked around the table to where he stood by the door. "The person you want to talk to at the SFPD is Lieutenant Kittredge. That will save you a call to Wong and he'll be able to…"

"Release the body?"

"Yeah."

"Here," he said, and pushed the wadded handkerchief into my hand.

22

HIVE TIMES

I stepped out onto Mission Street with the intention of returning to the office to enlist Gretchen's help in researching the Hive's Dream. I figured they had to have some sort of internet presence, and when it came to the internet, Gretchen would be a thousand times more likely to dig something up than I would. Then I realized that Kim might already know something about them and that it would be better to start with her—then it dawned on me that I hadn't been in touch with her since I found her friend Tuyen dead in the bathtub of the residence hotel. I felt like a gold-plated heel. It was bad enough that Tuyen was dead, but I should have been the one to break it to Kim rather than the cops or the five o'clock news.

I hurried up Mission to Second Street, cut over to Post, then jogged another half mile or so until I reached the nail salon. It was just after 4 p.m. when I arrived, and I was flustered and breathing hard—not exactly the composed demeanor I wanted to project when I spoke to Kim. I would have loitered outside to catch my breath, but there wasn't any point. Kim was leaning against a parking meter on the sidewalk in front of the salon smoking a cigarette. When she saw me, she stubbed out the butt and came over to where I was standing.

"I've started smoking again," she said in a deflated voice.

"I didn't know you'd quit."

"Yeah, about five years ago."

"You heard about Tuyen."

She nodded. "On the radio this morning."

I suddenly didn't know what to do with my hands. I started to slip them in my pockets, then I let them drop back at my sides. "I should have got in touch immediately. It's just—it's just there's been a lot going on."

She stared at me as if we were on stage and she was waiting for me to produce a forgotten line. "Don't stand there like a statue honoring the confused. Comfort me. Hug me or something."

I stepped over to hug her and nearly lifted her off her feet. She weighed almost nothing. "I'm sorry for the loss of your friend and for letting you hear about it from someone else."

"It's not your fault," she said into my sternum. "Tuyen was probably dead before I even asked you to check on her. What I need now is for you to do what we talked about—chop some rooster necks." She punctuated her point with a sharp squeeze.

I squeezed her back and slipped out of the embrace. "Yes, well, about that. Is there someplace we can talk? I could use some more of your help."

She sniffed and gave a wan smile. "We could talk while I give you a pedicure."

"Ah...no."

"Then let's adjourn to the executive suite."

She led me through the salon door past the client chairs and the soapstone Buddha to another door in the rear of the building. She flung that open to reveal a cramped break room with a folding table and a couple of folding chairs. A rice cooker and an electric tea kettle sat in the middle of the table surrounded by women's magazines with their mailing labels torn off. The whole space smelled faintly of miso soup.

Kim took the chair farthest from the door and gestured for me to take the other one. She pushed magazines to the side and rested her hands on the table. "Tell me what you found at Tuyen's first. The news story was pretty sketchy."

I recounted the story of finding Tuyen and Mrs. Kongsangchai in the bathtub. I was tempted to leave out the part about Tuyen being tortured, but I wanted to hear Kim's ideas about it. I tried to slide it in with a vague reference—and it slid in about as quietly as the Rose Bowl Parade.

"Torture," Kim nearly shouted. "What kind of torture?"

I shifted in my seat, making the folding chair squeak. "With a heated blade."

"How exactly with a heated blade?"

"That's enough detail, I think."

She took hold of bunches of fuchsia-colored hair on either side of her head. "You are really going to have to chop some necks now."

"You don't know the half of it. It looks like they've kidnapped my client and they may have done the same to her."

"Your client? I thought you were trying to find out who killed your friend."

"I am. But this client is really my friend's client. He was working on an investigation for her when he was killed." It felt odd calling Angelina a client at this point, but I didn't see any value in detailing the story for Kim.

"Shit. This is even scarier than I thought. It's not going to blow back on me, is it?"

"No. I've kept your name out of it. With the cops *and* Wo Hop To."

"You've talked to them—Wo Hop To?"

"Yeah, and I've changed my mind. I don't think they had anything to do with it."

"I told you. This is too fucked-up. They just want to make their money and be left alone." She smoothed her hair back down around her ears. "Why was Tuyen tortured?"

"I was hoping you could tell me. She knew something her killers wanted, I guess. And it was something she didn't want to tell them."

Kim stared down at the table and shook her head. "I've no idea. She didn't know anything—except maybe the best time to stick her finger up a guy's butt when giving him a hand job."

I cleared my throat. "I don't think that's what they were after. Let me ask you about this other thing then." I explained what Thompson had told me about the Hive's Dream renting out the secret room at Golden Fingers. "Does that ring a bell?"

"Maybe. You remember I mentioned that another girl at Golden Fingers told me about a polysexual family or club or something using the room? I think that's them. I don't remember the name exactly, but it had 'dream' or 'dreamy' in it."

"Can you find out for sure?"

"I can try." She pulled out a cell phone from a pocket in the apron she was wearing, hunted and pecked on the screen for a moment, then dialed a number. A moment later, she said something in what I assumed was Vietnamese.

There was a lot of give and take on the phone for more than five minutes. I amused myself by perusing the articles in the magazines: "It's Okay to Change Your Man (Because Secretly He Wants You To)" and "My Gyno Talked To My Vagina—And Other Doc Shockers."

Kim eventually signed off with a not very Vietnamese "Ciao" and looked over at me. "Picking up any tips?"

"Not really, but I'm beginning to think there's more to being a woman than I realized."

"Well, duh. But it doesn't have anything to do with what you'd read in those magazines."

"What'd you find out?"

"The group isn't exactly who I thought they were."

"But it's the same people—the Hive's Dream?"

"It is. It isn't a single poly family, though, or even a local swinger's club. They are a worldwide affiliation of poly families."

"Kind of like the Masons for pervs?"

"Sort of. The local branch is probably the one that talked to Mrs. Kongsangchai about renting out the room on an exclusive basis. My friend didn't know anything about that, though."

I thought about Chris's note and how he'd described Brendan and Andreas as being part of a family. "If it's an international organization, would out-of-town members get reciprocal privileges?"

"Sure, I think that's the point of it. That and the monthly newsletter. You have some out-of-towners in mind?"

"I do. But while they've been able to locate me with ease, I haven't been able to pin them down. If I could talk to someone with the local branch, I might be able to trace them."

"Then it's a good thing my friend made an outcall to a local Hive Dream daddy. According to her, he lives in a place on Arguello."

The Arguello Boulevard address Kim gave me turned out to be just across the street from the monumental Temple Emanu-El. I had a cab drop me a block away, walked to a spot by the entrance to the temple, and stood in the gloom scoping out the property. The house was tall, narrow, and vaguely English with a peaked roof, overhanging windows with tiny rectangular panes, and a jutting columnar chimney.

I wasn't quite sure what I was going to say when I rang the bell, and while I was mulling over the options, a car with an Uber sticker pulled up. A guy in a peacoat and watch cap got out and trudged up the brick stairs to the second-floor entrance. Less than five minutes later, another Uber driver delivered a young woman in a short wool skirt and a clingy sweater. When a third Uber pulled into the narrow driveway, I decided that a party was in progress and I had better make an appearance. I jogged across the street to the idling car, arriving just as the rear door popped open.

A tall woman wearing a hooded cloak stepped out. In the dim light, it was hard to see what she was wearing underneath, but whatever it was seemed to consist mainly of leather and metal studs.

"Well, well," she said in a husky whisper. "What do we have here?"

I didn't know what to say to that, so I kept my mouth shut.

"I haven't seen you before. Are you with a family or...?"

"Or?"

"Or are you a party favor?"

I almost winced. "Is there a third option?"

She laughed. It was a deep, throaty laugh that didn't seem to go with her soft speaking voice. "You are either with a family or you are a paid guest."

"I'll take the Fifth on that," I said, and gestured toward the house. "After you."

She hesitated for the briefest moment, then sauntered up the drive, her cape billowing out behind her. I followed a safe distance behind, and we clunked up the stairs together, me in my pointy ankle boots and her in her even pointer knee-high boots with stiletto heels.

At the door, she turned to block my path. With the benefit of the porch light, I got my first good look at her face. She had blonde hair and deceptively innocent features: large green eyes, an upturned nose, and a pouty cupid's-bow mouth painted a velvety matte red. I put her in her midforties. "Let me guess," she said teasingly. "You used to be in porn. Gay or straight?"

"You're jumping—"

"Or more to the point, top or bottom?"

"Like I—"

"Or vers. I think I would like it best if you were vers. In fact, I'm quite sure Robert wouldn't have hired you if you weren't vers."

"Robert didn't hire me."

"Then what are you doing here?"

I obviously didn't have many choices for a cover story. "I'm trying out for the family."

She laughed again and flung open the door. "Fresh meat."

I followed her across the threshold and closed the door with exaggerated care, hoping that she would take the hint and flit off on her own. No such luck.

"Come on now," she chided. "I'll give you the tour. Robert hasn't added to his family in quite some time. What's your name?"

"August," I admitted finally.

"August—Augustus. An appropriately debauched Roman name. Normally, we don't play at members' houses, but we've lost our hive space so Robert volunteered to host. But there are some rules, so please pay attention." She gestured to a large room at the front of the house. "This is the main play area—the main *public* play area."

On the hardwood floor in front of a gas fireplace was a fluffy rug with bolsters sprinkled across it. Various pieces of furniture—coffee and side tables, wingback chairs, a four-foot-high sculpture of a boy playing a flute—were pushed back against the walls to provide more maneuvering room. And maneuvering in that room were three clusters of writhing bodies: a female with two males, two males and a female, and a bigger group of three males and two females. As Kim had indicated earlier, they were not all beautiful people, and several of the men were downright flabby.

One of the participants moaned and another squealed loudly. "It looks like things are off to an early start," said the blonde woman. "Come on, I'll show you where we keep the provisions."

She led me past a stairway, down a short hallway, and into the kitchen. It had the standard granite counters and stainless-steel appliances that a million other places had. On an L-shape counter by the entrance were two large bowls filled to the brim with condoms and things that looked like McDonald's ketchup packets. But they probably weren't unless McDonald's was distributing lubricant. A phalanx of little glass bottles with colorful labels was arranged to one side of the bowls, and on the other side, a pile of lollipops in equally colorful wrappers. I recognized the bottles as poppers, but I wasn't quite sure what to make of the lollipops.

She stopped in front of the counter. "Rule number one—all play is safe." She reached into the condom bowl to retrieve a handful and pushed them into the satchel bag she was carrying. "The corollary of rule number one is that all play is smooth play, either naturally or with assistance." She took a handful of lubricant packets from the other bowl and dumped them into the bag. Then she smiled at me with a cat-ate-the-canary grin.

"And the other junk?"

"You really don't do this playing dumb thing well, do you? These are poppers, of course," she said, pointing at the bottles with a red-tipped nail. "I'll give you a pass on the lollipops since you might not have seen them before. They're THC."

"You mean dope? Marijuana?"

She laughed again. "That's right. There are all sorts of new products available since it became legal in California. But a word of advice—if you'd like to indulge, go slow. It takes a lot longer to kick in than it does when you smoke. You don't want to lick a second one down to the stick without seeing how the first affects you."

"You liked saying 'lick' and 'stick,' didn't you?"

"I did. Now, see anything you need? I've got us covered on rubbers and lube. Maybe some poppers?"

I didn't know much about poppers, but I did know that some gay men inhaled them before anal sex. "Maybe later."

"Sure. The night is young. Come on, I'll show you the cloak room."

We retraced our route to the entryway, then took a left into a room on the side. It was furnished like an office or study, but it had several rolling clothes racks with hangers parked in the middle. I recognized the peacoat of the guy I'd seen enter the house and the wool skirt and sweater of the woman who followed. There were also shoes on the floor and bags with smaller items slung over the hangers. "Here's another important rule," said my guide. "All clothes you intend to take off go here. No leaving underwear or socks wadded up in the corner for Robert to find tomorrow morning."

"What do you mean *intend* to take off?"

"Some of the traps like to leave on knee-high socks, short skirts, or bustiers to emphasize their femininity."

I looked at her with what must have been a stupid expression.

"You do know what a trap is, don't you?"

"Sure. Of course." I learned later that it was internet slang for androgynous anime characters and people who cross-dress.

"And I, on the other hand, like a little support." She whipped off the cloak to reveal a garment made of black leather straps, O-rings, rivets, and metal studs. It encircled her throat, crisscrossed her bare breasts, and formed a cage around her torso. Garters in front and back held up black stockings, and at her crotch, a built-in harness held a triangular nylon pad with a large O-ring in the center.

I was pretty sure I knew what the O-ring was for, and it didn't take long for her to confirm my suspicions. After hanging up her cloak, she reached into her bag to take out two black dildos, which she held right in front of my face. One was large and the other even larger.

"Pick your pleasure," she said in her husky whisper.

I took her hand by the wrist and lowered it. "Let's not get ahead of ourselves. I like a little foreplay first."

"Of course you do."

"Would I be correct in assuming that you are head of one of the poly families?"

She tapped me on the chest with the dildos. "Now you're getting it. We have three families here tonight. Robert, as you know, is daddy of one, I'm the mommy of another, and Sid is the daddy of the third. And mommies and daddies have special privileges. We each have a bedroom upstairs reserved for private play. Now why don't you get undressed and we'll go to my room?"

She had a lovely body, but I had no intention of going anywhere with her. She scared the bejesus out of me—and I needed to stay focused on the reason I'd crashed the party. "Do you know a daddy named Brendan by any chance?"

"No, no Brendans. Why?"

"No special reason."

She put her dildos back in the bag and smiled. "Let me help you off with your jacket."

"Shouldn't I check in with Robert first? Let him know I'm here?"

"No need. You've already checked in with mommy, and if I know Robert, he's in his room entertaining a crowd. I'm different. I like to start the evening with a little quality one-on-one time."

I patted the lapels of my jacket nervously. I was wearing the Luger in a holster underneath, and there was no way I was letting her take it off. "Let me make a quick pit stop first. Bathrooms are upstairs?"

She laughed. "Yes, they are. I see what you're doing. You're going to sneak a Viagra or a Cialis from your jacket pocket. Fine. Go ahead. I'll be waiting upstairs—third door on the right. The bathroom is the first on the left."

I nodded without making eye contact as if she'd caught me out and hurried past her to the staircase. I went up two stairs at a time, and instead of turning left for the bathroom, I went right for the first bedroom. I decided my only play at this point was to barge in on Robert and grill him about Golden Fingers, the Hive's Dream, and out-of-town members. I put my ear to the door, listening for sounds of activity within.

Just as I was reaching for the knob, the bathroom door behind me clicked open and an individual wearing pink-and-white-striped stockings, a pink skirt, a pink bra, and a short turquoise wig stepped out. From what "mommy" had told me, I realized with a jolt that I was looking at a trap.

I realized with a further jolt that this particular trap was none other than Angelina's friend Jeff. I recognized him before he recognized me, and I wasn't taking any chances this time. I shoved him back into the john, crowded in after him, and kicked the door closed.

He tried to squirt past me, but I blocked his path with one arm while I slipped the Luger out of its holster with the other. I pointed the barrel right at the little clasp between the cups of his bra.

"I've had trouble unhooking these in the past, but I've never tried shooting one off."

23
FAMILY TIES

"Fuck you," said Jeff, after taking a long look down the barrel of the gun.

"I'll have to pass. I've already had a better offer."

As if on cue, a loud tap sounded on the bathroom door. "August? August, are you in there?"

I reached back to compress the button lock, keeping the sight of the Luger centered on Jeff. "Tell her you'll be out in a minute," I whispered.

I could see the wheels turning in his head as he considered his options, but eventually he barked, "Occupied" and I heard the click of boot heels down the hall.

"So, Jeff, imagine my surprise. What are you doing here?"

"What does it look like I'm doing?"

I gestured at his clothes. "I don't think you want my answer to that question. Do you know our host—Robert?"

A long pause. "Yes."

I let my hip rest on the counter of the double vanity that ran along the right wall. A glass shower stall took up most of the left, and a space-age toilet with a console of buttons hunkered in the corner.

"Then you're a member in good standing of the galactic order of bee fuckers?"

He reddened and clamped his jaw shut.

"Are you?"

"Yes, I belong to the Hive's Dream. But belittling me, my gender fluidity, and my affiliations isn't going to earn my cooperation. I would have thought a man whose best friend was gay would be more woke."

I didn't know exactly what "woke" meant in this context, but I got the gist of what Jeff was saying. "You knew Chris?"

"Yes, I did. He was a nice guy. I liked him."

I took a step forward, and Jeff retreated, pressing into the towel racks along the back wall. "Who shot him?"

He brought his hands up in front of him, palms held out. It was a gesture that seemed partly intended to signal ignorance and partly to ward me off. "I don't know. I can guess, but I wasn't there."

"Brendan—or Andreas."

He gave the slightest nod. "Yes, probably," he whispered.

I closed on him. He laminated himself farther into the wall, contorting into a space between the towel racks and the toilet-paper holder. "How do you know them?" By then I was shouting.

A lip quiver—then nothing.

"You're in Brendan's family, aren't you? You're all members of the Hive's Dream. That's how you got access to the room at Golden Fingers. And that's how Angelina and her sister got sucked into all of this. She said you were her friend, but you were the one who put Brendan onto her. Do you know that he's kidnapped her—that he tortured her like he tortured and killed two other women who worked at Golden Fingers?"

I reached for Jeff's throat with my free hand. He shot both of his up to take mine by the wrist, but I was stronger and ended up pinning him to the wall. All the anger, hurt, and humiliation I'd experienced since returning to San Francisco coalesced in an overwhelming urge to crush his windpipe.

"Wait," he hissed, his whole body trembling. "It's not my

fault. I didn't have anything to do with it, I promise. This—this is not what Chris would have wanted."

Mentioning Chris again was the smartest thing he could have done. I still thought Jeff was guilty of something, but Chris had always served as a governor on my worst impulses, and Jeff was right when he suggested Chris wouldn't have approved. And more to the point, there was no advantage for me in throttling Jeff to death at a polysexual orgy. I needed him. He was my only conduit to Brendan.

I pushed off him and stepped back. He sucked in a rasping breath, then bent over in a coughing fit. Someone pounded on the bathroom door, and a voice—male this time—said, "Are you okay in there?"

"Get lost," I called over my shoulder.

Jeff eventually straightened, and leaning heavily against the vanity, he brought his gaze up to mine. Tears had washed out his eye makeup and were now glistening among the dusting of glitter he had applied to his cheeks. "Jesus," he said.

"Jesus nothing. Even if you aren't culpable, what are you doing flouncing around at a party when a guy you said you liked is dead and another of your friends is being held captive? How about doing something useful like reporting the crimes to the police?"

"It's not that simple."

"Of course it isn't. Nothing is simple with you, is it, Jeff? How did you know Chris?"

"You were right about my being part of Brendan's family, but I'm not anymore. I left after I came to town with him and Andreas."

"After you told him that Angelina was coming to see her sister."

"No, it wasn't like that. Brendan just said we were all going to take a vacation together."

"Right."

"I didn't have any idea what Brendan was after at that point."

"And what did you find out later?"

"That he wanted the scroll. The Kerouac scroll."

"Which Angelina's sister had whether she knew it was in the wall of her house or not."

"I guess."

"There's no guessing about it."

"But I did introduce myself to Chris after I got to town. I thought he looked...interesting."

There was something in the way he said 'interesting' that caught my attention. "Wait a minute. Are you telling me you and Chris had a thing?"

He nodded.

"And you had sex?"

He drew himself up, projecting a kind of tattered dignity. "Yes."

"The night he was murdered?"

"Yes, but we'd been together before. He came back to my hotel that night after we had dinner together."

"And what happened then?"

"He left. He told me he was meeting Brendan later that evening, but I didn't know the details."

"Could the meeting have been at Golden Fingers?"

"I guess."

I threw up my hand. "The daddy of your polysexual family books the local hive room for a roll in the honey—or whatever droll phrase you people have for it—and you aren't invited? You don't even know about it?"

"I'd already broken with the family by then. I didn't know what was going on, but Chris said I wouldn't want to be caught up in it. In fact, he encouraged me to leave town."

"Then why didn't you?"

"I was worried about Angelina."

"Does your idea of being worried translate into mooning around outside her hotel in the rain?"

He shrugged.

"She told me you were attracted to her, too."

"What of it? Do you know what the word 'polysexual' means?"

"Why did you follow me—then bolt when I braced you at the hotel?"

"I wasn't sure who you were. Chris had mentioned you, but you didn't look like he had described. You were better dressed for one thing."

That was sadly ironic. It took Chris's death to get me to dress in a way he would have approved of. I shook my head. "You're just making this up as you go along, aren't you? The only part of what you told me that makes sense is your getting together with Chris. The rest of it is gobbledygook. You're either confused or you're hiding something."

He reached down to the toilet-paper dispenser to tear off a few sheets, then dabbed at his face. "I'm not confused and I'm not hiding anything. I can't help it if the truth is more complex than you'd like."

"So now you're saying I can't handle the truth. Nice." I looked at him for a long moment. His resemblance to Chris seemed even stronger than when I first spotted him following me on California Street.

He fidgeted under my stare. "What? What is it?"

"It's decision time. Do you want to help Angelina?"

"Of course."

"Then I need you to get a message to Brendan. Tell him I have the scroll and I'll trade it for Angelina's safe return."

"But…"

"But what?"

"I thought Brendan already had the scroll."

I sneered. "There. Right there. Your saying that proves that you do know more than you're telling me. Brendan has a dummy. A fake that Chris manufactured. I have the original."

"Okay…"

"If I let you go tonight without turning you into the police, will you get that message to Brendan? Tell him I want to meet?"

"Under one condition."

"What?"

"Put down the gun. Please. You're scaring the hell out me."

I holstered the Luger. I'd forgotten I was still holding it, and we were long past the point where I needed it to control him. "Done. Now, when can you get the message to him?"

"Right now, if you like."

"How?"

"I'll text it to him, silly." Jeff leaned forward to pick up a pink Hello Kitty clutch purse that was lying on the vanity.

I had a sudden attack of prudence and snatched the purse before he could get hold of it. I undid the snap, half expecting to find a matching pink Hello Kitty carry pistol inside. I was relieved to find only money, cosmetics, a card with a magnetic strip that looked like a hotel key, and a cell phone. I passed the bag over to him with a self-conscious smile. "Just checking."

"Paranoid much?" he said, and took out the phone. He used the fingerprint sensor on the back to unlock it and touched the contacts icon.

I was watching him do this when I realized I didn't really have any way to be sure he sent the message to the right person. "How do I know you're really texting Brendan?"

He snickered and held up the phone for me to see. The screen showed the name "Daddy" and a picture of Brendan beside it. "Satisfied?"

"Yeah. Just make sure I can see you select his number to send the text."

I watched as he pressed a number with a 778 area code and started typing.

Riordan has the real scroll. He wants to trade it for Angelina's return. Contact him at this number to discuss:

"What's your cell?" Jeff asked.

I gave him the number and loomed over him as he transcribed

it into the message and pressed send.

"Happy?"

"Almost. Where are you staying?"

"A cheap hotel on Lombard Street."

"Text the name of the hotel and your room number to me. And paste Brendan's number on the end of the message."

He gave a dramatic sigh, but my phone dinged a moment later.

"What now?"

"Now is where I give you the warning. I don't know what your angle on all this is, but from this point forward, I'm not forgiving anything. Everything counts. If you cross me or play any sort of trick, I will find you and punish you. Severely. Maybe Chris told you enough about me for you to understand what that means."

He licked his pink-glossed lips and swallowed. "He told me you'd killed people."

"That's something to think about, isn't it? We're going to walk out of the bathroom now. You can go back to your party if you like but don't leave town and don't change hotels without telling me. You and I are working together on this, and I like to keep tabs on my partners. *Comprende?*"

He swallowed again. *"Comprende."*

I held out an arm to indicate that he should go out the door first. He went past me, opened the door, then lingered on the threshold. He turned and gave a small wave and wandered down the hallway to the right. I heard one of the bedroom doors open and assumed that he was rejoining a party previously in progress.

I slipped out a moment later, cruised down the hall and the stairs without seeing anyone, then paused at the entryway. I looked over to the play area. There, with her back to me, knees dug into the carpet, was "mommy" riding someone hard with a slap, slap, slap against his ass.

I shook my head and hurried out the front door. *But for the grace of God...*

24
FILM AT ELEVEN

My phone woke me at an ungodly hour the next morning.

"Get your ass down here," Lieutenant Kittredge growled.

"Where's here?"

"Look out your window."

I rolled out of bed in my underwear and crept up to the window that fronted Post Street. There, smack in the middle of the bus stop, was an obvious unmarked police car. Kittredge was leaning against the near side of the car, a donut in one hand and his cell phone in the other. He waved at me with his donut hand.

"Did you get one for me?"

"Of course not. Just get the hell down here."

I started to ask if I had time for a shower, but he hung up halfway through the question. I decided to take that as a no. I went to the bathroom to do the best I could with a washrag and some deodorant, then threw on last night's clothes.

Kittredge was already behind the wheel by the time I made it down. I got in next to him as a bus rumbled up to the stop. The driver gave a fulsome toot on his horn, which Kittredge acknowledged with an equally fulsome bird flipped over his shoulder.

"Nice," I said, as he pulled away.

"Sharing is caring."

"I'm sure that's how the SF Muni sees it. Where're we going?"

"The Performance Kitchen."

"Can you expand on that a bit?"

"Some kind of theater, apparently."

"Okay."

"What's more important is that it's on Turk Street just across from the SRO where you found Mrs. Kongsangchai and the Do girl from Golden Fingers."

"Ah."

Kittredge took a hard right on Mason, chasing a pedestrian back onto the sidewalk. "And what's even more important is that they have security cameras."

"And these cameras cover the SRO as well?"

He brought his finger to his nose. "Now you're getting it. One of my men interviewed the staff during a canvass of the neighborhood and found out about the cameras. He learned they retain the old videos for a week before recording over them, and he had them go back four nights to the time we think the two women got shot—"

"And tortured."

"Yes, and tortured. And he found some footage of the women going into the apartment."

"That's it?"

"No, there's more. The footage shows them going into the apartment closely escorted by two men who might have been holding guns."

I slapped the dash. "All right. Can you see their faces?"

"Briefly—or so I'm told. They've got the footage cued up for us, and I'm hoping you'll be able to identify the mystery men who took a shot at you outside your apartment."

Who the men were less of a mystery to me now, but I wasn't admitting that to him. "Multiple shots," I insisted. "They took multiple shots at me."

"I admire that about you, Riordan. When you cook up a story, you stick with it. Right down to all the fantastic little details."

"It can't be that fantastic if you're having me watch a video to confirm it."

Kittredge wheeled the car onto Turk Street, then coasted into a loading zone in front of a three-story cotton-candy-pink building with a neon marquee. He shoved the transmission into park. "We are watching the video to see if you recognize the men. Exactly where you ran into them is an open question."

"What about the slugs I collected? Have you had them analyzed to see if they were fired by the same gun that killed Chris?"

He popped open the door. "They've been analyzed all right— but we'll talk about that later. Come on."

We went up to the double glass doors of the building. Lettering on the glass said that the Performance Kitchen was a space for art and community, and that the box office opened forty-five minutes before showtime. Kittredge tried the door handle anyway. It was locked.

He tapped on the glass with his class ring. Eventually, a rail-thin woman in her late thirties with brittle, kinked hair materialized from the gloom at the back of the building. She undid several locks on the door and pushed it open a crack.

"Yes?"

"Lieutenant Kittredge with the SFPD. Are you Mattie Dahlsheim?"

"Yes."

"Detective Donaldson spoke with you."

"Yes. Please follow me."

She led us past a box office with a sliding-glass window and through a curtained doorway. The room behind it was tiny, cluttered, and filled with a musty smell. Posters from old shows were Scotch-taped to the walls, and what I assumed were props from the same shows were stacked in piles on the bare concrete floor. A shelf about waist height ran along the back wall. A TV monitor cycling through various views inside and outside the building sat on the shelf next to several boxy electronics and a wireless keyboard.

Mattie threaded her way around the props to the shelf where she picked up the keyboard with a bony hand. She dropped into a decrepit office chair and wheeled it around to peer up at us. "Do you mind if I sit? I've been up all night getting ready for our opening."

"A new show?" I asked. "What's it called?"

The woman smiled and leaned forward in the chair, showing the first flicker of life since we came in. *"Autoimmunity and the Body Politic."*

Kittredge's eyes bored into me as I asked, "And what's it about?"

"Well, that's a hard question to answer in just a few words. It's an interpretive dance dramatizing the circle of toxicity our communities have endured since the rise of capitalism, the patriarchy, and institutionalized religions."

"Does it have a cappella singing? The lieutenant really likes a cappella singing."

"No. There's screaming but no real singing."

"Too bad."

"Can we get back to the reason for our visit?" Kittredge asked tightly. "I understand you have video that might be helpful to an investigation."

Mattie sighed and pulled the keyboard closer in her lap. "Your Detective Donaldson certainly seemed to think so. I've made a copy of the segment to prevent it from being overwritten."

"When is it from?" asked Kittredge.

"It starts at about 1:22 a.m. five days ago. I should mention that it's really six videos—or the feed from the six cameras we have on the property."

Kittredge grunted. "But not all of them are outside, are they?"

"No, only three. Two are in front, and one is in back. But there's a gated parking lot in back, so we don't have much issue there. I can switch between the feeds during replay to focus on the ones I believe you're interested in—the two that look down on Turk Street across to the hotel."

"Let's see."

She pressed a key. The monitor switched from a live feed to a frozen checkerboard of six images taken at night. Each had a time stamp of 01:22:16:3 in the lower right corner. It was obvious which two came from the cameras at the front of the building. The entryway to the Sobrarbe was visible in both. Harsh flood-lights on the building were throwing spidery shadows across the sidewalk and the street. But one camera appeared to be at a higher vantage point than the other.

"Where exactly are the cameras?" I asked.

"One is on our roof line. That's the feed you see in the upper left corner. The other is above our front door—the feed next to it. I'll start the playback, then we can switch between these two as we like."

She tapped another key, and the time stamps began spinning forward in fractions of a second. Nothing happened for a long moment, then a dark SUV rolled into view. The driver pulled to a stop just before the loading zone in front of the theater. Turk Street was one-way running right to left, so the driver was on our side. After killing the lights and the engine, he popped the door and stepped out. He kept his back to the cameras as he closed it, but when he hustled around the front of the car, his profile came into better view.

"Stop," I said. "Can we isolate this from the closer camera?"

Mattie paused the recording and fiddled some more with her keyboard. The screen switched to a full-frame view from the camera above the theater door and gave us a good look at the driver's face. It was pale and foxy-looking with something of a Slavic cast to it: Andreas, the number one son of the family. With the benefit of the bigger picture, I could see the faint glint of a gun held down low by his side.

"Well?" asked Kittredge.

"That's definitely one of them." I didn't want to get into the daddy-and-son business, so I added, "The sidekick, I think. The other guy seemed to be in charge."

Mattie nodded. "There's another man in the car. You'll see him in a second, but the view isn't as good."

"Roll it," said Kittredge.

She went back to the checkerboard view and hit play. Andreas finished going around the front of the car and opened the rear passenger door. He pulled someone out, then two more people slid out in quick succession. It was hard to see exactly who or even what sex they were at first. The view of the theater-door camera was blocked by the bulk of the SUV, and the roof camera was too high.

Once the group began walking across the street, however, the roof camera picked them up. Mattie showed it on the monitor in isolation without being asked. Accompanying Andreas was a shorter, chubbier man, and they were frog-marching a pair of females between them. One woman was taller and thinner with long hair—undoubtedly Tuyen Do—and the other shorter with bobbed hair: Mrs. Kongsangchai.

"That's the hooker and Mrs. Kongsangchai," said Kittredge.

"Yeah. But I really can't say anything definite about the other guy."

"There's a moment coming up," said Mattie. She let the recording run until the foursome crossed the street and Tuyen began fumbling in her bag for the keys to the front door. The shorter man turned to look behind them, perhaps worried about being observed. Mattie froze the frame. His face was not much more than a pale smudge, but I recognized Brendan from the lima-bean shape of his head.

"That's the other one."

"Are you sure? He's pretty far away," asked Kittredge.

"I'm certain about the first dude, and at least eighty percent on this guy."

"Yeah. Okay." Kittredge turned to Mattie. "I'll be sending a lab tech to take a copy of the recordings. We may be able to enhance the images."

She sighed and slumped back in the chair. "Fine. Just tell them to knock loudly when they come. I'll probably be napping in back."

"Thank you. You've been very helpful."

"Yes, thank you," I echoed.

"Yeah, yeah. The way to thank me is by supporting the theater." Mattie leaned forward to extract two postcards from the hip pocket of her jeans and held them out. "For the new show."

I took them both and passed one to Kittredge. The front of the card had a picture of an amorphous mass of people covered by a translucent sheet of plastic and writhing on the floor. A red light under the plastic flooded the scene with an eerie glow.

"Keen-o," I exclaimed.

Kittredge held his face in a neutral expression, grabbed me by the sleeve, and pulled me out of the room. "Keen-o," he mimicked under his breath as we went out the front door. "A cappella singing. You dick."

We stopped on the sidewalk by the front bumper of his car. The air outside felt clean and bracing after the musty funk of the prop room. "What about the bullets?" I asked.

Kittredge passed his postcard over to me without responding. I put both of them in the breast pocket of my jacket.

"Well?"

"Yes, the bullets. That's an interesting story. The ones you gave me were *not* fired by the gun that killed Duckworth and Corrine White."

"They weren't? How many bad guys could be going around San Francisco shooting at people with .22s?"

"Hold your horses. There's more. They *did* match the ones that killed the Do girl and Mrs. Kongsangchai."

I thought about it. "That still fits. Both guys had guns when I saw them. They took turns."

"Maybe. But there's still more. We ran slugs from both guns against our ballistics database. The ones from the gun that killed Duckworth and White matched a slug from yet another murder."

"What murder?"

"A rare-book dealer on Third Street. He was killed during a store robbery about a month ago."

I should have seen that coming. It had to be Fingerhut. If Corrine had taken the Kerouac manuscript to Fingerhut for an opinion after she found it, Fingerhut might have shared the information with Brendan and Andreas. The lure of a previously undiscovered Kerouac manuscript brought them to San Francisco—and somehow prompted them to murder Fingerhut. Either to keep the find quiet or because Fingerhut hadn't been able to deliver the goods.

Thinking all this took too long. Kittredge narrowed his eyes. "You've gone awfully quiet there, Riordan. Something ring a bell for you?"

I felt my face grow stiff from the effort of lying. "No, just trying to figure how the worlds of rare books and prostitution fit together."

Kittredge paused as a disheveled guy in baggy sweats and a backward baseball cap went by pulling a roller suitcase. When he had bumped out of earshot, the lieutenant cleared his throat. "They don't really fit, do they? But neither do Corrine White and her sister." He paused. "You haven't heard from her? Angelina, I mean?"

I shook my head.

"This is just my opinion, but I think if they were going to kill her, they would have done it in the hotel. They haven't exactly gone out of the way to cover their tracks. They want her for something."

"I hope you're right."

He shot his cuffs and brought his hands up to smooth the hair on either side of his head. "Yeah, well, there's one more wrinkle on the bullets. The ones from the gun that killed Kongsangchai and the Do girl might be magnums."

"Magnums? There's such a thing as .22 magnums?"

"You're behind the times, Riordan. There is such a thing, and they have more zip than a .22 long rifle, of course. Some even say they're powerful enough for concealed carry/self-defense, but I wouldn't go that far."

"But the slug's the same size, right? How do you even tell if it's a magnum versus a long rifle?"

"There's no definitive way. The ballistics guy says recovered magnum slugs are often more deformed than long rifles. It's a judgment call, but he thinks the ones you gave us show more deformation than you would normally get after hitting metal and masonry from across the street."

"So after giving me shit about my story on the way over here, you're saying you thought I was telling the truth all along."

"Not based on your word. But after the ballistics results came back, I did send the lab guys to check the front of your building. They found another round in the gutter and fresh chips in the grill and building facade."

"What do we gain by knowing they were shooting magnums— in at least one of the guns, anyway."

"Fuck if I know. But I'll tell you one thing, Riordan—you're still not coming clean in all this. There's something you're holding back. Something to do with the book dealer, maybe. If you want to save Angelina—and if you want to get these jokers for murdering Duckworth—you're going to have to play straight with me. This is coming to a head. I can feel it. You need to get out of the way and let me do my job."

My phone saved me from having to respond. With Kittredge glaring at me, I pulled it out to see who was calling. I answered, figuring I would tell Gretchen I'd call back in a minute.

I never got that far. Without bothering to say hello, she blurted out, "August, did you text me from the ICU?"

"Ah, no. You know I'm—"

"Then get your ass over here. Someone has trashed our office."

25
TEXT AND SUBTEXT

After a lot of grumbling about misuse of city resources, Kittredge dropped me off on Ellis Street at the back of the Flood building. I went in the arched entryway next to John's Grill and rode up to the twelfth floor.

The door to Duckworth Investigative Solutions was propped open, and Gretchen was just inside the threshold with a broom, sweeping what looked like shards of a broken coffee cup into the hallway.

She leaned the broom against the door frame when she saw me and marched back into the office. Reappearing a moment later, she thrust her phone under my nose. The texting app was open, and there was a message next to a picture of my much younger face.

i got beat up pretty bad. i'm in the icu at ucsf. my jaw is wired shut & can't talk.

"Where'd you get that picture? Is that from when we were still dating?"

"Leave it to you to zero in on the most important thing. That's the photo I have for you in my phone—yes, from a long time ago.

If they spoofed the number for the text message, the picture shows, too."

"Did you go to the hospital?"

"Of course. There wasn't any record of your being admitted, but it took time to establish that. Then I called a bunch of other hospitals, thinking you'd gotten it wrong in your delirious state."

"I've been known to do that. Why didn't you text me back?"

"I did. Several times."

"Oh. I must have missed the notifications."

"I finally decided to come back here in case you or the hospital called the office number."

"And you found..."

She unfurled her arm behind her as if she were revealing a game-show prize. "I'll give you a hint. It wasn't a free home makeover from HGTV."

I stepped around her into the office. The only thing that stopped it from being as bad as Corrine White's apartment was that they had less material to work with. Gretchen's chromium and glass desk was overturned and smashed, its drawers strewn around it like orbiting satellites. Her potted plants had been pulverized. Her Aeron chairs had been flipped over and her file cabinets toppled. A layer of file folders, documents, and Post-its covered everything like oversize confetti. Real confetti from the office shredder was thrown in for good measure.

I glanced at the door to Chris's office. "How's the other room?"

"Worse. They took all the computer equipment as well."

"That doesn't make any sense."

"Why not? It's the only thing of real value in the office."

I realized that Gretchen was behind the times, and I updated her on everything that had transpired since Ray and I had left for the storage unit.

Agog was the best description of her expression. "So they ransacked the place looking for the manuscript?"

"Yes, and I'll bet they searched the Post Street apartment again."

Gretchen tugged at the hem of her double-breasted blazer and shook her head. "This is bad, August."

"Well, it could be worse. We still have—"

"No, you're not getting it. It means they didn't want to trade. It means they don't want to give up Angelina."

I hung my head. "Or they're not in a position to give her up. But we can't let ourselves think like that. It might be they figured they could make a quick score and not have to deal with us."

"Maybe. I just hope your crazy friend did what you told him."

"Ray, you mean?"

"Yes, Ray. Have you talked to him since you sent him off with the scroll?"

"Ah, no."

"Well, goddamn it—isn't it about time?"

I fumbled out my cell phone, dialed Ray's number, and pressed the speaker phone option so Gretchen could listen in. It was so long before he picked up that I was certain the call had gone to voice mail. Even after he answered, the only thing we heard was muffled rustling.

"Ray, are you there?"

Still more rustling.

"Ray Heinzmann speaking."

"I know that. This is August. Where are you?"

A beat went by. "Oh, out and about."

"What does that mean? I expected you to lie low at the hotel. Did you drop off the scroll like I told you?"

He cleared his throat. "Well, about that. I stopped at a bar on the way to wet my whistle and accidentally left it in the booth. It was gone when I came back."

Gretchen stared at me with eyes bulging.

I shook my head at her. "Cut it out, Ray. This has gotten serious."

"It wasn't already serious? Yeah, I took care of it like you asked. You should have already received the, ah, means to redeem it."

"Okay. Why the roundabout phrasing?"

"Now who's not being serious? How do you know your phone's not tapped?"

Gretchen and I exchanged a look. She took hold of the sleeve of my sport coat and pulled me into the corridor.

"How do we know they didn't leave a bug in the office?"

"Jesus, you two are paranoid."

"What are you talking about?" asked Ray.

I explained about the office being searched and Gretchen's concern about a bug being left behind.

"She's right. That's even more likely than the phone being tapped. Much easier to do. I hope you didn't say anything about the disposition of the scroll while you were in there."

A frission of panic ran through me. I couldn't remember if I gave Gretchen the details of what I'd tasked Ray with or simply told her I'd asked him to put the scroll in a safe place.

She must have seen the panic in my face. "Relax. You just told me you asked Ray to stash it."

I let out a ragged breath. "All right. We need to up our game from now on. Ray, you said your last name when you answered. I want you to switch hotels and check into a new one under a different name. And stay away from us. We can't be seen together."

"No problem. I already checked out anyway."

"What?"

"Don't worry—it's all good. I'll update you when we can talk safely. I better go now."

"Wait—what are you up to?"

"Bye."

I put the phone back in my pocket and looked over at Gretchen.

"What was that about?" she asked.

"Knowing Ray, it's either something terribly clever and useful, or it's something eccentric and strange that only an eighty-something-year-old aerospace engineer would think of."

"I hope it's the former. I'm going to finish cleaning up, then I'll have the office swept for bugs."

"By who?"

She smiled. "You forget this high-tech stuff is our specialty now. We have a firm we work with. What about you?"

I brought my hand up to rub my temples. "Guess I'll go back to the apartment and see if they searched it. Then I'll wait. They've got to get in touch. They've done just about everything else."

Gretchen nodded and reached over to give my forearm a squeeze. "Be careful."

"You, too. And know that any future communications from me will be in person or, worst case, by phone. No texting."

"No texting."

It took me about fifteen minutes to cover the eight blocks back to the Post Street apartment. It seemed shorter because I couldn't get my mind off the treadmill of worry launched by Gretchen's comment about Brendan and Andreas not wanting—or being able—to trade Angelina for the scroll. My own explanation that they were trying for a quick score seemed less and less persuasive.

When I crossed Leavenworth for the final block of the journey, prudence overcame preoccupation, and I slowed my pace and slipped the Luger out of its holster. I held it down by my side, scanning the street for anyone aiming target pistols at me as I approached the door.

I managed to open the keyless entry system without being shot and stepped into the lobby. But as I crossed to the elevator, Andreas came around the elevator cage holding a silenced pistol with a fancy sighting system aimed right at my chest.

"Come on. He wants to see you."

I should have been pleased. It was exactly what I had been waiting for. But I was tired of being pushed around.

I brought the Luger up to cover his torso. "Would he like to see my vintage Luger, too?"

"Don't be stupid."

"I'm not the one who brought a peashooter to a gun fight."

"These are .22 magnums."

"These are 9mm hollow points," I said with more bravado than I felt. "They'll tear a fist-size hole in your guts."

Muscles at the side of his jaw bunched. "He just wants to talk."

"Talk where exactly?"

"He's waiting in a car parked around the corner."

"Fine, we can talk—but on my terms. Put the gun on the floor."

"This doesn't have to be a standoff."

"It's not a standoff. A standoff is where nobody has an advantage."

He drew his mouth into a line that looked a puckered scar and shifted his weight back and forth between his legs, trying to decide.

"Put. The gun. Down."

He broke at the knees and ratcheted himself into a squat, keeping his eyes on mine the whole time. He set the gun down gently, almost lovingly.

I gestured with the Luger. "Over to the door—and stay clear of me as you pass."

He did as he was told, giving me a wide berth. When he reached the entrance, he turned to look back at me.

"Eyes front," I snapped, then scooped up the pistol. "Let's go see daddy. This will put you in solid with him."

26
BIG DADDY

Andreas led me to a dark SUV parked on Hyde Street next to a hair salon named Kwon's that must have moved into one of the building's ground-floor storefronts after I left San Francisco as I didn't recognize the business or the Asian woman sitting in the customer chair blowing smoke from a cigarette at the ceiling. If she was the least bit worried about a guy herding another guy down the sidewalk with two loaded pistols in broad daylight, she didn't show it.

The windows on the parked SUV were tinted, but I could make out Brendan's profile in the rear.

Andreas stopped by the driver's door and peered back at me.

"You got the keys to the car?" I asked.

He seemed surprised by the question. "Yes, of course."

"Throw them in the gutter."

"What?"

"You heard me. Throw them in the gutter and get in the front seat. And keep your hands on the wheel at ten and two where I can see them."

Andreas let the keys drop by the front tire and popped the front door. I yanked the rear door wide open to draw a bead on a startled Brendan.

"Hiya, pops." I kept the Luger aimed at an indeterminate point between both men while Andreas got behind the wheel as instructed. I slid into the back seat and kept the door open a few inches so I could tumble out if circumstances warranted.

After savoring the shocked expression on Brendan's face for a moment, I chucked Andreas's pistol well out of reach on the floor.

Brendan laughed. "Well, well. What's this?"

"Nancy Pelosi took it off him with a dull butter knife, but I made her give it back."

He laughed again. "You may be—as some in the family have suggested—a few clowns short of a circus, but you still manage to entertain. Perhaps we underestimated you the tiniest bit."

"If that's your idea of buttering me up, it's not working. But answer me this—what's with the .22 caliber pistols? Why not something—"

"Bigger and blunter?"

"Yeah."

"Israel's Mossad, the most effective intelligence agency in the world, uses suppressed .22s for assassinations. If they are good enough for Mossad, they are good enough for us."

"There's a difference between clipping an eighty-year-old Nazi in his bed and shooting it out on the street."

"Possibly. The other reason is that we already had them to hand. One of our family activities is target shooting in our indoor range." Brendan settled back in the car's upholstery and brought both hands up to his ample belly as he regarded me. "All that said, you must realize we are past the point where guns have relevance."

"Then why did number one son pull a gat on me as soon as I walked through the door?"

Brendan shrugged. "Guns were the language we were speaking until now. I'm sure Andreas thought it wise to reestablish communication in the old medium before switching to the new."

"Which is?"

"Trade. Commerce. The exchange of one thing of value in return for another. If you were to kill Andreas and me with that very fine example of the Pistole Parabellum—commonly known as the Luger in the United States—that would also be the end of Angelina Evangelista. If we were to kill you, we might not ever take possession of the Kerouac manuscript, although I am less certain of the latter than the former. We might sill recover the manuscript without you."

"Don't bet on it."

"I'm not betting on it. That's why I'm here. I was eventually persuaded it would be more expedient to trade with you than continue along the course we were following."

"How do I know you have Angelina?"

He smiled a prim smile with lips that were small and almost obscenely plump. "Oh, we have her. And we are prepared to prove it."

"Who's we, exactly? Just you and Andreas? Where did you leave her?"

"There are other members of the family besides Andreas, me, and our prodigal son Jeff. Female members. Cisgendered females, to be exact. Angelina is safe with them."

I shook my head almost involuntarily. I was still having trouble with the idea of anyone wanting to be in a polyamorous family—particularly *this* polyamorous family.

Brendan seemed to read my thoughts. "There are many reasons people join. Some realize that success in the traditional sense hasn't brought the fulfillment they thought, and they go on a journey to find something more. The family is what they find. Others like the idea of being unconventional, of doing something supremely naughty. It can feel really good to do what others consider to be bad. Still others need a regimen or structure to their lives. Andreas is one of those. Did you know that he used to be a monk?"

I glanced at Andreas, who groaned, and said, "Brendan, please."

"Relax. It's all part of building trust before our transaction. Like dogs sniffing each other's behinds."

"Could you try a different metaphor?" I said.

"There's no need to be prudish. I can assure you that members of the family have done a lot more than sniff my behind. In fact, we are all connected by my sperm. By more than my sperm—by my DNA. Did you know that the receiving partner in any sexual congress retains DNA from the donating partner in their brain tissue? For life?"

A box truck belonging to a document-shredding company rumbled by, shaking the SUV and possibly saving me from reaching over to slap the supercilious expression off Brendan's face. "Sounds like junk science to me. But I'll bet you are one of those guys who donates to sperm banks just to see his progeny spread around the world."

"It's not junk science, I assure you. And, yes, as it happens, I was a donor to the Repository for Germinal Choice."

"The Repository for Germinal Choice?"

"The genius sperm bank."

"Of course."

"Sadly now out of business. Since I've given you a good sniff up my back side, perhaps you can return the favor. What in the world possessed your friend Duckworth to make a copy of the Kerouac scroll?"

"I've no idea. Apparently, he didn't trust you." I jabbed the Luger forward in a threatening manner. "A better question is why you killed him."

"I didn't. He was alive when I left the club."

"I don't believe it."

"Believe what you like. We were conducting a good-faith negotiation. I had no reason to kill him."

"Next you're going to tell me that you didn't kill the club mama-san or her employee."

He gave me an oily grin. "Yes, I freely admit to killing *them*. And that should tell you something. Why would I lie about the one and not the other?"

"Because the other was a close friend of mine."

"Well, there's that. I understand that you two used to work as a team. It strikes me that it was a mistake to split up. You both lost something vital when you dissolved the partnership—he, the ability to protect himself; and you, the ability to negotiate life's more serpentine labyrinths."

"Fuck you."

"You forget—I am the fucker, not the fuckee."

I growled. I was within an inch of emptying the whole eight-shot magazine of the Luger into him. The only thing that stopped me is that he seemed to *want* me to shoot him. I forced a deep breath into my lungs. "You said you were negotiating with Chris. For the scroll?"

"Yes, just like you and I are. The terms were different, of course."

"Had you agreed on a price?"

"No. I was proposing he accept a ground-floor interest in an ICO."

"An ICO?" The moment the words left my lips I regretted it. I'd just handed Big Brain another opportunity to show off.

"Initial Coin Offering. A cryptocurrency like Bitcoin. You know, making use of blockchain technology. The family is issuing one. We call it the Family Affiliation Token, or FAT for short."

"Let me guess. Chris wasn't interested in being paid in any of your FAT coin."

"No, and it was his loss, believe me."

"But he had a much bigger loss, didn't he? Just what makes this scroll so valuable to you people? I get that a previously unknown manuscript from Kerouac is worth some money. Maybe even a large sum of money—but it's not worth the suffering and death you've caused. I count five people murdered, and it wouldn't surprise me if there were more."

"No, five is correct," said Brendan, as if we were discussing a ball score. "But as I said, I am not personally responsible for all of them."

"You didn't answer the question."

"Why is the scroll so valuable? It's true that a previously unknown manuscript from Kerouac's typewriter is worth millions. But it's not the medium that we care about; it's the message. And the message is nothing less than revolutionary. The Beats were pioneers in polyamorism. Did you know that Dr. Alfred C. Kinsey interviewed most of them for his six-year study, *Sexual Behavior in the Human Male*? Those conversations were key to helping Kinsey understand that sexual orientation is not exclusively hetero or homosexual in most people.

"The Beats also preferred communal living. Many of them resided in the so-called Beat Hotel in Paris where William S. Burroughs completed the text for his masterwork, *Naked Lunch*. This new scroll of Kerouac's is even greater than that book. It combines and synthesizes all the experience and thinking about polyamorism and communal living into a prescription for life. It is to us what the Ten Commandments are to Jews and Christians."

A bunch of perverts living together didn't seem particularly new or revolutionary to me, but I didn't say that. What I said was "How do you know?"

"What?"

"How do you know that's what 'The Beat-hive' is about? If it's a previously unknown manuscript, how do you know what's in it?"

Brendan patted his fat egg of a belly and shook his head as if I were a slow learner. "I shouldn't have to remind you that I *have* seen a fragment of it in that elaborate copy your friend made."

"Yeah, but you were after it even before you saw it."

He let out an exasperated sigh. "Its existence is well-known among the Beat cognoscenti. For example, there's a clear reference to it in a letter from Kerouac to Neal Cassady. The family and I have been on a quest to recover it for years. And now we are on the cusp of doing so at last." He leaned forward. "But I want no further tricks from you. How can I be sure that you actually have the complete manuscript?"

"You can read it when we meet for the exchange. Don't worry— the ending is every bit as socko as the opening."

"Your sarcasm is tedious and small-minded. How can I be sure you have it *before* we go to the bother and risk of meeting?"

"I dunno. How do you want to be reassured?"

"Text me pictures of the typescript—clear pictures."

"Okay. But I'm not going to photograph the whole scroll. I'll send you a sampling."

"That is acceptable but make sure the samples include the text immediately after the portion we've seen and the ending. And I want to see the scroll from the side—to get a sense of its length."

"Fine. Now how about from my end? You said you were prepared to prove you have Angelina."

"Indeed we are." He chuckled merrily.

I don't know if that was a prearranged signal or if they had communicated by some nonverbal means, but Andreas wheeled around suddenly and brought a large-caliber revolver to bear at an uncomfortable spot between my eyes.

"I hope you'll approve of our car gun," said Brendan. "A Smith & Wesson .44 Magnum. It packs quite a wallop."

I tightened my grip on the Luger and licked my lips. They tasted dry and salty. Now we were in a standoff. If I shot Brendan, Andreas would shoot me. "I thought we were past the point where guns have relevance."

"We are—we definitely are," said Brendan. "I just wanted to be sure you respected that while we showed you our proof. With your permission, I'll retrieve my cell phone from the seat pocket in front of me."

I nodded, a horrible feeling of dread pressing down on me.

Brendan took out a phone, hit the power button, and turned the screen so I could see it. "Here you go—a nice picture of Angelina holding today's *San Francisco Chronicle* while she sucks my cock."

27
TAG, YOU'RE IT

I couldn't seem to get enough air. My pulse pounded in my temples like a pneumatic press, and the hand holding the Luger began to tremble, prompting Brendan to laugh.

"Jealous? You can't have polyamory with jealousy."

I knew I had to move or risk losing control entirely. I backed out of the car and stood raging on the sidewalk, my head and the muzzle of the Luger the only things still poking into the cabin. "You pig."

"Don't go away mad," Brendan said after I began to do exactly that, "And don't forget the pictures, Mr. Riordan. Text me the pictures and we can set up a time and place for the exchange."

I grunted in response, but he wouldn't have heard me. I was running by then.

I went two blocks before I realized that I was still holding the Luger. I holstered it and ducked under the awning of the 1920s-era Ben Hur apartments at the corner of Hyde and Ellis. Andreas and Brendan drove by a moment later, Andreas sneering at me as they passed.

It was time to call in the cavalry. I phoned Gretchen to set up a meeting with her and Ray. But when she mentioned that the Flood Building office had, in fact, been bugged, my paranoia went into overdrive. I didn't want Brendan and Andreas listening in on our conversation, and I didn't want them to even be aware of Ray's existence and his role in the case, which meant we needed a new place to meet. After a lot of back and forth, I hit on the idea of borrowing the break room at Kim's nail salon. Gretchen hung up to get Ray on board, and I called Kim to borrow the room.

After covering the receiver to check with someone else in the salon, she said, "It's all yours. Just be sure to slip a twenty in the tip jar at the reception desk. And I won't be around. I'm leaving now to do some freelancing."

I glanced up at the bas-relief of Roman chariots above the windows of the old apartment building. "I thought your freelancing days were over."

"Not that kind of freelancing, silly. I'm doing pedis for a bunch of girls at a bachelorette party."

"But nothing for the bachelors."

"That's right. Thank you for your interest. Do I detect the slightest bit of concern or jealousy?"

"No—I mean, yes. Actually, I don't know what I mean."

"Bye now."

The whole exchange had been silly, but it somehow lifted my spirits. When I stepped into the break room twenty minutes later, my rage and paranoia had dissipated, and I was ready to talk rationally about getting Angelina back.

Ray and Gretchen were already sitting around the flimsy card table, and someone had set the rice cooker and tea kettle aside. Ray looked up from the well-thumbed copy of *Elle Magazine* he'd been perusing, and said, "Take a lot of your meetings in nail salons, do you, August?"

I scraped the last available chair out from under the table and sat down. "No, but you have to admit it's good cover."

Ray made a scoffing noise. "For Gretchen maybe. Everyone laughed out loud when I came through the door."

"Boys," Gretchen said. "Let's skip the grousing and get started.

I think we can all agree the less time we're together, the better." She looked over at me. "You weren't exactly coherent on the phone. What happened with Brendan and Andreas?"

I gave an abbreviated summary of the meeting, nearly choking up when I came to the punchline.

No one said anything for a long moment. "Jesus," Ray finally said.

"Jesus has got nothing to do with it. The thing that really sent me off the deep end was that it was clear they'd staged the picture to make it look like it was done voluntarily. I'm sure they were holding a gun on her, but you couldn't see it and you couldn't read the expression on her face. Brendan was also dropping broad hints that, given enough time, she would join the family. Like a modern-day Patty Hearst."

"The poor girl," said Gretchen. "We've got to finish this. The sooner the better."

"No kidding. But first things first. We need to retrieve the scroll from the hotel, take some cell phone photos of it, and text them to Brendan. He won't set the time and place for the exchange until he's convinced we actually have the real deal."

Ray cleared his throat and did his beard-combing ritual. "It could be a trick."

"A trick? How could that be a trick?"

"You know what Exif is?"

I sighed. "You know I don't."

"It stands for exchangeable image file format. It's a way to store metadata about a photo *inside* the photo. You don't normally see it when you look at a picture online. You need a special tool or operating system utility."

"So?"

"So unless you turn it off, one of the pieces of metadata recorded when you snap a cell phone picture is the GPS coordinates of the location where the photo was taken. It's called geotagging, and the information is commonly used on social media sites to automatically label the exact location of, say, your exciting vacation photos taken in the South of France."

"But if we don't turn it off before we send Brendan the photos—"

"He'll know exactly where the scroll was when we took the photos of it. All you've got to do is type the coordinates into Google Maps and it'll pinpoint the location within a few yards."

"Then we'll have to turn it off."

Ray ducked his head. "Yeah, or we can clear it before we send the pictures."

"But if Ray is right," said Gretchen, "and Brendan is trying to trick us, it means he's still trying to get the scroll without freeing Angelina."

I slumped back in the folding chair, eliciting a plasticky squeak. "Yes. And now that I think back on the meeting, all of his bullshit about the family and why people join points to the same conclusion. He doesn't want to trade. He wants both the scroll and Angelina." I brought my hands to the back of my head, cradling it while I tilted back even farther in the chair and stared at the ceiling's grimy popcorn texture and drooping cobwebs. "It's too bad Chris didn't make another copy of the scroll."

"Why?" Ray asked.

I looked over at him. "Because maybe we could turn Brendan's trick around on him. He wants the geolocation of the scroll so he can break into wherever it is and steal it. What if we sent him pictures of another phony scroll taken in a place that we stake out? When he comes to nab it, we follow him back to wherever he's got Angelina and free her."

Gretchen made a face. "It sounds pretty dangerous, August."

"I don't think so. There aren't that many of them, and we would have the element of surprise. It would be a calculated risk, but it wouldn't be completely foolhardy."

She flashed an impish grin that made me think of better times. "At least on the Riordan scale of foolhardy, you mean."

I grinned back. "Yes, it's a little like centigrade and fahrenheit."

"All right," she said. "But why do you need another copy? You can use the real scroll just as easily. It would be too bad if we lost the original scroll, but it's nothing compared to Angelina's freedom."

"I agree about the worth of the thing. I don't give a rat's ass about it if we get Angelina back, but if things go south when we confront Brendan, using a copy as bait would let us retain a bargaining chip. We could still do the original trade as planned if we had to."

Ray cleared his throat again. "We *do* have another copy."

"What?"

"I made one."

"When?"

"I scanned the scroll—the whole scroll this time—before I dropped it off at the hotel. Then I used a modified version of the teletype we found at the storage unit to print a copy."

"So that's what you've been up to."

He nodded. He was trying to look humble and keep a straight face, but you could tell he was pleased with himself.

"'Modified,' you said. How?"

"Your friend Duckworth had a good idea to use the teletype. It's like a motorized typewriter. Only problem is, the output doesn't really look like a typewriter. It looks like a 1960s computer. I fixed that. I soldered the letters from the strikers of a 1930s Underwood portable onto the strikers from the teletype."

"Let me guess—Kerouac used a 1930s Underwood."

"Yep. I read that he borrowed it from Neal and Carolyn Cassady when he stayed at their house on Russell Street."

I brought my hands up to clap softly. "Bravo, Ray, bravo. But what possessed you to do it in the first place? You had no way of knowing we'd need a copy."

He shrugged. "I didn't exactly set out to make a copy. At first, I was only concerned about the scanning problem. The reason Duckworth had to make a copy by repeating only part of the text from the scroll was that it was so hard to scan a continuous roll of paper. I figured there had to be a better approach, so I did some research and found that one of my fellow old-fogy engineers had come up with one for a completely different application—copying player-piano rolls. This fellow used a capstan-driven transport designed with a single 300 DPI Dyna-CIS sensor and a MK4 hardware circuit board, all driven by a Windows—"

I waved my hands. "We'll take your word for it. So you solved the scanning problem. Then what?"

"Then I thought, well, why not print a copy with my scan— and while I'm at it, why not make one that would look even more like the original?"

Gretchen reached a hand across the table to each of us. "Boys, as much as I'm enjoying this technology-geek fest, don't you think we should get back to the topic at hand? Thanks to Ray's genius, we are blessed with an even more realistic copy of the scroll. How do we use it to bait our trap?"

"Let's think it through," I said. "Brendan will assume we've hidden the real scroll in a location we think is clever—one that we believe he wouldn't know to search. So we need to pick a location like that and photograph the copy there, leaving the Exif stuff in the photos like the dummies he's convinced we are."

Gretchen nodded. "Yes, and this location has to be good for us, too, doesn't it? It has to be easy for us to stake out without being observed."

"Right, so all the places he's already searched are out because we would have found them too risky to use at this point. The office and the Post Street apartment. The hotel where we have the real scroll would be bad for another reason. It would be hard for Brendan and his crew to break in without being seen by hotel staff, and we want him to be able to get to the scroll easily. But I think I know the perfect place—the storage unit. It's unknown to him, it's easy to break into, and it's easy for us to stake out."

"No," Ray said flatly.

"Why not?"

"I'm living there. Where did you think I went after I checked out of my hotel?"

I shook my head. "Another hotel is what I and the other ninety-nine percent of the population would have said."

"Too expensive. And besides, that's where I was doing all the work with the teletype machine."

"Then I give up. Where should we put it?"

Gretchen sat up straight in her chair. "I know. Back to the place where the real scroll was hidden. 29 Russell Street."

28
GATHER ROUND THE CAMPFIRE

"Again with the Little Debbie Banana Pudding Rolls, Ray?" We were parked in his Dodge Aries on Hyde Street across from the intersection with Russell Street. It was about 9:20 p.m., and in lieu of the perfectly good McDonald's meal I'd offered to buy him, he was now compulsively unwrapping and shoving into his face lard-infused sponge-cake rolls covered in squiggles of icing that he took from a box on the seat between us. The last time I'd watched him engage in this particular brand of self-toxification had also been a stakeout. It seemed to be a pattern.

"No worse than that Double Quarter Pounder with Cheese you ate," Ray said in a voice wheezy with pudding roll.

"You ever heard of Yellow Dye No. 5? That's known to cause hyperactivity in children. Those things are loaded with it."

"Yeah, I know. At my age, I could use a little hyperactivity."

He had a point, but he—and I—had actually been quite active since our meeting with Gretchen. We had retrieved Ray's copy of the scroll from the storage unit, taken it to 29 Russell Street, threaded past the crime scene tape to the second-floor landing and photographed it with my cell phone, being sure to leave suggestive bits of the surrounding background visible in the picture. Then I had texted the photos to Brendan along with a message demanding to set up a meeting for the exchange as soon as possible. It turned out that the camera app on my phone had been set to incorporate Exif, and we left it in the photos we sent.

Brendan responded with a smug message indicating he was "satisfied with the proofs we offered." That wasn't surprising as Ray's scroll did look very convincing—the only things he hadn't been able to replicate were the foxing on the paper and the yellowing, brittle Scotch tape.

Brendan followed with a proposed meeting time at nine the next morning at a location he would text me thirty minutes beforehand. His reply was so facile and lacking in details that I became convinced that the whole thing was a trick as Ray had suggested. I agreed to the plan in any case.

To finish baiting *our* trap, we put the scroll in an old toolbox and wedged the box between a pair of studs on the landing as if it had been left behind by a member of the construction crew. But the duplicate scroll wasn't the only thing we left behind. Ray mounted a battery-powered video camera high on another stud that provided a wide-angle view of the whole landing and some of the steps approaching it. The camera was part of the gear Ray used for his one true passion in life—model airplanes—and it could transmit a wireless signal to a monitor up to five miles away.

We weren't anywhere near five miles away, of course. We were just a half block up the street. Ray had a computer tablet receiving the live feed from the camera next to the Little Debbie box. So far, the only thing of interest we'd seen on the feed was a stray cat prowling up the stairs to sniff at the toolbox, his eyes glowing in the special low-light camera like a demon's.

In spite of my admonition, Ray tossed the wrapper of the previous Little Debbie Pudding Roll over his shoulder and rummaged in the box for another.

"You might want to press the pause button on your Little Debbie binge," I said, nodding at the SUV with tinted windows that was trying to park in front of the converted condos across the way. If I had any doubts that the car contained Andreas and Brendan, they were erased when the driver obsessively reversed and pulled forward in the spot to get the car positioned just so even though he was working with a good three feet of room on either side: Andreas, the anal-retentive heist driver.

Ray flipped over the tablet so the telltale glow from the screen wouldn't light up the interior of the Aries, and we both hunched as low as we could on the old bench seat. It was unnecessary effort.

Brendan rolled out of the car like the potentate of a prosperous kleptocracy, oblivious to his surroundings. Andreas fell in behind him clutching a tablet computer of his own, and they ambled up Russell Street, alternatively checking house numbers and glancing at the tablet.

"They're using the computer to confirm the GPS coordinates," Ray said.

"Yeah, I got that. But it shouldn't be that much of a mystery. They've been there before—when they murdered Angelina's sister. You'd think it would have left an impression."

Ray shrugged. "They are psychopathic killers, true, but they are *conscientious* psychopathic killers."

"I'm pretty sure that's worse."

"Probably."

Ray turned our tablet computer over to monitor the feed, but we picked up the sounds of their approach on the camera's microphone before we saw them. A board on the stairs squeaked, and Andreas said, "Upstairs? Where the body was? Isn't that a little dramatic?"

Brendan chuckled, and the top of his head became visible. "That's where I'm betting. Given his limited intelligence, he probably thought that this was the last place in the world we would check. Or that we would be deterred by the crime scene tape."

Both men came fully into view as they trudged up the rickety stairs, Brendan's torso gray and wavering in the ambient light and Andreas's blown out by the glare from his computer's display.

A step shy of the landing, Brendan pointed at the toolbox on the floor between the studs. "Hey, shine some light over there."

Andreas came up beside him and fiddled with the tablet, projecting a white-hot beam from a corner of the device. "It's a toolbox."

"As if any competent demo crew would leave their tools around to be stolen. That has to be it." Brendan hurried up to the box and kneeled on the bare boards to open it. "Bingo," he said with a new urgency in his voice. "What a cretin. It's almost too easy."

Andreas squatted beside him, pouring the tablet's light over the scroll. "Are you sure? Not another fake?"

Brendan feverishly unspooled the scroll, taking care not to let any part of it touch the floor. "Yes, yes," he mumbled to himself as he went, interjecting "My God, it's genius" and "What beautiful writing" when he came to passages he particularly liked. After running through almost the whole thing, Brendan slumped back on his haunches with a sigh. "What did I tell you? This is it. We have the full manuscript."

"Daddy knows best," said Andreas without the slightest trace of irony.

"Damn right. But Riordan wasn't a worthy opponent. Nothing like Duckworth—Duckworth was a different story."

"Yes, he was."

Ray glanced up from our tablet. "That's three times they've insulted your intelligence."

"Sure, but who's counting?"

"Time for your little chore. They'll be heading back to the car soon."

"Naw, they'll be patting themselves on the back for another twenty minutes." But I opened the glove box as I spoke and extracted another of the gizmos Ray had adopted from his model airplane hobby: a small GPS tracking device. "Where's the best place?"

"The tailpipe."

"Really? It won't get burned up?"

"No, I've got a special heat shield around it, and the tailpipe is less likely to be checked than the wheel well or under the bumper."

"Well, since Brendan prides himself so much on being a top, there is a certain irony in shoving this up his tailpipe."

Ray made a face. "Please, August. You need to be more respectful of my generation's sensibilities."

"Right," I said, leavening the word with irony. I popped the passenger's door on the old Dodge and hustled across the street to the back of the SUV, where I deployed the mission payload, griming my fingers with carbon in spite of the care I took. I stood and waited for a slug of traffic to pass, then jogged back to the Aries, where I resumed my seat beside Ray.

"Anything interesting happen while I was gone?"

"Nothing you want to hear about, except they've repacked the scroll in the toolbox and are already headed down the stairs. They seem to be in a hurry now that they've won the prize."

Sure enough, it wasn't a minute before we saw the pair of them hotfooting it down Russell Street, their long shadows under the street light stabbing ahead of them as they went. The parking lights on the SUV flashed as Andreas unlocked the doors remotely and Brendan dove into the back seat with the toolbox clamped to his middle as if it were a football. Andreas got into the driver's seat, started the car, and pulled out onto Hyde with reckless abandon—for him, at least.

Ray had returned to the tablet computer as soon as we saw them approach, and he had switched from the camera stream to an app that showed a map of San Francisco with a deep-blue background.

"Your doohickey working?"

Ray touched a menu at the corner of the screen and made a selection. A flashing dot appeared at our location on the map. "Yes. My doohickey is working. We can safely tail them from a mile or two back."

We'd had the inevitable argument about who was going to drive, so I was relieved to hear that my decision to let Ray get behind the wheel wasn't going to be tested by the requirement to do a close-up tail. "Okay," I said, picking up the tablet. "I'll call out the directions so you can devote your full attention to keeping all four wheels in contact with the road—and pointed in the right direction."

"Piece of cake," Ray said, and fired up the Aries, holding the key in the start position a second too long so the flywheel ground with a noise like a shovel scraping asphalt. "Sorry," he mumbled.

"Off to a flying start. They're still on Hyde heading south, so you need to do a U-ey."

Ray did a creditable job of executing a three-point turn, using the mouth of Russell Street for extra maneuvering room and only getting honked at by oncoming traffic once. As we rumbled down the gently sloping road with the cable-car tracks directly beneath us, I checked the tablet and saw the flashing dot turning off Hyde. "They are turning left onto Golden Gate about a mile ahead."

"What's that mean?"

"Too early to tell. They could be heading for one of the freeways."

"You think they're leaving town?"

"I hope not. This is going to be a lot harder if we have to ambush them on the road. But I don't think so. We know there are more members of the family. If they did drive here, there are other vehicles, and they'll want to rendezvous before they head up to Vancouver. Remember, they think they've outsmarted us. They've got plenty of time."

"But what if they're going to the airport? How do we—"

"Ray, just drive. We'll deal with it when we deal with it."

He grunted but said nothing more.

We followed them onto Golden Gate Avenue, but by the time we got there, they had already turned south onto Sixth Street. I was pretty sure that they were heading toward the freeway since Sixth feeds directly into the on-ramp for Highway 280 South. Unless Brendan and Andreas were badly confused, that eliminated driving north to Canada but still left the airport as a possibility.

We crossed Market Street and rolled down Sixth, passing a number of SRO residential hotels, many of them with homeless people huddled in the gloom by the entrances.

Andreas did as I expected and got on Highway 280 South, but I delayed telling Ray to avoid another what-if discussion. There were still plenty of San Francisco exits on the freeway they would have to pass before we would know if they were leaving town.

"The freeway," Ray said, as he stared at the looming on-ramp from the stoplight at Sixth and Brannan. "I was right. They're going to the airport."

"You're right about the freeway, but they've already gotten off."

"Where?"

"The Twenty-fifth Street exit into Bayview—Hunters Point, but they are still going."

Ray floored the Aries, provoking a crescendo of knocking and pinging, but the car barely accelerated.

As Ray wheezed slowly up the elevated on-ramp, I watched as Andreas executed a series of quick turns over the course of less than a mile. He went east onto Cesar Chavez, then south on Third, then veered southeast on Cargo Way, and finally took a couple of hard lefts onto Jennings and a street called Amador, where he stopped. I didn't know Amador, but the map told me it was very close to the Bay near the old Pier 96, which had been converted from a dock to a recycling center.

Ray drove on 280 to the exit for Twenty-fifth and followed the same circuitous route to where Amador intersected with Jennings. The area was thoroughly industrial, with a rail yard to the left and a rock-crushing plant to the right. And it was dark. Very dark. The tablet computer told me that Andreas had stopped another half mile ahead, surprisingly close to the point where Amador bent back to an intersection with Cargo Way. Unless he had gotten lost, I wasn't sure why he hadn't taken the more direct route from Cargo to his destination.

"Well, what now?" Ray asked, as we idled on the shoulder of the road.

"They've stopped just ahead. I don't want to go barreling up in this squeaky tub with the lights blazing and give ourselves away. We get out and walk. But at some point, you're going to have to hang back and let me handle it."

"I brought a gun."

"What? You brought a gun after giving me so much crap about sending me the Luger?" I pressed my elbow on the holster next to my ribs to feel the gun's reassuring bulk. "Where'd you get it?"

"Where do you think? From a gun store."

"Okay. I'm not going to say I'm sorry you have it, but you still have to hang back if I tell you."

"With pleasure."

Ray killed the lights and turned off the car, and we stepped out into the night. It was cool and damp so close to the Bay, and there was an unpleasant, almost tarlike tang to the air—most likely a carcinogenic solvent from one of the industrial yards, I reassured myself. We debated taking the tablet computer with us, but after watching Andreas and Brendan blunder around Russell Street with one, we decided the risk of their leaving the area without us knowing was outweighed by the risk of the light from the computer giving us away.

We trudged along the chain-link fence topped by razor wire that bounded the rock-crushing operation. At a curve where the road bent back toward Cargo Way, the fence ended, and we came upon a tall steel tower painted orange and white. It had a single light flashing on the top, but it seemed an odd place for a transmission tower. Ray noticed me staring.

"Aircraft warning light," he whispered.

I nodded, and we continued past a cement plant with mixers parked by the gate. Past that were warehouses and several honest-to-goodness trees, which looked as out of place as gazebos in the ninth circle of hell. Approaching the location where Andreas must have parked, we passed railroad cars on a siding and a cluster of storage tanks.

Up ahead, we saw an abandoned grain elevator with more than a dozen silos. There were tiny windows around the top of the silos, and the surface of the concrete walls was mottled and cracked with age. A decrepit chain-link fence surrounded the structure, but as I came up to the gate, I could see that there was no lock in the hasp.

Standing quietly on the cracked, weed-infiltrated asphalt by the gate, I heard a low rumble of male voices and a higher lilt of female laughter coming from beyond. A flickering light emanated from behind the grain elevator, but it was impossible to tell whether it came from inside the building or from a source in the yard that was blocked from my view.

I took hold of Ray's sleeve and pulled him closer. "This is where you hang back. If you hear shouts or shooting, use your discretion. If you see them drive out again, go back to the car and track them. Then alert Gretchen and call 911."

"Those are a bunch of swell options."

"Don't worry. They've boxed themselves in here, and they aren't expecting us. If I can, I'm going to disable their vehicles first, then we'll have our little tête-à-tête."

"Godspeed, John Glenn."

"Thanks."

I lifted the hasp on the gate and pulled it open a foot or so, then slid through. I moved quickly to the side of the grain elevator and poked my head around the corner.

A motorhome was parked head-in toward the building. Squatting, I could make out the wheels of another vehicle parked beyond the motorhome. The SUV, I assumed.

I slipped the Luger out of its holster, snicked off the safety, and crept up to the side of the motorhome. Its front bumper was nearly touching the wall of the grain elevator, and as I crouched by the front wheel, I came face-to-face with big-toothed animal graffiti spray-painted on the walls by someone who styled himself "Chili Dog."

I was tempted to let the air out of all the tires of the motorhome, but the voices were louder here and I was both worried I would be overheard and curious to know what was going on. In one of the most foolhardy moves I've made in a long career of foolhardy moves, I got down on my belly and combat-crawled under the RV.

I snaked myself over to the front wheel on the other side and peered around the edge closest to the grain elevator. There was a gap of about eight inches, and I could see a large opening to the building. In front of it sat some sort of gas fire pit in a ceramic bowl: the source of the light I'd seen earlier. Sitting around the fire pit were four or five people. I could see the feet of two of them, and I heard two or three more on the other side of the pit.

"There's no rush," said a voice I recognized as Brendan's. "Midday is soon enough. After all, no one is coming after us, and that would still give us time to get across the Oregon border by nightfall. We can use the morning to take care of a couple of final items. One is sending Riordan a text to confirm the time and place for the fictitious exchange even though he no longer has anything to trade in return for our fair Brigid. Ha-ha."

Our fair *Brigid*. Who the hell was Brigid? It took me a moment to figure it out, but the implication hit me with sickening vertigo. Lying flat on my belly on the grimy asphalt beneath the motor-home, I felt like I was spinning out of control, cold sweat popping from every pore.

"The other thing we need to do is dispose of the guns—all of them. I don't know what possessed you and Jeff to go rogue, Brigid, but a ballistics test on your weapon would implicate us in the worst of the murders. No one cares if a drug-addicted whore and desiccated pimptress die, but the others—well, that's a different story. You hear me?"

"Yes, Daddy," said Angelina.

29
SWEDISH ALL ALONG

I shot out from under the motorhome like a startled crawfish, shredding the elbows of my jacket as I went. I rolled to my side, pulling the knife off my ankle with my left hand while retaining the Luger in my right, then scrambled to my feet. My plan was simple. I was going to puncture the tires on my side of the vehicle, then charge around the other, blasting anything and everything in my path. I would switch to stabbing when I ran out of ammo.

I brought the point of the knife to the tire closest to me, but after barely scoring the arm of the Michelin man, I drew it back. Yes, my plan was simple, but it was also dumb—comically dumb. Even if I managed to survive and finish off Angelina, Brendan, and all his family, I would almost certainly be caught and charged for the crime. Ironically, it was Brendan and his many insults about my intelligence that made me realize it. As he had pointed out, Chris would have done better. I could do better, too.

Vibrating with impatience and suppressed rage, I trod in a herky-jerky stride around the grain elevator to the gate. As I slipped through it, Ray rushed out from the shadows.

"What happened?" he whispered, eyes wide in reaction to all the weaponry I still brandished. "Weren't they there?"

I ignored the question. "Angelina's with them. She's part of the family."

"You can't blame her. They coerced her either physically or mentally. It's Stockholm syndrome."

"You're missing the point," I hissed. "She's been Swedish all along. She killed Chris."

Nearly three hours later, I was once again standing in front of the grimy balustrade guarding the Bush Street overlook to Stockton. Ray and I watched as Cristabel and Hector locked the front door of Golden Fingers and trundled down the sidewalk pushing the cart of supplies they had used to sanitize the place after a day's worth of hand jobs.

As their white uniforms faded completely into the gloom, Ray turned to me, and said, "Explain to me why we're doing this again. Aren't you worried that Brendan and the family will get away?"

I elected to focus on the latter portion of his question because I hadn't actually explained the purpose of this exercise. I wasn't sure he would help me if I did.

"I heard them say they're not leaving until midday." I looked down at my watch. It was closing on two in the morning. "That's more than ten hours from now. And even if they do take off early, your GPS tracker is still on their SUV. We'll know where they go."

"I'll stipulate that your answer is factually correct. Why doesn't it make me feel any better?"

"That's a personal problem, Ray. Let's get this show on the road. Time for you to head to the pay phone."

"You don't want me to wait till after you do your bit?"

"No. Make the call as soon as you get there. We don't need to do any real damage. We just need to make a point."

"If you say so," he said, and shuffled down the concrete staircase leading from the overlook to Stockton Street. He was heading through the Stockton tunnel to a Chinatown vegetable market with another of the few remaining pay phones in San Francisco in front of it. Given the rate at which he walked, he probably wouldn't arrive until after I had done my "bit."

I picked up the baseball bat and wine bottle I had left on the sidewalk by the balustrade and followed Ray down the staircase to Stockton and the entrance of Golden Fingers.

The frosted-glass door took several whacks with the baseball bat before I'd smashed an opening in the upper quadrant big enough for what I intended. I dropped the bat and retrieved the wine bottle. I'd dumped the wine in the parking lot of the convenience store where I'd purchased the bottle and substituted gasoline mixed with motor oil. The cork I'd replaced with a wick made of a ripped-up dish towel I got from the same store. I used a disposable lighter to set the wick on fire. It burned with a fat, lazy flame that gave off heavy smoke visible even in the dim light.

Careful not to cut or burn my arm, I threaded the bottle into the hole in the door and gave it the old alley-oop. It shattered on the lobby's concrete floor, and flame engulfed the room with a satisfying whump. I tossed the bat in after it—and ran.

I scrambled up the stairs to Bush Street, then hurried west on Bush until I came to the short alley where I'd left Ray's Dodge Aries facing outward. I jumped in the driver's seat and peeled off the gloves I'd been wearing, fumbled out my cell phone, and dialed the number Mr. "Wong" had given me. The line picked up and I heard a grunt.

"This is August Riordan. I need to talk to Wong."

Another grunt.

"It's urgent. I need him to call me back as soon as possible." I recited my number.

There was a long pause and the sound of someone hacking. When the hacking stopped, a heavily accented voice said, "Okay, Irish, I tell him." *Click.*

I tossed the phone onto the seat and cranked the starter to resuscitate the Aries. It caught on the third try, and I edged out onto Bush. Although there were almost no cars on the road, it still took time to execute the tortuous series of turns on one-way streets required to reach where Ray was making his 911 call. When I pulled up, he was pacing nervously in front of the pay phone.

"What took ya?"

"Arson can't be rushed. Did you make the call?"

"Yeah. The woman I spoke with seemed particularly disappointed I wouldn't identify myself."

"Go figure."

Just then, two discordant noises reached our ears. One came from inside the car—my phone ringing—and the other from outside—the plaintive wail of a siren. I hoped the latter was the fire truck Ray had summoned because I really didn't want to completely torch Wong's business—or damage the adjacent buildings for that matter.

I hurried the Aries over to a space in front of a fireplug, but the car stalled before I could even get the shifter into park. "Riordan," I said breathlessly after I snatched up the phone.

"This had better be good." Wong sounded like he wasn't used to being woken up in the middle of the night.

"Part of it's good. I found the people who killed Mrs. Kongsangchai and my friend."

"I'm struggling to see what part of that wouldn't be good. And why you needed to call at two in the morning to tell me."

"I tailed them to Golden Fingers."

"And?"

"And they tossed a Molotov cocktail through the front door and set the place on fire."

"What? You didn't stop them?"

"They were too fast, and I was outgunned. There were at least four of them. I did call the fire department." I felt Ray stirring beside me. He had to see where this was going.

"That's it? You called the fire department?"

"And I tailed them back to where they are staying."

The line was silent for a long moment. "Why?"

"Why what?"

"Why are they doing this to me? Who are they? What's their motive?"

This was the bit I was worried about. There was no way I could tell Wong the real story. It would be completely incomprehensible to him. "I've no fucking clue. They are from out of town and they are into kinky sex. That's all I know."

Wong made a skeptical noise in his throat. "How did you get onto them? How did you even know to follow them?"

"I didn't. My friend did—the one who was killed. I found a 'if something happens to me' letter that he left for me." That part was true at least. "He laid out his suspicions about them and told me where he thought they were staying. I managed to find and question one of them without revealing my connection to you or my friend. That's how I discovered the little I know about them."

"This is all too vague, Riordan. You could be making this up entirely."

"I didn't make up the fact that Golden Fingers is burning. And I didn't make up that they are armed with .22 caliber target pistols. Target pistols that, if the police recovered them, would produce rifling marks that exactly match the slugs that killed my friend and your Mrs. Kongsangchai, not to mention your other employee and two more people besides."

Wong drew in a heavy breath. "And how might the police recover these pistols?"

"Suppose, for instance, they were investigating multiple shootings involving out-of-town victims at an abandoned industrial facility in the Hunter's Point neighborhood. They might come upon the pistols at the crime scene and bag them as evidence."

Wong's voice turned several degrees colder. "What is the address?"

I told him about the grain elevator on Amador.

"And you are there now?"

"I'm close," I lied.

"Is there a place where you can keep them under surveillance without being seen?"

"Yes, they've boxed themselves in." I described the general area to the east of the gate.

"If others approached from the west on Cargo, these kinky out-of-towners would be blocked in?"

"Yes."

"Then go to the location and wait for my men. They will come from the other end of Amador."

"Okay."

"And Riordan?"

"Yes."

"The police have gunfire locators in the area. There won't be multiple shots unless we can't avoid it. There will be multiple throat cuttings."

Ray reluctantly agreed to come with me, but now he was curled up in the back seat of the Aries. He made it clear that he wanted no part of what happened next. I had risked bringing the Aries well past the point where we had parked last time so I could see the gate of the grain elevator's yard from behind the wheel.

Waiting in the car with the chilly vinyl of the seat against the skin of my neck, I had too much time to think. I also began to doubt the wisdom—and the morality—of what I'd set in motion. If revenge was a dish best served cold, then at least the preparation of it was better done at a fast boil. If I could have taken everything back from the time I crawled out from under the motorhome, I might well have done it.

At 3:37 a.m., a white panel van swept up to the gate, its driver unconcerned with stealth. Six men in dark clothing tumbled out and rushed the gate, guns and large-bladed knives glittering in their hands. They flooded into the yard, went around the back of the motorhome, and disappeared from view.

I rolled out of the Dodge and stood by the front bumper, not even bothering to draw my gun. There seemed little likelihood that the men with the knives would need my help.

I strained my ears for any sound coming from the yard. I might have heard a door yanked open or a soft thud of bodies, but there were no shots or cries. If people were dying, they were dying swiftly and silently.

Then a lithe figure shot through the gate like a fish darting through narrows. She had dark hair with sweeping bangs and wore nothing more than a T-shirt that came to midthigh. Her feet were bare, and she made little gasping noises as she sped across the roadway. *Angelina.*

As she moved toward me, I saw she was carrying the toolbox with the fake scroll. I pushed away from the Aries and stepped forward to grab her in a hug that lifted her clean off the ground. She tensed and squealed at first, then went soft in my arms when she recognized me.

"Oh, August," she said in my ear. "Thank God."

I set her down hard, giving her a little shove to push her away from me. I yanked the toolbox from her hands. "Hello, Brigid."

She sucked in a sharp breath, and the whites of her eyes flashed beneath her bangs. "No. I'm Angelina. *Your* Angelina."

"I know you killed Chris."

"No. Why would I?"

"He was onto you, or you thought Brendan would be arrested for the killing. Or both."

"What're you talking about?"

"I'm talking about sneaking up on him while Jeff kept him occupied and firing a .22 caliber slug into his skull. And doing the same to your sister—if Corinne White was even your sister."

She reached for me. "How can you say these horrid things? I thought you cared for me."

"And I thought you cared for me."

"I do, August, I do. Let's get out of here and I can explain everything. There's nothing we can do now for Corinne and Chris. But we can still be together."

The man with the filed incisors Wong had called Uncle Yuen appeared on the road behind her, silent on slippers with cotton soles.

"Can we still be together when you learn the scroll in the toolbox is another fake and that you'll never get your hands on the real one?"

"What do you mean?" She swallowed with difficulty, and she made her voice softer, more entreating. "I only took the box because Brendan attached so much importance to it. Please, we need to go." She eyed the strip of road between the car and the fence, calculating her chances.

"You're not going anywhere."

She was tensing for a sprint past me when Uncle Yuen snatched her from behind.

"No, August," she screeched. "Don't let them do this."

"Let them? I arranged it." And I no longer had any doubts about it.

She flailed in his arms, flinging obscenities at me as he carried her backward. "You stupid, stupid old man. You don't know how sick to my stomach it made me to sleep with you, staring at your graying hair, the wrinkled skin on your chest, the crooks of your arms, the—"

I don't know if Uncle Yuen knew enough English to understand what she was saying, but he mercifully clamped a hand over her mouth and manhandled her under his arms as if she were a roll of carpet.

He turned to give me a quick nod before slipping through the gate. The last thing I saw were her bare white legs windmilling through the night.

30
ONCE IN A WHILE FOREVER

Chris was buried in the Mountain View Cemetery in Oakland. Somehow he'd managed to score a family-size crypt in the main mausoleum, which had been sold out for years and was home to the industry titans Henry J. Kaiser and Warren A. Bechtel who had collaborated on construction of the Hoover Dam.

While I didn't think Chris had built any dams, I was pretty certain that neither industrialist had been buried in drag. As stipulated in his will, the service was open casket. The casual observer would have noted Chris's copper-blonde wig styled in a chignon and his smartly tailored Chanel suit with a retro cut. Someone with an eye for the right sort of details might have realized that he looked an awful lot like photos of Eva Perón lying in state.

After the service, there was a wake. That was how I ended up at a table in the back of a nightclub in the Castro with Gretchen, Ray, and Kim while a raucous party featuring 1970s disco music convulsed in the main room.

Ray leaned forward to take a sip of his beer, then slouched back into his chair. The black suit he had picked up from Goodwill was too big, and the slouching widened the gap between his shirt and jacket collar and puckered the fabric below the shoulder seams.

"When I go," he announced, "please don't subject me to anything like this."

"Don't worry," I said. "You'll outlive us all. It's more likely you'll be arranging services for me."

"Besides," teased Gretchen, "you'd look good in a Chanel suit."

"You might go with a different wig, though," I suggested.

"Screw you." Ray grinned, then the smile faded and his face took on a solemn look. "I still can't believe she did it."

"You're talking about this Angelina/Brigid person?" asked Kim. "She killed them all?" Although the fuchsia hair was a little jarring, she looked quite elegant in a belted dress with darts at the sides emphasizing her trim figure.

"She didn't kill them *all*," I said. "Kittredge told me that one of the guns they found matched the slugs recovered from Chris, Corinne White, and Fingerhut. That gun had her prints all over it, so it's a safe bet it was hers. Brendan's gun matched the slugs taken from Mrs. Kongsangchai and your friend."

Kim pursed her lips and said nothing.

"Andreas had his own target pistol, and I assumed at first that he and Brendan had split the killings between them, but none of the slugs matched his gun. Angelina and Brendan were the heavy hitters in the family."

Gretchen sniffed and dabbed at a tear at the corner of her eye. There had been plenty of crying at the funeral service, but we had promised to treat the wake as the celebration of life Chris wanted. Gretchen drew in a deep breath and brought both hands to the table. "Okay. I get all that. But if Angelina was simply after the manuscript, why did she hire Chris? And why make up the story about her missing sister?"

"One was justification for the other," I said. "She made up the story about her missing sister—who wasn't her sister at all—as an excuse to hire Chris. The actual reason was to find the manuscript. He didn't know at first that he was looking for the manuscript, but she hoped that if he dug around long enough he would turn something up.

"Brendan said Angelina and Jeff had gone rogue, attempting to cut the rest of the family out of the picture and take the manuscript for themselves. My guess is that they somehow intercepted a message from Fingerhut that alerted Brendan to Corinne's discovery of the manuscript during the remodel of her house. No doubt Corinne had taken it to Fingerhut to get it authenticated and appraised. But once Angelina arrived in San Francisco, she proceeded to intimidate and kill the only two people who knew anything about the scroll. She realized Brendan and the rest of the family would be on the trail soon, so she needed help."

"Then why did she kill Duckworth?" asked Ray.

"We'll never know for sure. If Chris told her he had found the manuscript, he would have become expendable—especially if he also told her he was negotiating to sell it to Brendan. She may also have hoped that Brendan and his family would be arrested for the murder, effectively taking them out of the picture."

"Maybe Chris was onto her?" Gretchen asked.

"I threw that in her face the night at the grain elevator, and she denied it. But even if Chris had suspicions, he couldn't have been certain. He didn't mention anything about her in the note he left for us, and he trusted her enough that she was able to creep up on him and shoot him in the back of the head."

Gretchen brought her hand to her throat and sighed. "And hiring us was just a continuation of her idea to hire Chris."

"Sure. She didn't have anywhere else to turn. Only with us—or me, at least—she had the added advantage of being able to use her sex appeal. With Chris, it was Jeff who did the seducing. Jeff was also attracted to Angelina so she was able to subvert his loyalty to Brendan."

Kim stirred her drink. "I don't know what everyone saw in that emo tart anyway. You need to develop better taste in women."

I looked over at her and smiled. "I'm working on it."

"Hey," said Gretchen, "we were once a couple, too."

"Yeah, and you left me for a urologist."

"Urologists make good money," Kim said. "I have a question. What happened to this manuscript you keep talking about. The real one."

Gretchen, Ray, and I exchanged glances. It had been the topic of considerable debate. We had no idea who it belonged to legally. Corinne White's heirs? She had no close ones. The child she was pregnant with when she left the architecture firm had died during birth, and she'd divorced her husband. Kerouac's estate? From what we could tell, it was confused and still hotly contested, complicated by, of all things, a forged will.

In the end, the overriding consideration was that it was simply better for us if the thing wasn't made public for years—many years. Kittredge and the police had no idea about the scroll, and it had never been mentioned in the press coverage of the case. As far as anyone knew, a bunch of crazy Canadians had come to town and wreaked havoc with no clear motive. One of them, a girl whose real name was Brigid, assumed a false identity and claimed kinship with Corrine White for equally nebulous reasons. They had all been murdered just as mysteriously.

"Apart from being buried in drag and all, Chris's will had another unique feature," I said. "He wanted a time capsule— actually just a large safe deposit box he had at a bank—placed in the crypt with his coffin, and he requested that his crypt be opened and the contents of the box revealed fifty years later."

"So you put it in the box," said Kim.

"Yep. If Corrine White hadn't remodeled her house when she did, the scroll would have remained hidden for many more years. Putting the scroll in with Chris is the closest we could come to honoring Kerouac's original intentions without getting ourselves in trouble. Not that we can ever know exactly what Kerouac intended when he stashed the manuscript in the house."

"What else was in the safe deposit box?"

"Gretchen and I didn't look."

"Why not?"

"I think we were afraid it might have something about—" My phone started to ring. I pulled it from my jacket pocket and checked the caller ID. I didn't want to talk to Wong, but I knew I eventually I would have to.

"We were afraid it might have something about us. I better take this."

I stood from the table and walked as far away from the disco music as I could get. "Hello," I said tentatively.

"Is that 'Love Rollercoaster' I hear in the background?" asked Wong. I was surprised he even knew it.

"Yes, I'm at a wake for my friend."

"Certainly a change from 'Danny Boy.'"

"Refreshing, isn't it?"

"I called because I've reached the conclusion that you misled me, Riordan. That you used me to accomplish your own agenda."

"I thought we had the same agenda."

"Only to an extent. I do not like being used. In fact, I hate it. I'm sorely tempted to retaliate. Do you know why I haven't?"

I leaned against the paneled wall of the room. "Is it the letter I gave my lawyer to forward to the police if anything happens to me?" I had toyed with the idea of taking it further: ratting him out to Kittredge, confident I could spin a version of the story that kept me from being implicated.

The line was silent for a long moment. "You're not nearly as clever as you think. The reason I haven't retaliated is that I feel confident this 'Canadian Sex Family,' as the papers have dubbed them, *is* responsible for nearly all the violence against me. The murder weapons were recovered as you promised. I received further collaboration from employees who recognized several of them from their visit to Golden Fingers the night your friend Duckworth was killed. I even discovered a hidden room in the basement that would help to explain their presence. Were you aware of the room?"

"Possibly. But if I was, I learned about it by following a lead you suggested."

"Mrs. Kongsangchai's son."

I let that one drift with the breeze.

"Since he wouldn't have talked to me directly, perhaps you owe him confidentiality. But there are other things that don't add up. When I first met with you, you said that you were working for a client—the same client who had hired Duckworth—and that this client had been kidnapped. Now I find that this client was actually part of the family."

"I didn't know that when we met. She had me fooled—just as she had fooled Duckworth."

"But to what end? I have the definite sense that a piece of the story is missing—some underlying motive that drove all their behavior. It's almost as if my business was collateral damage."

"I don't know why you would say that."

"One very good reason is what Uncle Yuen told me about the night of the raid on the encampment. He doesn't know enough English to understand what you said to her, but he told me that you stopped this so-called client from escaping. That you took a toolbox she was carrying. What was in that box?"

I knew this was coming and I was ready. "Sex toys."

"You're kidding."

"I wish I were. I had hoped it was money or something valuable. It wasn't. It was just a bunch of strap-ons. I dumped them in the Bay as soon as I could. Look, I admit I had the same idea as you— that there was something valuable they were after. But I didn't make a damn thing off this case. I only lost a good friend. You can do a forensic audit of my finances and have me followed around for the next five years to see if I come into any unexplained wealth. But you won't find anything. If they were after something, I don't know what it was."

Wong let out a heavy sigh. "All right, Riordan. Just know this—I *will* be watching you. If I were you, I'd steer clear of Chinatown and my businesses."

"And if I were you, Wong, I'd stop threatening the man who

can implicate you in six murders—"

I was talking to a dead line. He'd hung up well before I'd finished. I put the phone away and looked up to find Kim smirking at me.

"If you are done talking shit to the head of the Wo Hop To, I'd like to dance." She took hold of my wrist.

"To this?" I pointed vaguely in the direction of the main room. "'Boogie Oogie Oogie?'"

"You think you're too cool to boogie?" she asked, quoting a line from the song.

The tune was more apt than she knew. "Boogie Oogie Oogie" was the only disco number that Chris and I used to perform when we played together at clubs. Composed by Taste of Honey lead singer and bassist Janice-Marie Johnson, it featured an elaborate—and much sampled bass line—that gave me a chance to shine on the electric bass, and just as importantly, provided Chris the opportunity to boogie around the stage in slinky costumes (as Johnson did) when he sang the tune.

We had to partner to re-create Johnson's chart-topping performance—just as we had partnered, one final time, to avenge his death.

"I'm not too cool at all," I said to Kim, who pulled me toward the pulsing beat. I waved for Gretchen and Ray to join us, and soon we were all "up on the floor" boogieing as Chris used to do.

ACKNOWLEDGMENTS

Deepest thanks go to fellow writers Sheila Scobba Banning, John Billheimer, Anne Cheilek and Ann Hillesland for reading early drafts and providing invaluable feedback.

And to entrepreneurial Down & Out Books publisher Eric Campbell for carrying the torch for independent crime fiction high and proud.

To David Hough, for his superlative copyediting. And to Rick McMahan, for his knowledge of ballistics (although any and all errors are my own).

And most of all to my wife, Linda, who passed away before this novel reached press. None of these books would have been possible without her—she made sacrifices for me and encouraged my often ill-starred ambitions, she was supportive and nurturing, and she took care of me in a way that no one has since I left my parents' house. I don't know how I will write, much less live, without her.

MARK COGGINS' work has been nominated for the Shamus and Barry crime fiction awards and selected for best-of-the-year lists compiled by the *San Francisco Chronicle*, the *Detroit Free Press*, and Amazon.com, among others. His novels *Runoff* and *The Big Wake-Up* won a Next Generation Indie Book Award and the Independent Publisher Book Award respectively, and his *The Immortal Game* has been optioned for a film.

MarkCoggins.com

BOOKS

On the following pages are a few
more great titles from the
Down & Out Books publishing family.

For a complete list of books and to
sign up for our newsletter,
go to DownAndOutBooks.com.

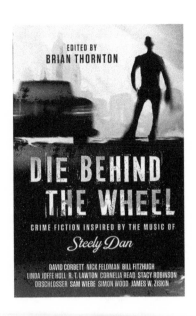

Die Behind the Wheel
Crime Fiction Inspired by the Music of Steely Dan
Edited by Brian Thornton

Down & Out Books
June 2019
978-1-64396-016-6

What's the end result of a crazy scheme to match some of music history's most evocative and memorable songs with twelve of today's most entertaining writers? You're looking at it.

With this collection there's no need to chase the dragon, tour the Southland in a traveling minstrel show, or drink Scotch whiskey all night long. You've already bought the dream.

Covering every game in the Grammy-winning catalog of Donald Fagen and Walter Becker—collectively celebrated as Steely Dan—these compulsively readable stories will stagger the mind of ramblers, wild gamblers, and—of course—the winners in the world.

Swann's Down
A Henry Swann Mystery
Charles Salzberg

Down & Out Books
May 2019
978-1-64396-011-1

At skip-tracer Henry Swann's weekly business meeting with Gold-blatt at a local diner, his inscrutable partner drops a bomb. He wants to hire Swann to help out his ex-wife, Rachael, who's been swindled out of a small fortune by a mysterious fortune-teller, who has convinced the gullible young woman that she's made contact with her recently deceased boyfriend.

At the same time, Swann receives a call from an old friend and occasional employer, lawyer Paul Rudder, who has taken on a particularly sticky case…

Countdown
Matt Phillips

All Due Respect, an imprint of
Down & Out Books
April 2019
978-1-948235-84-6

LaDon and Jessie—two hustlers who make selling primo weed a regular gig—hire a private security detail to move and hold their money. Ex-soldiers Glanson and Echo target the cash—they start a ripoff business. It's the wild, wild west. Except this time, everybody's high.

With their guns and guts, Glanson and Echo don't expect much trouble from a mean son-of-a-gun like LaDon Charles. But that's exactly what they get. In this industry, no matter how much money there is for the taking—and no matter who gets it—there's always somebody counting backwards...to zero.

It's Not My Cult!
A.X. Kalinchuk

Shotgun Honey, an imprint of
Down & Out Books
March 2019
978-1-948235-71-6

Anthony Dosek, after unwittingly creating a flying saucer cult he would rather forget about, goes to live with his cousin and his wife. Anthony's ruthless second-in-command would rather Anthony not forget his followers, and in trying to create a founder-martyr that will increase cult donations, this wannabe Iago dispatches a cynical former veteran and his naive sidekick to make that martyrdom happen.

In the meantime, to make amends, Anthony tries to reconnect with the mother of his child that he fathered while leading the cult.